Knock Off

Knock Off

RHONDA POLLERO

KENSINGTON BOOKS
KENSINGTON PUBLISHING CORP.
http://www.kensingtonbooks.com

KENSINGTON BOOKS are published by

Kensington Publishing Corp.
850 Third Avenue
New York, NY 10022

All Kensington titles, imprints and distributed lines are
available at special quantity discounts for bulk purchases for sales promotion, premiums, fund-raising, ed-
ucational or institutional use.

Special book excerpts or customized printings can also
be created to fit specific needs. For details, write or phone
the office of the Kensington Special Sales Manager: Kensington Publishing Corp., 850 Third Avenue, New York,
NY 10022. Attn. Special Sales Department. Phone: 1-800-
221-2647.

Kensington and the K logo Reg. U.S. Pat. & TM Off.

ISBN-13: 978-0-7582-1558-1
ISBN-10: 0-7582-1558-4

First Hardcover Printing: March 2007
First Mass Market Paperback Printing: February 2008
10 9 8 7 6 5 4 3 2

Printed in the United States of America

For my wonderful husband, Bob, and my precious Katie Scarlett—thanks for giving me time, space, encouragement, and M&Ms.

In loving memory of Kyle McKinley Pollero (1985–1999)—I know you'd be proud of me.

You're never out of money until your
credit cards are maxed out.

One

If I could find a way to deep-fry chocolate, my life would be whole.

Or at least that's what I told myself as I parked my BMW in its regular spot in front of the law offices of Dane, Lieberman and Zarnowski. I often muse about food when I'm in a funk.

It was a beautiful, sunny April morning, making it really hard for me to get excited about going to work. Okay, so I rarely got excited about going to work regardless of the weather. Then again, who does? I grabbed my adorable new Chanel bag, and with a quick, surreptitious glance, checked to be sure I was holding the pale pink bowling bag correctly. I was, and tugged it onto my shoulder.

It would be freaking embarrassing if my coworkers noticed the big black smear of God-only-knew-what on the lambskin leather. The smear would out me. I'd bought the damaged purse at the outlet in Vero Beach. I would take my secret vice to my grave.

No one would ever know that I, Finley Anderson Tanner, am a . . . *discount shopper.* And my other really huge fashion secret—I'm a tribute to Slightly Irregular. My wardrobe is a collection of the unloved cast-offs from the factory and/or the snagged and stained seconds discarded by the trendy stores, then sold at deep discounts. Thanks to the smudge, my new purse was marked down low enough to fit in my budget.

Well, that wasn't *exactly* true. I didn't have a budget so much as a propensity to carry just enough credit-card debt to force me to acknowledge that I have little if any shopping self-restraint.

Well, not just shopping. My excesses seem to be limitless, guided only by my overwhelming desire to have it *now. It* can be anything. Anything I can pay for in installments, that is. My favorite word is *preapproved.* I especially like it when it's stamped across a solicitation for yet another credit card.

So, that's how I morphed into a twenty-nine-year-old woman who doesn't technically own anything. My apartment is rented, my car is leased, and if we still had debtors' prisons, I'd be serving life without parole.

Which is the reason I'm dragging myself into work when I'd far prefer to be headed for the beach on this spectacular South Florida Monday. I'd much rather be lying in the sun, listening to tunes on my almost paid-off iPod, wearing my five-percent-down, custom-made, barely there, body-hugging bikini and matching sarong, ignoring all the warnings about the dangers of sun exposure in favor of a bronze, blonde-complexion-flattering tan. Debt sucks.

Especially for a person like me, who—of my own volition—has gone from moderate riches to heavily financed rags. The only high point of my week thus far has been finding a great deal on a solid screw-down crown on eBay for my build-it-from-parts Rolex project. Hey, everybody's gotta have a hobby. Over the past year, I've acquired the pink mother-of-pearl face and a sapphire crystal. I figure by the time I'm thirty-five, I should have enough parts to assemble the watch of my dreams.

For today, I'm dependent on my really cute Kuber to let me know that I'm more than twenty minutes late.

Stepping into the ornate lobby of the firm made my watch irrelevant. I was instantly given the evil smirk by Margaret Ford. As always, the fifty-five-year-old receptionist was stationed behind the crescent-shaped desk, pen poised, Bluetooth tucked into her right ear.

Margaret's crooked and overly thinned brows arched disapprovingly. "Nice to see you, Finley."

Liar, liar, pants on fire. I knew Margaret was the source of the unflattering nickname bestowed on me at the firm. It wasn't all that original, either. I think I was in elementary school the first time someone put my initials together and called me Fat. The only difference between then and now was that in elementary school, the kids called me Fat to my face. The receptionist and her pudgy posse didn't have that kind of nerve. I greeted her politely, then asked, "Any messages?"

She shuffled through the neat stack of pink notes, looking completely put out by my very reasonable request. Then again, Margaret always looked put out whenever she was forced to deal with me. With a less than subtle "*Humph*," she passed four messages and a thin folder across the polished mahogany desk. "Mr. Dane left this for you to review. The client will be here in"—she paused for effect—"twenty minutes."

Twenty minutes? Damn. Barely enough time for a decent couple of cups of coffee. Still, I smiled, thanked her, and collected the stuff before heading toward the elevator.

The Estates and Trusts Department of the firm occupied the entire second floor of a six-story building in West Palm Beach. Several secretaries—oops—administrative assistants were arranged in a cluster around various fax machines, laser printers, networked computers, and incessantly ringing telephones. None of them so much as looked up when I passed, exiting to the right and heading down the corridor toward my office.

Thanks to one of those plug-in things, my space smelled faintly of mango. I went about my usual morning ritual—flipping the light switch, opening the blinds to my stunning view of the parking lot below, turning on my coffeepot, then jiggling the cordless mouse to awaken my hibernating laptop.

I slipped my purse into the desk drawer and reached for the telephone. Maudlin Margaret took messages only from people who were too impatient or too incompetent to leave a voice mail.

"You've reached the desk of Finley Tanner. Today is Monday, April second. I'm in the office but unable to take your call right now. Please leave a message, and I'll get back to you as soon as possible. If you need immediate assistance, please press zero for the receptionist."

I checked my voice mailbox and scribbled the gist of the message from the court clerk regarding the D'Auria estate.

Being far too impatient to wait for the coffeemaker to finish, I filled my mug with coffee sludge before turning my attention to the file I'd brought up from Reception.

It was unusual for Victor Dane to assign a case to me. He was a civil trial attorney and I was an E&T paralegal, so rarely—thank God—did our paths cross. Victor is a total asshole. Worse even, an asshole with money, dyed hair, and a passion for man-toys. His latest toy is a black Hummer. *A freaking Hummer!* I shook my head at the thought. Who needs a Hummer in the flattest state in the country? The same guy who has his nails buffed and his teeth bleached at regular intervals, I suppose.

So, thanks to Vain Dane, I opened a new document on my computer and began entering the data before Stacy Evans arrived. I had gotten as far as the basic information off the death certificate before my intercom buzzed.

"Yes?"

"Mrs. Evans is here. Should I send her in?"

"Yes, thanks."

I stood and went toward the door to greet the grieving widow. It was something I'd grown pretty good at during the past seven years. Florida had a goodly amount of grieving widows, most of whom fell into two general categories. Real widows were normally over sixty and devastated by their loss. Faux widows ranged in age from mid-twenties to early forties and had dollar signs embossed on their pupils.

One look at Stacy Evans told me she was a real widow. Her slender shoulders were hunched forward, and her sunken green eyes were red and puffy. She looked frail and fragile.

After showing her into my office, I discreetly moved a box of tissues to within her reach. "I'm Finley," I began, bracing myself for the possibility of a crying jag. "I'm very sorry for your loss."

"Thank you," she responded in a flat voice. She

clutched a large leather tote to her chest. Two thick manila folders peeked out from the bag.

"Would you like some coffee? Tea? Water?"

She shook her head. Mrs. Evans was a golfer. She had the brown, leathery skin, a no-frills haircut, and wore those horrible little socks with tiny golf tees rimming the ankles.

I'm going to hell. Here this woman was in the throes of despair and I'm ragging on her socks.

I pointed at the files she held, prompting, "Mr. Dane asked you to bring along your late husband's will?"

I took a sip of Kona macadamia nut coffee while she eased the folders from her tote. She placed them on my desk but seemed reluctant to completely surrender them to me. Instead, she placed her palms on top of them and met my eyes. "My husband didn't die."

I almost choked on my own spit. I had a copy of his death certificate. Marcus Evans was very dead. So dead, in fact, that he'd been cremated. Now I understood why Vain Dane had passed this woman off to me instead of meeting her himself. Weenie.

"Mrs. Evans," I said, donning my most compassionate expression, "perhaps you'd be more comfortable if we put this meeting off for a little while. There's no hurry, and it sounds as if you need—"

"He was murdered," she injected, her face suddenly animated. "Marc would never fall asleep behind the wheel of a car. And he most certainly wouldn't do it at nine in the morning."

"Accidents happen," I suggested gently. Bad idea. The woman across from me suddenly looked seriously pissed.

"Young lady," she began, her colorless lips pulled taut, "do not dismiss me. I may be old, but I'm not senile." She took in a deep breath and let it out slowly. "I tried to tell Victor my husband was murdered during our telephone conversation."

Victor? *Oh, crap.* It would have been nice for Vain Dane to tell me the woman was a personal friend. Time to backpedal. "Mrs. Evans, I'm sorry if I've upset you."

"My husband's murder upset me," she fired back. "You are just annoying me."

"I'm truly sorry." I sat back against my vented leather chair, folding my hands around my now tepid coffee mug as I bought some time. "Why don't we start from the beginning?"

"Marcus was murdered." She took a sheet of paper, neatly typed on both sides, from one of the files and slipped it across my desk, then remained as still as a statue while I scanned it. The official accident report. If there was something wrong, it sure as hell wasn't jumping off the page at me. I figured maybe I was just having a prolonged blonde moment, so I read it again. That seemed to please Mrs. Evans.

At nine-o-five on the morning of March twenty-seventh, Marcus Evans had driven his Cadillac off I-95, down an embankment, and landed—roof down—in a canal just south of Jupiter. The official mechanism of death was drowning. The manner of death was accident.

Mrs. Evans wasn't senile so much as she was just plain wrong. Or maybe psycho? All I knew for sure was Vain Dane had handed her off to me. Which was just the kind of thing I should have expected.

"Have you spoken to the police?" I asked with due seriousness—due, that is, to my boss being a chicken-shit, cowardly asshole for palming his psycho friend off onto me instead of handling it himself.

Eyes narrowed, Mrs. Evans pursed her lips. Apparently I wasn't the first person to ask. "They dismissed me." Waving one hand—the one sporting a five-carat, emerald-cut diamond—she deposited her bag in the second chair and leaned closer to me. "It had to be murder," she said, speaking in a conspiratorial tone.

In the library? With a wrench? By Professor Plum? "Was the car examined for mechanical defects?" *Have you been examined for psychological defects?*

Which wasn't really fair, I had to admit. The woman was *grieving.* I got that. But couldn't she have worked through that before coming to see me? It was hard trying to have a rational conversation with someone who wasn't in the here and now. I felt bad for her, but, really, she should be telling this story to the police— Oh yeah. They didn't believe her, either.

It took everything in me not to sigh. I folded my hands on my desk and gave her my I-am-hanging-on-your-every-word look that I'd perfected over the years. I was pretty good at it. I'd used it frequently during bad dates.

"Not by the police," she said flatly. "Something about the witness statements supporting their theory that it was an accident, and they claim that no further investigation is warranted. I had his car towed to Palm Beach Motor Specialists on Okeechobee Boulevard," she explained. "I need you to arrange for an expert to inspect it. Again. Marc took care of his car. Never missed a single service appointment. Someone tampered with something, maybe the brake lines. I don't know what, specifically, but something must have been done to the car, and I fully expect you to get to the bottom of it."

Stacy smoothed her hand over her functional

yet expertly coiffed pale brown hair while I tried to think of the best course of action.

I read the determination in the set of her jaw that was mirrored in her narrowed eyes. I also reminded myself that she was a personal friend of the senior partner. Which meant my first priority was to appease the client. It didn't matter that my investigatory skills were pretty much limited to researching clear title to effect a transfer of real property. For two hundred dollars an hour, if she wanted me to do a Nancy Drew, so be it.

"I should make copies of what you have," I told her, watching the tension drain from her shoulders as I spoke. I pulled a retainer agreement from my desk drawer and passed it to her. I recited the high points of the agreement by rote. "This case may necessitate the hiring of a private investigator as an independent contractor," I explained, "any of those charges are considered separate from and not included in the hourly rates charged by Dane, Lieberman and Zarnowski."

"What about you?" she asked pointedly.

"Excuse me?"

"Well, why was I relegated to a paralegal? Shouldn't a real lawyer be handling a murder case?"

Yes, I thought, *a murder case would be handled by an attorney. The paranoid delusions of a grieving widow are, however, my cross to bear.* "I work under the direct supervision of an attorney," I told her as I started affixing "sign here" flags to the signature lines on several forms with a little more pressure than necessary. "Mr. Dane is and will continue to be personally involved."

"That's acceptable, then," she said after a brief pause. "I expect regular updates on your progress. I'm taking my husband's ashes up to New Jersey this afternoon for the memorial service." She pulled another neatly typed sheet of paper from her tote. "These are all my contact numbers with the dates and times most convenient for you to reach me."

Paranoid, grief-stricken, and anal. Great combination.

"Do you have a cell phone or a pager?"

I was a little surprised. No one had ever asked me for that information. "I have voice mail," I offered. "I check my messages regularly—"

"I prefer a direct number," Mrs. Evans said in a way that pretty much said it wasn't so much a preference as a requirement.

Grabbing one of my business cards, I hated myself as I scribbled my cell number on the back. Something told me giving Stacy Evans unrestricted access to my life was something I would definitely live to regret.

By lunchtime that prophetic thought was fact. Stacy had called no fewer than three times. Once on the office line and twice on my cell. Now, as I walked slowly down Clematis Street, on my way to meet my friends Becky, Jane, and Olivia, my purse was vibrating incessantly. I checked the incoming number, recognized it as Stacy's, and refused to answer. She might be a close, personal friend of Vain Dane, but I wasn't her indentured servant. At least not between twelve-thirty and two. Which was my definition of the forty-five-minute lunch hour.

The best part about being a estates and trusts paralegal was the relative freedom. No one ever questioned my absences from the office, so long as I grabbed a few folders and mumbled something about filing things with a court clerk. No one seemed to notice that my "meetings" were almost always linked to mealtimes. Or if they did, they didn't say anything, which suited me just fine.

Downtown West Palm Beach was crowded, but that was about to change. Locals claim there are two seasons in Florida, summer and snowbird. Summer lasts from February through the first week of November. Snowbird season lasts roughly from Thanksgiving through Easter, defined mostly by caravans of RVs clogging I-95 as their occupants flee winter in search of a milder climate to wait out the snow melt.

For year-round residents like me, it means parking lots filled beyond capacity, long grocery-store lines, and forget trying to get a prescription filled. The pharmacy is apparently some sort of Mecca for the sixty-five-and-older crowd. Easter is late this year—two additional weeks of "Season" before they head back to their homes and families.

A horn blared, startling me. I ducked to avoid a low palm frond as I maneuvered past a white-haired woman and her walker. I know I should feel compassion. Respect my elders, yada, yada, yada. But, in my defense, whoever made those rules was never cut off on the highway by a ninety-year-old whose reflexes no longer included a glance in the rearview mirror before a lazy lane drift.

I allowed myself a subtle vanity check as I neared the corner at North Olive Street. Sushi Rok was a trendy, relatively new Asian/Japanese seafood place that catered to the business crowd. It was a good choice for lunch, since the tourists tended to avoid this place in favor of the more casual spots that welcomed shorts, T-shirts, and scrunchies.

Okay, I had to admit, while I loathed every second I spent in my gym, the results made it all worthwhile. Especially now that I was entering the danger zone, when my body started acting like a cereal-box disclaimer: some settling may occur during shipment.

Spring meant one thing to me—Lilly Pulitzer. I'd paired my seventy-percent-off-because-of-a-lipstick-smudge hibiscus pink cardigan tied around my shoulders with a—gulp—full-price patchwork dress in her signature citrus colors. Since the cotton span-dex dress was both form-fitting and left my arms bare, I did have to give a little mental nod to my stump-necked personal trainer, Neal, who pushed me mercilessly. While I was giving silent praise, I also thought of my wonderful dry cleaner, who man-aged to turn the smudge into little more than a faint ghost near the jeweled neckline of the worsted cashmere sweater.

The ensemble, paired with my new purse and strappy sandals, was, I decided, really, really flatter-ing. Lilly *is* the blond woman's best friend.

The restaurant was fairly crowded. A low buzz of overlapping conversation was punctuated by the clinking of glasses and tableware. Shoving my sun-glasses up on my head, I scanned the tables for my friends. It took just a second for me to spot Olivia, casually waving her hand.

I weaved toward the table, checking out the men in the room on single-woman autopilot. Well, I wasn't completely single. And the pilot in my life is actually Patrick. Thinking of him should have made me happy, giddy . . . something. Something more than *comfortable*.

I sighed heavily as I joined Olivia and Becky. "Jane's late?" It was a rhetorical question. Jane was always late. Jane would die late. Olivia was on her Blackberry, so I directed my greeting to Becky.

Becky sipped on peach iced tea. Her dark brown eyes were hidden behind orange-tinted glasses. Rebecca Jameson and I have been friends since college. She's a junior associate at the firm, a contracts specialist working under the watchful eyes of Ellen Lieberman, only female partner and all-around über-bitch.

I'm the one who convinced Becky to apply after she graduated with honors from Emory Law School. I'm also the one who suggested she focus on some area of the law other than contracts. Becky didn't heed my advice, which, it turns out, worked in her favor. For some unknown reason, Becky and Ellen actually work well together. As well as anyone can work with Ellen, who, incidentally, believes the road to success requires draining all estrogen from her being. Ellen Lieberman is all drab suits, Birkenstocks, and gray roots.

Becky was dressed in taupe slacks and a cotton blouse in her favorite shade of orangey red. "Nice top," I complimented.

"Thanks," she replied, twisting her long hair into a knot as the midday sun streamed in from the window at her back. "Coffee's on the way."

I smiled, grateful that my friends loved me enough to anticipate my continual need for caffeine.

Turning my attention to Olivia, who was slipping her latest and most favorite electronic toy into her purse, I said hello, then asked, "How is Garage Boy?"

Olivia's perfect mouth turned down at the corners. "He is not a boy."

"He lives in his parent's garage," I pointed out. "He's thirty-six. He doesn't have a job. He's—"

"An asshole," Becky finished unapologetically. "Geez, Liv, cut him loose and find a real man."

"Like you?" Olivia returned smoothly. "Your last date was when? Your high school prom?"

Becky smiled, since we all knew the assessment wasn't all that far off. "I'm building a career. There'll be plenty of time to find Mr. Right later."

"Later, huh?" Liv asked. "Like when you're alone in your apartment, about to hit fifty, watching reruns of *The Gilmore Girls*, while you devour an entire box of Moon Pies and are surrounded by sixteen cats?"

"Do not mock the Moon Pie," Becky cautioned as she glanced around the restaurant. "It's my comfort food."

"Ladies?" I interjected, knowing full well the constant barbs could go on indefinitely. Becky and Liv enjoyed teasing each other. Probably because they were polar opposites.

"That was an e-mail from Jane," Liv said. "She can't get away."

Becky and I both gave little groans, then immediately grabbed our menus. I was vacillating between the yellowfin tuna special and California rolls when the waiter arrived with my coffee.

"We're still waiting for the fourth?" he inquired. Predictably, he spoke predominantly to Olivia. It used to bother me, her getting all the male attention. Now I understand they can't help it. Olivia is just *that* pretty. Exceptionally pretty. She has exotic coloring and flawless features. At first glance, most people think her violet eyes are fake—those horrid contact lenses created in hues not known in nature. They're real, as are her high cheekbones, bowed lips, tapered neck, ample boobs, small waist— Hell, her whole five-seven, size-two body is just a thing to be envied.

"Actually, it will just be the three of us," Liv supplied. She batted her lashes. Flirting was as natural to her as breathing. "Could we have a few minutes?"

"Certainly, ladies," the waiter said. "I'll run and get you another cucumber water while you decide."

He was attractive enough to warrant my glancing over the top edge of my menu to assess his butt. "Too skinny," I murmured.

"Too short," Liv added.

"I'd do him," Becky announced.

"You've been celibate too long," I said with a sigh. "You'd do anyone." I looked up at my tablemates. "Thanks to your recent color change, Becky, we now look like we belong on *Petticoat Junction.*"

Becky twirled a lock of her recently tinted red hair. "I'm Betty Jo. Wasn't she the red-haired one that ended up with the cute crop duster? Speaking of pilots, how is Patrick?"

I shrugged. "Fine. He's due back late tonight." Again I hated it that thinking about him did little to inspire my fantasies. On paper, he was *the* guy. The *one.* The man of my dreams. He was thirty-four, moderately tall, blond, blue-eyed, and a pilot. Perfect, right? His income potential is on target; he's intelligent, funny, and athletic; we like a lot of the same things—the beach, movies, restaurants, etc. Genetically, he's the ideal person to father my children. There's just no . . . magic.

I long ago abandoned fairy-tale *special,* but I'd like it a lot more if I felt my heart flutter when I opened the door. Or, the alternative, toe-curling sex. The sex was okay. Patrick was considerate enough to be . . . methodical. Methodical was satisfying, but it didn't exactly inspire passion. When I'm with Patrick, all the foreplay is accomplished in a determined, specific order. It's like sex has a preflight checklist that he has to complete before he can achieve lift-off.

I frowned and laid my menu on the table to await the return of the server.

Liv reached over and patted my hand. Twin chunky bracelets clunked against the tabletop. "Still no fireworks?"

I shook my head. "Not even a spark."

"It won't get any better," Becky commented. "In my experience, bad sex is not like good wine. It doesn't improve with time."

"When was the last time you had sex?" Liv asked. "Bad or otherwise?"

"I'm trying to remember," Becky drawled. "Let's see, it was on a sofa after my boyfriend's parents went to sleep. No, wait! That was *you*."

"Tease me all you want, Betty Jo," Liv responded. "At least I'm not wedded to my work."

"Weddings *are* your work," I inserted. "Speaking of which, any good bridezilla stories to share?"

Liv is a much sought after wedding planner, with clients on both sides of the bridge.

I should explain that "the bridge" is the section of Okeechobee Road that crosses the Intracoastal Waterway, separating West Palm Beach from the super-rich, invitation-only world of Palm Beach. Old money, like the Posts, the Flaglers, and the Kennedys, mix reluctantly with the new-money residents.

New money is something of a misnomer, since nothing much in Florida predates 1924. Nothing but the family fortunes used to build some of the most incredible oceanfront mansions on the East Coast. Along with offering primo golf and deepwater slips for personal yachts, Palm Beach is an event haven.

Liv and her partner, Jean-Claude DuBois, had turned Concierge Plus from kid's party planners into *the* premiere wedding coordinators in the area. Now they were branching out into coordinating other things, like some of the elaborate balls that raised funds for a diverse list of charities.

Still, the wedding mishaps were my personal favorites. Probably because I derived some sort of childish, perverse comfort knowing that if I wasn't happily walking down an aisle, no one else was, either. Which makes no sense whatsoever, since I really don't have any burning desire to embrace hearth and home. Not yet.

Lunch was pretty uneventful. Good food, casual chit-chat, and a lot of laughs. I prepared to leave feeling recharged, ready to tackle the remainder of my day.

Becky and I waited with Liv until the valet brought her champagne-colored Mercedes convertible around to the front of the restaurant. Unlike me, Liv was making really great money, but, like me, she spent freely.

Becky was probably earning three times my salary, but her only vice was clothing, so she had more money in the bank than any of us.

As soon as Liv pulled away from the curb, Becky turned and said, "I heard Victor sent a case your way this morning."

"Yeah." I recounted my strange meeting to Becky before scrolling through the messages on my cell phone. Stacy Evans had called two more times during lunch. I glanced at the time on the screen. According to the schedule she'd given me, she was just about to board a plane for Newark. With any luck, she'd land a few minutes after I was done for the day.

"What does she expect you to do?"

If you don't love your job,
then you'd better love your paycheck.

Two

Becky's question was still haunting me as I returned to work. I would have pursued it with her, but we followed an unwritten rule when it came to work and socializing. We always part company at least two blocks from the office so no one, meaning Margaret, would catch on that I took leisurely lunches with a junior associate. Margaret long ago appointed herself chief of the employee police. She wouldn't approve of an attorney and a paralegal having lunch together. Especially if said lunch exceeded the time allotted by company policy.

In reality, I think Margaret is just miffed that there's a support-staff hierarchy. Specifically, she's pissed that I'm higher up on the food chain than she is. Frankly, I wear better shoes than she does, too. Not that that's hard. I shuddered at the thought of Margaret's shoes. And forget that I actually have a degree and she doesn't. In Margaret's world, lawyers are gods, and the rest of us should all be judged solely on seniority. Which would work out pretty well for her, since she's been sitting at the reception desk for thirty-one years.

I shivered uncomfortably. The mere thought of sitting at the same desk for more than a quarter-century made me want to gnaw through my wrist for a vein.

Not that I was making a lot of headway in the move-up-and-succeed department. There was no vertical move for me. Unless, of course, I took my mother's counsel and went to law school. Right! Like taking on hundreds of thousands of dollars in student-loan debt to do basically what I do now makes sense. If I'm going to be in debt, it's going to be for important things, like Lulu Guinness stuff.

Much as I didn't want to dive headfirst into the uncharted waters of the Evans case, I figured I should get started. For one thing, I was pretty sure Stacy would be calling me in the morning, if not the very instant she touched down in Newark. And, on a more immediate note, Victor Dane was in the building and might get some wild idea about checking up on my progress.

I knew he was in because his stupid seven-foot-wide Hummer was hogging up a good portion of the parking lot.

Seated back at my desk, I tapped a pen against the blotter as I tried to formulate the best plan. Florida had very user-friendly probate laws, so it only took me forty-five minutes to fill out the forms necessary to open an estate. Stacy had already signed the forms on her visit to the office that morning.

Normally, I would run to the clerk's office, get Letters of Administration, then start an inventory. Once I had that in my hand, I'd meet with one of the tax associates and formulate a plan for trans-

ferring title to the surviving spouse. The point of
all the paperwork was to make sure the client's tax
liabilities were minimized and to recommend the
best way to preserve assets based on the age and
needs of the beneficiaries.

But this case wasn't normal. Not at all. I didn't
have the first clue how to investigate a murder, let
alone a non-murder murder.

So, I read Mr. Evans's will. Nothing sinister in the
twenty-page document. The usual things were covered—basically all the real and personal property
went to his wife, with the exception of a specific
bequest to his son. The ten-percent ownership in
Evans & Evans Jewelers retained by Marcus Evans
upon his retirement transferred directly to his son,
Abram, in accordance with a partnership agreement.
I flipped through the papers provided by Stacy,
found the partnership agreement, and slapped a
bright pink Post-it note on it. I scribbled a message
that I needed to send this to the Contracts Department, standard practice to ensure everything was
in order and in full compliance with the laws of
the State of New York, where it had been drafted.

All that stuff was well inside my professional comfort zone. But I still wasn't sure how to approach
the whole "my husband was murdered" thing. I
needed help, so I pulled out my firm directory and
started running down the alphabetical list of names.

I dismissed three of the paralegals out of hand. I
knew two of the litigation assistants were in trial, so
they wouldn't be available to give me a crash course
on murder investigation. The third non-possibility
was Debbie Gayle. She was on maternity leave. Again.
The woman was like a freaking machine. Three kids
in four years. Two of them were born in the same
year but weren't twins. God, what did she do? Have

sex in the backseat on the way home from the hospital? I conjured up a mental picture of Debbie. Pretty, if you could look past the sleep-deprived, dark circles under her eyes. Her short, no-fuss brown hair was always slightly mussed, as if she'd had only enough time to run her fingers through it. Very little makeup. Then again, if I had three kids under four, I'd be hard-pressed to shave both my legs on the same day. I couldn't remember the last time I saw Debbie without a yucky blob of baby barf down her back. It was enough to make me rethink the whole having-children thing.

I cringed when I got to the next possibility. I rolled my chair back in order to refill my coffee cup, my eyes still fixed on the company directory. Maybe I was hoping that if I stared at it long enough, her name would morph into something else. No such luck.

Very few people intimidate me. Mary Beth is one of those few. In fact, she is at the top of the make-me-feel-like-a-lesser-lifeform list. Mary Beth is one of those people who can do everything and do it perfectly. She's the Martha freaking Stewart of legal assistants—without the felony conviction, of course. To make it worse, she's very, very nice. It would be easier if she was a snot, but she isn't. Aside from being genuinely kind, she volunteers for everything. Not only does she never forget a coworker's birthday, she bakes cakes, circulates cards, and organizes all our holiday parties.

Her office is a thing of beauty. Mary Beth even made her own curtains. "Curtains," I muttered with a grudging smile, sipping on my coffee. The fact that she can sew is annoying enough. The fact that she redid her own office at no cost to the firm is just . . . *wrong*.

I knew she'd help me. Mary Beth doesn't know how to say no. But it would also mean I'd be on her radar. Mary Beth wouldn't stop at helping me with the Evans case. No, she'd keep helping. Her help would spread into other areas. It would start innocently enough—interoffice e-mails to check on my progress. Then it would escalate. She'd drop by to offer tips and helpful hints. After that would come the invitations to the dreaded home parties. Recipe swaps, storage-container parties, and, worst of all . . . faux-jewelry sales.

I cringed at the thought of spending an evening pretending I liked competing with other women by seeing how many words I could make out of *gold plated* in sixty seconds or less. I imagined myself frantically scribbling log, old, dog, late, tall, blah, blah, blah, all in the name of winning a not-available-in-stores pot holder or set of plastic coasters.

My fingers hovered over the keypad of my phone. Was it worth it? Was I willing to consign myself to the fiery pits of home-party hell, all in the name of investigating a noncrime? As much as I loathed the idea of risking a weekday evening trapped in the nether regions of cream cheese hor d'oeuvres, it was my job.

Mary Beth answered her extension on the third ring. Her voice was annoyingly perky. Kind of like an overeager cheerleader on speed.

"This is Finley down in Estates and Trusts."

"Hi, Finley!"

I could almost see her painting a poster that read GO TEAM! BEAT STATE! in brilliant primary colors. I explained my situation as I listened to the sound of her flipping through her Rolodex.

"I've got just the person for you," she gushed. "His name is Liam McGarrity."

I wrote the name on a Post-it, along with the phone number she provided. "Thanks."

"I'll go ahead and send you an e-mail with my new case tracker as an attachment," Mary Beth offered. "It's user-friendly and has all the pertinent investigation contacts, including a recommended timeline that automatically computes your billable hours along with outside contractor costs. I'd be happy to come down and—"

"I'm good," I interrupted. "Thanks so much. Sorry, Mary Beth, I've got another call," I lied. My e-mail dinged her incoming message almost before I had a chance to disconnect the call.

After opening the document, I swallowed more coffee along with a groan. I didn't see myself filling out a fifty-plus-page checklist for a simple car accident. Scrolling down, I made notes on people to contact and other highlights. Thanks to Stacy, I already had the police report. According to Mary Beth's tomelike bible, I also needed the hospital records, an autopsy report, and a background check on Marcus and his family, friends, and business associates.

I sent a quick e-mail to thank Mary Beth. Unlike my colleague, I didn't include an animated happy face with little hearts coming out of its ears in my reply.

The letters of request didn't take much time, so when I was finished, I dialed the number for Liam McGarrity. While I listened to the phone ring, I thought about his name. It sounded masculine and—

"McGarrity."

Forget the name. The voice was very deep, very sexy. Which meant he was probably a middle-aged, balding redhead with a bulbous nose and chewed fingernails. It was one of those cruel jokes of nature. Men, in my experience, are like God's little Mr. Potato Head projects. If they're smart, they're ugly. If they're funny, they're snide. If they're cute, they're jerks. For every positive, there's usually an offsetting negative that makes them . . . *men.*

"Hi. This is Finley Tanner from Dane, Lieberman."

"Yeah. I got a call from Mary Beth."

I rolled my eyes. Her efficiency was daunting. "Yes, well, um, I need some—"

"A mechanical review on the car and a complete background."

"Well, yes. Seems like Mary Beth covered everything."

"She always does," he agreed. "I've got a thing this afternoon that might run long. I'll be by in the morning. Say, nine?"

A "thing"? What the hell is a "thing"? "Say ten," I suggested, knowing the odds of my actually being at my desk would be better then.

"See you at nine, later."

Later? Surfer vocabulary. I was ready to lay odds that his "thing" was the afternoon high tide. A pudgy redhead on a surfboard wasn't a pretty mental image.

But it stayed with me through the remainder of the day. It followed me to my car and still irritated me as I slipped behind the wheel.

"Damn, damn, damn," I muttered, finally focusing on my commute just in time to realize I'd passed the exit to my mother's posh digs. Traffic was at a virtual crawl, so I briefly considered pulling onto the shoulder and reversing my way back to the off-ramp. Except that the shoulder was closed because of construction. And—oh, yeah—it's illegal.

Normally, I would have blown off the chore of watering my mother's plants. But she was due back from her husband hunt this weekend, and I needed to inventory the damage. My mother's cruises were costing me a flipping fortune. She was currently steaming her way back from twenty-eight days in the Mediterranean, and if I didn't start replacing plants soon, I'd never be able to hide my inattentiveness. It was a small price to pay. Way better than admitting that in the month she'd been gone, I'd watered her prized orchids exactly twice.

I'm such a wrong person for this chore. The only kind of flowers I like are *delivered*. Her plants seem to sense this. It's like the little bastards make a suicide pact the minute they see me walk through the door. Leaves drop, buds rot. It isn't pretty.

The whole "water my orchids" thing is penance. Yet another way my mother has to subtly remind me that I'm a failure. My brown thumb is legendary. My sister, Lisa, on the other hand, could breathe life into firewood.

But Lisa is in New York, finishing her residency and planning the September wedding of the century. It isn't just a residency. No, Lisa wouldn't settle for *just* becoming a doctor. Nope, she's spent the last three years specializing in pediatric oncology. My mother likes to tell anyone who stands still about her daughter who is going to cure childhood cancers. It works kind of like this:

Total stranger, "Do you have any children?"

My mother, "Yes, I have a beautiful daughter, Lisa. She graduated at the top of her class from Harvard Medical School. She was on a complete academic scholarship. Lisa is engaged to marry Dr. David Huntington St. John IV. He's the son of Georgia State Supreme Court Justice David Huntington St. John III. Lisa and her fiancé plan to have a fall wedding—at the family estate in Buckhead, of course—because David IV is spending the summer in Central America donating his time to Doctors Without Borders. Oh, wait . . . yes, and I have another daughter, whose name escapes me at the moment."

I swallowed my own pettiness. Truth be told, Lisa is a decent person, and David IV seems like a great guy. It's just that the better they are, the worse I look to the rest of the world in general and to my mother in particular.

It doesn't help that my mother is Cassidy Presley Tanner Halpern Rossi Browning Johnstone, former rising star for the Metropolitan Opera. Cassidy is actually a stage name, made legal for a hundred bucks back in the seventies. She thought it sounded better than her birth name, Carol—more exotic and more in keeping with her destiny.

My mother had a beautiful voice. Her promising opera career was cut short by nodules on her throat. The removal of those nodules turned her amazing voice into something less than what is required of a star soloist. So she embarked on a second career—serial marriage.

It worked out pretty well for me. My mother's first husband was Jonathan Tanner. I was eighteen months old at the time. He adopted me and treated me like his very own. Which was a good thing, since I didn't find out he wasn't my biological father until I was thirteen. And I only found out then because I had snuck into my mother's lingerie drawer because I wanted to know what a two-hundred-dollar bra looked like. That's when I found my birth certificate and my adoption papers.

Until then, I was told that my name—er, *names*— were old family names on my mother's side. Technically true. Finley and Anderson are both family

names, just not members of her family. They're
the surnames of the two men my mother was sleeping with when she got pregnant with me.

Maybe it should have bothered me, but it didn't
because Jonathan was a great dad. Ironically, even
though we didn't share any DNA, he never treated
me any differently than Lisa. My mother was the
one who blatantly showed favoritism. It wasn't that I
was unwanted. It was more a function of Lisa being
so perfect. Lisa was an easy child. I was the challenge—the kid who, when told the stove was hot,
had to touch it just to make sure. My dad saw it as
spirited. My mother found it irritating.

I'm guessing that's why, after fifteen years, I still
miss him. Jonathan was a great guy and a hard act
to follow. I'm sure he's why my mother likes being
married.

She's currently on the prowl for husband number six, which is how I got stuck with the chore of
watering the self-injurious orchids. While she's off
expanding her search to include other continents,
I have to drive seven miles out of my way to tend to
the plants. Ten miles if you count the U-turn,
which I will.

Thanks to three profitable divorce settlements
and two sizable estates, my mother has a stunning
condo on Singer Island with breathtaking views of
the Atlantic. It's a twelve-story building accessible
only by decree of the ever present security guards
posted on the overly air-conditioned side of double glass doors.

I parked in a spot marked DELIVERIES ONLY, ALL
OTHERS TOWED, got out of my car, then climbed up
the polished stone steps. A large, ornate fountain
sprayed the walkway with a fine mist. A crew of
landscapers were busy changing the flowers. I

must admit, it was a practice that didn't make a lot of sense to me. Routinely, perfectly good plants were dug up, tossed in the back of a truck, and replaced by other plants in different colors. They were plants. Who cared? Someone on the owner's association had too much time on their hands. They treated the foliage as if it was the important accessory, removed and banished like last year's out-of-favor fashion item.

The guard buzzed me in, nodding a general recognition before he made a notation of my arrival on his clipboard as I strode toward the elevator. My heels clicked and echoed against the marble walls of the two-story atrium lobby.

The elevator always smelled faintly of the vapor trails left by previous riders. I sniffed, recognizing the scent of tuberose, jasmine, and orange blossom blend as Annick Goutal Gardenia Passion.

My game of guess-that-perfume only got me as far as the fifth floor. I shifted from foot to foot, bored and anxious while the elevator slowly rose toward the penthouse. Even though my mother wasn't here, I suffered a moderate failure-as-a-daughter attack. Strange how that happened.

I could be completely confident in all other areas of life, yet I crumbled when it came to all things "mother." I had this vision of myself, stepping off her elevator, certain that I had a big neon sign over my head flashing I SUCK! It was a mother-daughter thing. Mothers had this amazing ability to make you feel sixteen and lame even when they were thousands of miles away out at sea. The little telepathic bitch-slap did little to lighten my mood.

A mood that careened down when I opened the door and started counting dead plants. Just for fun, I considered running out and buying chalk, coming back and outlining their little plant bodies, and treating the whole place like a massive botanical crime scene. That would be my idea of fun. My mother would take it as yet another example of my irreverent propensity to treat her disrespectfully.

So I dropped my purse onto one of three ornate sofas in the living room and moved past the pricey and mostly headless marble statues that had scared me senseless as a child, finally ending up in the kitchen.

My mother's penthouse was nearly five-thousand square feet, more than three times the total area of my apartment if I added my parking spot into the equation. Large windows, balconies, and sliding glass doors made you feel as if you were standing in the clouds above the ocean.

The space was very Mom. The decor was formal, floral, and—I glanced around just to check—organized. In a futile attempt at triage, I filled the copper watering pail and went plant to plant, drizzling water onto hard soil. It wasn't working. The water just rolled off the caked dirt into the saucers.

Fortunately, while I suck at plant care, I know people. The day after my mother left, I took photographs of the plants on my cell's camera. A great reference for getting their little plant doppelgängers. It was my backup, a pretty foolproof plant-care system.

Time for Plan B. Luckily, my mother left the stakes in the pots, identifying each plant by color and variety. I wrote the information on a sheet of paper, then guestimated the height. I have a great relationship with Ricardo, who has a cute plant stand up in Juno Beach. One phone call and I can replenish the plants by Saturday morning, hopefully without my mother being any the wiser.

List tucked inside my purse, I left the penthouse

and headed back to my place. I thought about stopping at the store for something to make for dinner but then decided not to bother.

My modest, rented apartment is on the ground floor of a complex in Palm Beach Gardens. It has a decent-sized bedroom and bathroom, but I chose it mainly for the walk-out patio. Ignoring the statistical reality that I was something like twenty times more likely to be robbed in a garden apartment, I opted for this place because the patio made it seem bigger.

I changed into a pair of shorts and a T-shirt, then made some coffee and opened my refrigerator. Chinese takeout and a jar of mustard. My pantry wasn't much better. The only thing that didn't require cooking was a box of stale Lucky Charms. One of the greatest joys of living alone is the complete freedom to eat Lucky Charms by the handfuls straight out of the box. Paired with an excellent cup of hazelnut coffee, I was all set for the evening.

I flipped through the channels, stopping only long enough to see if something grabbed my interest. I was feeling restless for some reason. It wasn't the caffeine or the sugar. Given my generally poor eating habits, my body was used to the nutritional void.

There were a few framed pictures on top of my entertainment center. I focused on the one of Patrick and me taken two months earlier when we'd slipped over to the Bahamas for a weekend. We did look perfect together—all blond, blue-eyed grins set against a tropical backdrop. I smiled. It had been a nice trip. Patrick and I traveled often, and he always picked romantic, beachy locations. He took great care to make sure the hotel was just right, the room was just right, the view was just right, the wine was just right, the sex was just right.

Raking my fingers through my hair, I knew I should feel more appreciative. What woman wouldn't kill for a guy who was so considerate?

Me. But, I told myself, *In the world of dating, the evil you know is always better.* "He isn't evil," I mumbled. I could make a long list of Patrick's plusses. Unfortunately, none of them compensated for the fact that if I was being totally honest with myself, I had to admit I was growing bored.

I crunched another handful of cereal into my mouth just as my cell phone rang. Half-expecting it to be Patrick, I glanced at the Caller ID, but the identification was blocked.

"Hello?"

"Miss Tanner?"

The last time a person called me "Miss" I was twelve and standing in front of the headmistress's desk about to suffer the consequences for being late to class . . . *again.*

"Yes."

"This is Stacy Evans."

"Yes, ma'am," I said as I quickly tossed my Lucky Charms aside as if she could actually see me stuffing my face with marshmallow stars, hearts, moons, and clovers. "How was your flight?"

"I've been trying to reach you all afternoon."

"I was in and out," I supplied.

"What have you learned?"

That giving you my cell number was totally fucking nuts. "I've completed all the paperwork, and I'm meeting with an investigator in the morning."

"Why did you put it off?"

Off? I'm thinking less than a twenty-four-hour turn-around is pretty damned impressive! "It was the first time that was convenient to both our schedules."

"I'm not paying you for convenient. I'm paying you for results."

"I understand that. I will be in touch as soon as I've met with Mr. McGarrity." That should have been the end of the conversation, but it wasn't. Mrs. Evans spent the better part of ten minutes chewing me out for not returning her phone calls, for not keeping in touch, for basically everything shy of global warming.

After I hung up, I made a mental note to make sure I added the time spent on the phone call to my billing sheet. I went into the bedroom and pulled out my laptop. It's pretty much just for e-mails, photographs, and shopping, but every now and again—like now—I actually do some work from home.

I plugged in all the wires and cables, then went online and Googled Marcus Evans. His obituary was the first thing to pop up. Nothing new there. The next few entries were just what you'd expect. Photographs accompanying articles regarding various charitable events in and around Palm Beach attended by Mr. and Mrs. Evans. I scrolled down, finding an article that seemed marginally more relevant.

It showed a picture of the Evans family standing in front of a store in New York. The article described the successful and profitable jewelry business Marcus had built from really humble beginnings. Along with retail, Evans & Evans did commission pieces for an impressive clientele. But Marcus had retired years earlier, maintaining little more than an advisory presence in the business. According to the article, his son, Abram, carried on the family enterprise with great acumen.

"None of this has anything to do with a car accident in Palm Beach," I said with a sigh as I scrolled down through the next few mentions. I wasn't sure what I was looking for, mainly because I was convinced there was nothing to find.

My heart skipped when I saw the next to last listing. Having clicked the link, I was frustrated by a series of registration processes that made me jump through hoops before I could read the text of the article. Mild interest had turned to genuine curiosity as I waited for the server to grant me permission to access the newspaper archive.

Patience isn't one of my strong suits, so I drummed my nails on the edge of the computer as the annoying little hourglass spun and twirled on the screen. We can fly probes to Mars, but I can't read a newspaper article from three years ago without a screen name, a password, and a reminder-tip question just in case I couldn't remember said screen name or said password. Amazing.

Finally, a copy of the article came up. I read it over, looking for some reference to Marcus Evans. It was a long article. I must have missed something, so I read it again.

Irritated, I used the *Find* key. No Marcus Evans, no M. Evans, no Evans, period. No jewelry, no business, not even a mention of New York or New Jersey. I tried searching for golf, charities, pretty much anything I could think of that might somehow link my guy to the story. Nothing.

I was vaguely familiar with the story, though. My firm had represented Kent Hall, M.D., in the medical wrongful-death suit filed by the estate of Brad Whitley. The jury had completely exonerated the renowned transplant surgeon. So what, I wondered, did the Hall trial have to do with my poor dead jeweler's car accident?

Men are like a great pair of shoes in the wrong size—no matter how much you love them, they can't be fixed.

Three

"He was a juror," I excitedly told Becky when we met for coffee the next morning at our favorite coffee shop a couple of blocks from the office. Nancy Drew had a break in the case. "Marcus Evans was a juror on the Hall trial." I was quite pleased with my minimal detecting skills.

Becky's brow furrowed for a second as she sipped her chai tea. "The Hall case? That was the doctor who did the heart transplant on the rich guy who died anyway, right?"

I nodded. "Brad Whitley," I said. "Forty-three-year-old real estate developer. He had"—I paused to consult my notes—"cardiomyopathy. His only chance was a transplant. Crappy luck that he finally got the transplant and then got nailed by some funky postop infection. Killed him."

"That's some pretty cruel karma," Becky agreed. "Was there any negligence?"

We both knew that a jury verdict, especially one

in a medical malpractice suit, didn't mean squat. That whole "jury of your peers" thing pretty much flies out the window when you're talking about complex medical procedures to people who, on average, have the same medical IQ as a bag of hair.

Normal people find a way out of jury duty. Jobs, family obligations, and general hardships are just some of the claims used to get out of the civic call to service. In a case like the Hall trial, potential jurors run for the hills. Can't say as I blame them, either. It's hard to ask someone to commit to sitting on a trial that could last for weeks, if not months. All for the whopping sum of roughly twenty dollars a day.

So, in Palm Beach county, at least, juries are composed of people under seventy—you get an automatic pass if you're over seventy—who are the unemployed, the underemployed, the never-employed, professional students, housewives, retirees, and the occasional true believer who actually answers the call to duty regardless of the personal cost.

"I'm going to review the file today," I said. "After I meet the redheaded-surfer-slash-investigator." I glanced down at my watch and gave myself a little mental pat on the back. It was only eight-twenty and I was ready to get to work.

"That trial was, like, um, three years ago," Becky reminded me. "What's the connection?"

I shrugged. "Probably none. But at least I have something to say to Mrs. Got-Finley-on-Speed-Dial Evans."

"If Dane had a relationship with the Evanses, how did Marcus end up on a jury where Dane was defense counsel?"

"That bothered me, too," I admitted. "I won't

know until I read the transcripts." I stood, taking my half-finished latte with me. "Can you do lunch today?"

"No." Becky sighed. "I've got meetings. Are we still on for dinner tonight?"

"Seven o'clock, the fountain at City Place." Waving as I walked, I headed out and strolled the two blocks to the office.

There was a chill in the morning air. Well, chilly to me. I consider anything under eighty degrees a major cold front. But there was hope in the bright orange sunshine slowly rising above the buildings. By lunchtime I'd be able to shed my denim jacket and show off my Tom K Nguyen embroidered tulle blouse. I got it at a serious discount on my last trip to The Mall at Wellington Green because some poor soul in my size had torn the ribbon tie, allowing me to score the blouse for just under one hundred pre–sales tax dollars. Tacking the ribbon back in place had taken me less than five minutes even with my limited sewing skills.

My new blouse was so terrific that it acted like a force field, protecting me from the nasty glare Margaret shot my way when I arrived at work.

"I think my watch is running slow," I told her sweetly. "Got the correct time?"

She gave me a dark look as I went for the elevator.

Even her snarl couldn't rain on my "I'm here early" parade. Not just on time, mind you—early. The last time I was early to work was when the hot repair guy was there fixing one of the state-of-the-art, computerized, automated copy machines that jammed more often than it worked. I greeted my coworkers as my uncharacteristically cheery mood carried me into my office.

I shrugged off my jacket and looped it on the hook behind the door before flipping on my coffee-pot and settling into my chair. Pulling the list I'd made the night before from my purse, I unfolded the wrinkled sheet of paper and went over it again.

My voice mail was clear, which was good. By nine-o-five, I was scanning my e-mail and feeling the first wave of annoyance wash through my system. Liam McGarrity was late. Worse yet, his tardiness was screwing with my unusually sprightly mood. And here I'd made a point of being on time.

Most of my e-mails were easily dispatched with minimal effort on my part. Including, as expected, a chatty little note from Mary Beth offering, yet again, to help me. What I didn't expect was the curt, single-line e-mail from Victor Dane, commanding my presence in his office at noon. I groaned. My really great morning was turning to shit.

I put in a request for the Hall transcripts from the fileroom, marking it *urgent* just because I could. I did the other things on my list that didn't require input from the investigator, who was now a full twenty minutes late.

My latte was history and I was on my third cup of coffee by the time Margaret buzzed my line to inform me that McGarrity was on his way up. Not that I'm anyone to talk, but the fact that he was almost an hour late didn't bode well. Grabbing a sticky note, I made myself a reminder to keep a close eye on his billing. It wasn't my money, but that didn't mean I was going to pay for late.

The scent of cologne and soap arrived a few seconds before the man. I noticed two things right off the bat. He wasn't redheaded and he wasn't middle-aged.

There are few times in adult life when you have a purely primal response to a man. This was one of mine. My guy-dar picked up and tracked him as he came through the doorway. It wasn't that he was classically handsome. He was more the casual, rugged type. In a fraction of a second, I sized him up as dangerous—the kind of guy you're attracted to even though you know, going in, it will be a disaster.

"I'm Finley," I greeted him, extending my hand in his direction and silently praying I wouldn't do something stupid, like leap over the desk and tackle him.

"Liam," he returned, not shaking my hand so much as gripping it for an electric second.

The deep, sensual voice was even more of a distraction when I was looking into his clear gray-blue eyes. Who knew he'd be Baldwin-brother black Irish? I was expecting an unattractive redhead with freckles and a paunch, and here I was faced with the very real possibility of drooling on my new blouse.

Lazily, he lowered himself into the chair opposite my desk and slapped a folder in front of me. The sound was enough to clear my man-fog. I asked, "What's this?" Pulling the elastic band off the folder, I glanced inside. Several hand-labeled files were organized in neat order.

"Copies of all the pertinent reports, hospital, M.E., preliminary background checks, and the responding-officer's notes."

Okay, I was duly impressed. "What about having the car inspected?"

"I'm on it," he answered easily. "That coffee private, or can I have some?"

Coffee, water tea, . . . me. "Sorry, sure."

Turning in my chair, I opened my credenza to grab a second cup. Bypassing my big, bright pink emergency mug, I grabbed one of the emerald-colored cups embossed with the firm's logo. "Cream? Sugar?"

"Straight," he answered.

Are you? I wanted to ask. Of course he was. He was too scruffy to be gay. No self-respecting gay man would wear stone-washed jeans, a blue cotton shirt, and a crooked tie. There wasn't so much as a hint of product in his black hair, nothing to smooth the wayward lock off his forehead. I wanted to run my fingers through it. I wanted to do a bunch of other things that I think are still illegal in twelve states. But I settled for pouring his coffee.

"What do you know about the Hall trial?" he asked.

I slid the cup to the edge of the desk, childishly avoiding the potential brush of the fingertips. Until I knew his fatal flaw, I didn't want to feel that zing. I knew he had one. My best guess at this point: he's one of those guys who makes you think you can fix him. He had a hooded, George Clooney-ish kind of gaze.

I came of age to that look. The whole "I'm open to it if only the right woman comes along" expression that Doug Ross used to give long-suffering Carol Hathaway. Mentally, I reminded myself that *the look* had driven Carol to suicide, so it was probably best for me to switch gears and focus on the case.

"I know Marcus Evans was a juror."

He tossed me a little half-smile. "Very good. This firm defended Dr. Hall."

"I've already requested the transcripts. I don't remember much about the case, except that it made the news every night until the verdict came in."

Liam brought the mug to his lips, paused, and looked at me over the rim. "Rich folks usually make for good ratings."

"I met Brad Whitley once," I mused. "Correction, I didn't actually meet him. More like I passed him leaving The Breakers."

"Go there often?"

I couldn't get a sense if he was mocking me or making conversation. I hate when that happens. "A friend of mine did his wedding."

"And?"

"Nothing," I said, wondering now why I'd brought it up in the first place. "When do you think the car inspection will be completed?"

"My guy will give me first impressions later today if there's something obvious and suspicious." He drained his cup, rose, and set the mug on my desk. "If this is a wild-goose chase or if the tampering is sophisticated, then it could take a couple of weeks."

"What about the background checks? Did anything jump out at you?"

He shook his head and slowly let out a long breath. "On the surface, your dead guy's squeaky clean. Good husband, good father, good businessman, charitable. Model citizen."

There was a decent amount of cynicism in his tone that I admit made me a little curious. "You think he had some sort of double life?"

His broad shoulders strained against his shirt when he shrugged and shoved the hair off his forehead. "He'd have to if that's what got him killed. Random victims are pretty rare. Murder is up-close and personal."

"So he probably wasn't murdered?"

"If he was, you're dealing with a slick killer. I know the officers who responded to the accident. They're good cops."

He was framed in my doorway, leaning against the jamb as he checked the fancy Breitling chronograph watch on his tanned wrist. I was impressed for a second time. Watch-envy washed over me.

"How do you know the police officers?"

"Used to be a cop," he replied. "I've got another thing," he added. "I'll be in touch."

Again with the "thing." For a large man, he moved fluidly. I was half-tempted to jump up and watch him walk down the hall, but that would be just too obvious.

Instead, I spent the remainder of my early-for-me morning catching up on my open cases. The D'Auria estate accounting was due in less than a week, and I still had a math error making me crazy. There were a few other odds and ends that needed my attention as well, and I wanted my desk to be clear when the transcripts arrived. Thinking about them, I sent an e-mail to the file clerk, asking when I could expect action on my "urgent" request.

I got an instant reply letting me know the files were on their way. So, having some free time, I logged on to eBay and hunted for Rolex parts. I found a box in excellent condition and entered a bid, but the item auction didn't end for another seventeen hours.

I also called the orchid guy and told him what I needed. It was annoying to hear he was going to tack on a rush-order fee of ten percent over retail, but I wasn't in any position to argue. He knew it, I knew it, so I coughed up my credit-card number and kept my irritation in check. Orchid replacement was going to cost me roughly as much as a pair of decent sandals at the Dillards' semiannual shoe sale.

The transcripts arrived at eleven-fifteen, and I dove into them as if they were cheesecake and I was seriously PMSing.

Trial transcripts are the most mind-numbing reading on the planet. Which probably explains why television shows depending on actors reciting them are about as interesting as watching C-SPAN at three in the morning. It isn't *Perry Mason* or *Matlock*. The people aren't ever scripted, and the lawyers aren't usually brilliant. In fact, the process is technical, and jurors often nod off during lengthy objections. Hell, some even nod off during actual testimony, though that's never indicated in the transcripts.

The content was daunting—lots and lots of medical terms and names of complex surgical and diagnostic procedures that had me reaching for dictionaries and searching the Internet for some semblance of understanding. Volume one covered jury selection, opening statements, and the first morning of testimony. Looking over at the eleven boxes stacked neatly against the wall made me want to rethink my approach.

My computer alarm chimed at a quarter to twelve, reminding me of my high-noon summons to Dane's office. Needing a break, I typed the names of all the jurors and witnesses to check after my meeting. I just needed to see if anything popped. I didn't expect to find anything. For a trial of this magnitude—a multimillion-dollar verdict at stake—jurors are vetted pretty thoroughly by both sides.

Carrying a pad of paper, I headed for the elevators, not thinking about the time and that they would be loaded with people heading off to lunch, so would be running really slowly. In a quick change of decision—it wouldn't do to be late—I turned for the stairs instead and climbed the four flights up to the executive office suite.

As I entered the office doors, I felt like Dorothy when she stepped into Oz. Posh carpet, buttery-soft leather furniture, stunning fresh floral arrangements greeted me. I tried to think of the last time I'd been up here. My last review, maybe, when Ellen Lieberman had reamed me out for not taking enough initiative. My stomach knotted at the memory. Ellen's assessment had cost me a bonus. A contemplated bonus I had already spent. Twice.

Little good, in my experience, ever comes of a visit to the boss's office. But since I didn't have any other option, I greeted the executive receptionist, whose name I totally blanked on, and took a seat to wait.

And wait and wait. My stomach was growling, and I was jonesing for coffee. Lunch was secondary to my coffee need. It had been forty-minutes since my last caffeine hit, and I was starting to feel the effects. I considered asking if I could reschedule, but I was afraid to.

As time ticked on, my nerves frayed to the point that I was tapping my foot. That earned me a disapproving glance from the executive sentry.

"Do you have any idea when Mr. Dane will see me?" I asked, the words spilling out of me in one rush of breath.

"He's still on a conference call."

That will last the rest of my lifetime? C'mon, I thought, *where's the sisterhood? We're all underlings here—toss me a crumb. Something I can hang my hope on.* Nothing. She continued typing as if I was invisible.

I straightened my blouse, wishing now I had

grabbed my jacket to cover the start of perspiration stains I was sure would morph into big, ugly wet blotches at any second.

Nearly an hour later, I was ushered inside the spacious masculine office of Victor Dane. The walls were covered with professionally framed diplomas, certificates, news clippings, and various other accolades and statements of appreciation. Dane was seated at the far end of the room.

He didn't look up as I entered and took the long walk toward him. An ornate pen was in his left hand, poised above an inch-high stack of papers.

Do I say something? Clear my throat? Remain silent? Throw myself out the window? It's hard not to be intimidated by him. Mutely, I remained in the room with God, watching Him autograph copies of the Bible.

"Sit."

I did as instructed, quelling my urge to ask for a liver treat for my obedience. He continued his task, drawing out the painful silence.

My eyes darted around the room as I pretended to be interested in photographs of Dane with various celebrities and the elite of Palm Beach. One of the few things I liked about the man was his cologne, it was Burberry and reminded me of my dad.

Dane, I grudgingly admitted, had a great sense of style. His suit was subdued, hand-tailored brown silk, paired with a camel-colored shirt that had his monogram on one cuff. For an older guy, he was pretty dapper. If only there wasn't that glare coming off of his buffed nails. I hate buffed nails on a man. They cross the invisible line between pampered and prissy.

I cataloged the things on his desk: an antique Tiffany desk set, a bottle of water, three file folders, and several pink messages scrawled in Margaret's precise handwriting. There was a matching mahogany computer station forming a wide semicircle around to his right. His laptop was open to a geometric screen saver making liquid shapes that changed at preset intervals.

The wall behind him went up three feet, then a to-the-ceiling window opened on a stunning, panoramic view of the ocean. I had to look beyond his artificially darkened hair to see the ships dotting the horizon. I would have given anything to be out at the beach, lying in the sun, instead of waiting for whatever unpleasantness was coming my way.

It had to be something bad, I decided as I clutched my pathetic-looking pad. Dane didn't issue invitations unless you did something really, really good or really, really bad. It had been a while since I had done anything spectacular, so it had to be the latter.

Hello? Growing old here! I thought, feeling my heart pounding in my chest.

He looked up then, tethered to a telephone by a ear bud. He smiled, something I hadn't expected. "Sorry I kept you waiting, Finley."

"Not a problem," I said.

"I wanted to thank you."

I leaned forward, thinking I had misheard him. "For?"

"Taking on the Evans matter. I know Stacy can be . . . difficult."

"We're fine," I told him. "She's just convinced her husband was murdered."

He sat back, stroking his chin. "You do know that's ludicrous?"

Got that on the first try. "Yes, sir."

"Where are you on the estate?"

I was really impressed by the professional way I ticked off all the things I had done thus far, finishing up with, "A mechanic is going over the car as we speak." Only he probably got a lunch break.

"Don't spend too much time on this," Dane cautioned, returning to his task. "Copy me on any relevant information."

It was a dismissal, so I stood, then lingered at the edge of his desk.

Eventually, Dane lifted his brown eyes to meet mine. "Yes?"

"You were the lead attorney on the Hall case, right?"

"Uh huh," he answered, clearly bored by me. "And you're wondering how Marcus sat on a jury if we had a personal relationship?"

"Yes."

"We didn't. Marcus and Stacy retained me a year after the trial. Is there anything else?"

"No, thank you." I backed out of the room.

I strolled back to my office, feeling pretty good about my meeting. That was as close as Dane ever came to praise, so I'm already thinking of ways to spend my holiday bonus even if it is only April.

I'd earned a nice lunch, but for once, I had no desire to leave the building. I was on an employee high, so I thought I should make good use of it.

I detoured down to the vending machines on the first floor and, armed with four packs of M&Ms, I went back up to my office. I noticed that I had three messages from Stacy Evans. Grabbing the receiver, I started to call her, when I noted the list of names on my computer screen. Why not do a quick search on the remaining jurors' names? Then I would start on the witnesses. It would give me one more thing to report to Mrs. Evans.

Cutting and pasting the relevant information between the Internet and my list of names, I was on my way to preparing a pretty decent memo for the client. Then I could get back to reading the transcript and continue feeling really impressed with myself.

I was moving along at a pretty good clip when I entered the fifth juror's name from my list. The first hit was a three-month-old obituary. Another member of the jury had died. According to a corresponding, brief mention in the *Post*, José Vasquez, a landscaper, had been killed in a freak work-related accident. Okay, I shouldn't laugh, but, honestly, it was hard to keep a straight face when I was reading about a guy being crushed while planting a palm tree. Talk about your freak accident.

Only two names remained on my list. One was a drama student at FAU who, according to the critic who wrote the article, was so talentless that she made Paris Hilton look like Meryl Streep. The other was Graham Keller, the jury foreman.

Keller was a fifty-eight-year-old man who—I swallowed—was also dead. Also an accident. Also within the last three months.

The hairs at the back of my neck prickled. I let out a breath and whispered, "Something is very wrong."

Never blow your girlfriends off for a guy.

Four

It was Wednesday, and in just three short days I was beginning to change my opinion about Stacy Evans. As in, maybe she wasn't a delusional widow with nothing better to do than bug me. Maybe there was something to her theory that her husband had been murdered after all. Hell, I hadn't even started checking out the trial witnesses and already the bodies were piling up.

My fingernails clicked against my keyboard as I cyber-hunted for more information on Graham Keller, the third dead juror. There was a tingle of excitement in my stomach. A normal person would equate it to that sensation you feel when you know you're about to get great sex. Me? It's more like the thrill I get when an eBay auction for one of my coveted Rolex parts is about to end and I'm still the high bidder.

Unlike the poor landscaper crushed by the palm tree, the details of Graham Keller's demise were pretty standard fare. According to the newspaper, he simply keeled over during a performance at the Kravis Center. I grimaced when I discovered the death occurred during intermission on the opening night for a touring company's production of *The Marriage of Figaro.*

My reaction was a sad commentary on my character because the response wasn't empathy for the dead guy. Oh no. It was pretty much a function of my own personal experience.

Mom dragged Lisa and me to various operas on a regular basis when we were growing up. Fully expecting her daughters to share her love of opera. Lisa does. I so do not. Particularly not *Figaro*. For me, it's three and a half hours of sappy romance set to music. Don't get me wrong, I like romance as much as the next girl. I just prefer the *Sleepless in Seattle* kind. About an hour into the opera, my hand starts to itch, and I've got to battle the urge to rush the stage and bitch-slap the Susanna and/or Figaro character, just for being so stupid.

So the notion of a quick and painless death at intermission held some sort of perverse appeal for me. Lucky bastard didn't have to sit through the second half.

"Stop it," I chided myself softly. A therapist could probably have a field day analyzing the correlation between my loathing of opera and my relationship—or lack thereof—with my mother and sister.

Shaking my head to clear my errant thoughts, I returned my focus to Keller's sudden death. His age was listed as fifty-eight—pretty young to just drop dead. Again I thought there was a possibility that Stacy Evans wasn't a complete loon. Three dead jurors in three months is pretty damned suspicious.

Even to an underachieving estates and trusts paralegal.

My shoulders slumped when I reached the last line of the article just above a grainy photograph of the deceased. There'd been a autopsy. The M.E.'s office determined that Keller had suffered a massive coronary. Natural causes, damn it.

In the bizarre and wonderful world of the medical examiner, once homicide and suicide are ruled out, a heart attack is technically considered an accident. Which I suppose makes some sort of sense. It's not like anyone would intentionally have a coronary.

That knowledge didn't do much to support my growing belief in the jury conspiracy. As some of the enthusiasm drained out of my system, I leaned back against my chair, tapping my index finger against the edge of the desk. Graham Keller's face was smiling at me from the computer screen, giving me the creeps. Even the dead guy was taunting me over my as yet unsubstantiated suspicions. I could almost hear him clucking his tongue. Common sense and reasons I'd seen thus far dictated that Keller, Vasquez, and Marcus Evans had all died from explainable causes or accidents.

But I still couldn't get past the tingle in my gut. *Something* wasn't right. Me, probably. There was a distinct possibility that I was making a mountain out of a mole hill. I knew the M.E. had reviewed the Evans and the Keller deaths and hadn't found anything suspicious.

Reaching for the phone, I figured it was worth a shot to check on the Vasquez accident. Just one last shot, and then I'd leave it alone. I flipped through my Rolodex, absently aware of the fact that I was about due for a manicure. My polish wasn't chipped or anything, I'm just a firm believer in preventive personal beautification.

My call was answered on the third ring.

"Hi Trena," I greeted, relieved that she was the one I'd reached.

Trena Halpern, one of the clerks over at the morgue, and I have chatted dozens of times. She's my go-to girl when I need a rush on duplicate death certificates or a heads-up that the M.E.'s findings might cause me some grief. A lot of insurance companies won't pay out benefits if the deceased committed suicide, so Trena has become a valuable contact over the years. She's nice, and generally comfortable telling tales out of school, mainly because I did simple wills for her parents gratis.

"Hi, Finley. How are you?"

I could almost see her twisting strands of auburn hair around her forefinger. Then again, I'd develop a lot of nervous ticks if I spent eight hours a day surrounded by dead bodies.

"I'm good. You?"

"My nineteen-year-old daughter just had her nipple pierced. My son wrote a pro–gay marriage paper for his English class. Wasn't real popular with the nuns at St. Ignatius Boys Latin."

Whoa. Wrong question. "Uh, sorry."

"Not as sorry as he is. I grounded him until he gets his first gray hair because I lost a half day's work so the principal and the priest could lecture me on family values. They worked in a dig about me being the problem. They seem to forget that my husband divorced *me*." Trena let out a long sigh. "So, what can I do for you?"

"I'm working on an estate." *Technically true.* "I'm hoping you'll share anything you've got. Totally off the record, of course."

"I've already, er, shared with one person today, so sure. Got a name?"

"José Vasquez," I said, then read off the date of death I'd gotten from the obituary.

"Hang on."

I cradled the phone between my cheek and shoulder as I rolled my chair over to the tower of boxes. Remembering the juror questionnaires were in the top box, I quickly found the file and took it back to my desk.

José's was the second one in the pile. While I waited for Trena, I scanned the three-page document. The most notable thing about José's answers was poor penmanship. I deciphered enough of it to know that he was a naturalized citizen who'd come to the United States from Guatemala. He was married to Rosita, had four young children, and had started his landscaping business just a year before the Hall trial.

According to his answers, he'd never been arrested, never served on a jury. His closest and only connection to the justice system was a cousin who'd been convicted of spousal abuse in the late 1990s. José had taken the time to scribble in that he'd been a witness against his cousin.

"Got it," Trena said, slightly out of breath. I heard the sound of papers being shuffled before she continued. "Died as a result of closed trauma to the chest and head." More shuffling of papers. "The only two witnesses said he was guiding a royal palm into position when it fell and crushed him. Injuries consistent with witness statements. Ruled an accident."

"Were there tox screens done?"

"Blood alcohol level was nil," Trena said. "Why? Did your guy have a history of drug abuse?"

"Not that I know of."

"Well, if you're going after his insurance company, we've got a vial of his blood in the freezer. Don't wait too long. Oh, I can fax you a copy of the police report if you want. Save you a trip to the Riviera P.D."

"That would be great. Thanks."

I made some notes after I hung up the phone. If José's accident wasn't really an accident, I needed to talk to the witnesses.

At that thought, I rolled my eyes and swallowed a groan. What did I know about interviewing witnesses? Forget interviewing them, I wasn't even sure how to find them. I was pretty sure I couldn't pick up the phone and dial 1-800-WITNESS.

But I did have Mary Beth's e-mail attachment, better known as The Complete Guide to Litigation Management. Pulling up the long document, I did a quick search and found a bulleted list of questions. They were divided into categories—law enforcement, eyewitnesses, forensic witnesses, character witnesses, alibi witnesses, blah, blah, blah.

After some cutting, pasting, and sorting, I created a more manageable document that I could use, assuming I could track down whoever was with José when he died. I could probably find his wife fairly easily, but I didn't really relish the idea of popping in on the Widow Vasquez. At least not yet.

Hearing a tap on my open door, I looked up to find one of the interns standing there with a small stack of papers in her hand. I wasn't a hundred percent sure I knew her name. I don't usually have time to learn their names. Interns only stay at the firm for about three months at a stretch.

I'd dubbed this one—only in my thoughts—Bad

Hair Girl because she had the worst cut I'd ever seen. The color was great, pale brown with natural blond highlights. The kind of highlights I pay a small fortune for every six weeks or so. But the functional bob pretty much negated the gift of perfect color. And she had bangs. Bad ones. They were far too short, making her face look too round. She had a nice shape and a propensity for wearing plain skirts and tailored shirts. She was tall, five-ten, maybe. Something she compensated for by always wearing flat shoes.

Or, I thought, feeling a little guilty at my unflattering mental inventory, maybe she just wore them because her feet hurt. Lord knew the partners treated the interns like servants. They spent a big part of their stints at Dane-Lieberman filing motions and running errands. Bad Hair Girl spent a lot of time ferrying exhibits to and from the printer. I'd seen her often, dragging heavy mounted charts, graphs, and photo blowups up and down Clematis Street.

None of that explained why she was in my doorway, since she was assigned to Vain Dane.

"Hi. Connie, right?"

"Cami," she corrected. "Short for Camille."

"Sorry. Cami."

"No problem. Everybody gets it wrong." She thrust the pages in my direction, still not crossing the threshold into my office. "This fax just came for you."

Getting up, I walked around my desk and took the pages from her. "Thanks. How'd you get stuck with fax delivery duty?"

"I do what I'm told," she said, her tone tinged with a small amount of frustration. "Fax delivery today, pencil sharpening tomorrow."

I smiled up at her, surprised by the sharp humor. "Not loving your duties?"

"I've got a four-point-oh GPA, an almost photographic memory, and next year I'm going to be the editor of the *Law Review.* I'd imagined my first internship would be a little more, um, challenging."

It's a learning experience, not an appointment to the Supreme Court. "It'll look good on your résumé," I assured her.

"Mind if I ask what you're working on?"

"Wheel-spinning," I said, returning to my desk and offering her a seat at the same time. Procrastination is, after all, one thing I excel at.

"A lot of that going around," Cami agreed as she folded her long, lean body into the seat.

After giving the faxed pages a cursory glance, I returned my attention to the intern. Her hazel eyes were darting around my office, finally settling on the framed photograph of Patrick and me.

"Your husband?" she asked.

I shook my head. "No, boyfriend."

"I've had exactly one date since I started working here. It's hard to meet men when you're stuck here until the wee hours of the morning and the weekends are devoted to indexing transcripts."

Feeling a kinship to the overworked woman, I offered her some coffee. She declined. I refilled my mug and gripped it with both hands as I brought it to my lips.

"Your case?" she prompted.

"Well, *case* is a bit of a stretch," I admitted. "It's more like appeasing a grieving widow who is convinced her husband's death wasn't an accident. Said grieving widow should be calling any time now for her hourly update."

"Mrs. Evans?"

The hairs on the back of my neck prickled and stood on end. "Yes. How'd you know that?"

She shrugged. "I'm a trial junkie. I saw the name on the fax and remembered that José Vasquez was on the Hall jury. I was the one who put together the Evans notes to pass along to you for Mr. Dane last Monday. I remembered Marcus Evans was on that jury, too. So I just figured there is some sort of connection."

I decided right that second that Bad Hair Girl was a little scary, and definitely not anyone I'd want to piss off. "Good guess."

"Too bad they're both dead. Mr. Vasquez seemed like a nice man."

I was more than a little stunned. "You met him?"

"All of them," Cami admitted. "I sat in on the trial. It was the summer between my sophomore and junior year at college. I was tending bar at night, so my days were free. I was considering applying to law school, so I attended a few trials just to see if that was really what I wanted."

"How'd you meet the jurors?"

"They weren't sequestered or anything. I'd run into them at lunch or outside the courthouse during breaks. One of them, Daniel Summers, even hit on me once."

Glancing over at the boxed transcripts, I thought Cami might be my way around reading the hundred or so volumes. Hmm. Maybe she could be my personal Cliffs Notes. It was worth a shot.

"Was there anything hinky about the trial?"

Cami shook her head with conviction. "Everyone from the orderlies to the anesthesiologist present at the transplant surgery testified that Dr. Hall did everything right. Then there was a parade of witnesses from the post-op ward who insisted Brad Whitley's infection came on fast and furious. Nothing short of a miracle could have saved him."

"So why did the wife sue?"

"Grief. Sara Whitley sobbed through her whole testimony. I got the impression that she just wanted her husband's death to be someone's fault."

"Sounds a lot like Mrs. Evans." *Which means that I need to stop looking for something that isn't there.*

Cami stood, smoothing the creases from her linen skirt. "Good luck, Finley. If you ask me, the kindest thing you could do for Mrs. Evans is to tell her the truth." She pointed toward the fax on my desk. "Telling her about José Vasquez being dead will only make things worse."

Cami was probably right. The best thing I could do for Stacy was to convince her to let it go. I was just about to call the fileroom to have them retrieve the boxes when my phone rang. With my luck, it was probably the Widow Evans demanding an update. Well, I'd give her one. An honest one. It was time for her to accept that her husband's tragic accident was exactly that—an accident.

"Finley Tanner," I practically growled into the receiver.

"Wow, you're in a mood. Caffeine withdrawal?"

Hearing Patrick's voice salved my irritation. "Sorry. Hi. When did you get in?"

"Really late last night."

That explained why he hadn't called. I absently started twirling a pen between the fingers of my right hand. I began our well-practiced game by asking, "So, where'd you go this time?"

FedEx flew all over the world. Patrick never told me his itinerary. Instead he brought me thoughtful gifts from whatever countries he'd hit during his trips.

"I'm holding something you can wear and something to eat."

Just to get his blood boiling, I said, "Mmmm, I'm thinking edible panties."

"Now that you mention it, so am I," he teased, his tone dropping several seductive notches.

I was grinning now. The whole Evans mess began evaporating from my thoughts as I threw myself further into the game. I'd missed him. He was my rock, my . . . All of a sudden I had a vision of a big iron ball and chain dangling from around my neck. Was there some kind of subconscious passive-aggressive thing in me that thought of Patrick as some sort of albatross around my neck? That couldn't be right. He adored me.

I rubbed my tired eyes. "So, what's the plan?" Patrick always had a plan. Most women would find that impressive and considerate. I did, too, most of the time. Though I wouldn't have complained if he'd done the occasional spontaneous thing.

Anyway, what was the alternative? Returning to the depths of Single Hell? Pass, thanks. In my opinion, dating is a lot like interviewing for a job you don't really want but feel compelled to go after.

"Dinner and sex."

I laughed quietly. "I'm supposed to meet the girls tonight for dinner."

"You get to see them all the time," he reminded me. "Can you get out of it?"

"Sure," I said on a sigh. I knew full well that I'd get a mixture of grief and support from Becky, Liv, and Jane. I was going to break one of the cardinal

rules of girlfriendom. A last-minute ditch in favor
of a man. They'd understand, of course. They
knew Patrick and I had to work around his schedule but I'd still be charged with a misdemeanor
friendship violation.

"You should come by here first," he said. "I want
to give you your presents before dinner. I've made
reservations for seven, so you'll need to be here by
six-thirty."

I glanced at the small clock on the right-hand
corner of my computer screen. Amazingly, it was
already after one. Hard work certainly made the
time pass.

"I can do that."

"Six-thirty," Patrick repeated, knowing full well
that I had a small propensity for being late. "Six-
thirty-one and you don't get your presents."

I felt a twinge of excitement at the thought of
being with Patrick again. Knowing him, he'd made
reservations at Fendu. He knows how much I
adore their food, and the ambiance is to die for.

I spent the next half hour begging off my commitment to the girls. Then I used my lunch hour
to run to Macy's for something new to wear that
night. I found an adorable strapless black dress
and some really cute satin and rhinestone sandals
in just under forty minutes. I talked the clerk
down on the shoes because one of the stones was
missing. The dress was fifteen percent off, but only
if I opened a new Macy's account—which I did.
Like I need another Visa card, but, hey, for fifteen
percent off, it was worth the hassle of filling out
the tedious form.

I grabbed a coffee on my way back to the office,
stopping only long enough to put my purchases in

my car. Margaret issued her usual faux smile, and I felt her eyes on my back as I slipped into the elevator.

I was looking forward to my date with Patrick, and I was growing curious about my gifts. His choices are always personal—he certainly knows how to set the mood for a romantic reunion. A guy like Liam McGarrity wouldn't know how to make plans for a romantic reunion.

Where did that come from?

Libido meltdown, I decided as I returned to my office. I could make a list a mile long as to why I should put Liam in my "don't even go there" file. But something about those ice blue eyes kept drawing me back.

Putting my fantasies on hold, I sat at my desk and checked my e-mail. I nearly groaned when I saw the one from Mary Beth. She was inviting me to a scrapbooking party at her house Thursday night. Tomorrow. Shit.

After hitting REPLY, I struggled to find a polite way to tell her to kiss off. I didn't want to lie. First, I'm a terrible liar, and I'd get caught. If I said something like "I'm visiting a sick friend," Mary Beth would want details, then she'd send flowers and probably host a fund-raiser. I could try the general "other plans" excuse, but a week from now she'd inquire about those plans and I'd probably choke and forget whatever lame-ass thing I'd said.

Thing. I smiled. "Thank you, Liam," I mumbled as I typed in my reply:

Thanks, Mary Beth, but I have a thing on Thursday. Maybe next time. Regards, Finley.

The "thing" was convenient as hell. Vague but effective. One problem solved. Now on to the other thorn in my side.

Pulling out the file, I dialed Stacy Evans and felt almost giddy with relief when the call went straight to voice mail. I told her I was sorry I'd missed her and that I'd be in touch in the morning.

My e-mail dinged. It was Mary Beth, letting me know she was sorry I couldn't attend. Beneath her name was a smiley face with big tears spilling down that made a loud splat sound as they fell.

Stacking the information about José Vasquez off to one side, I went back to the D'Auria estate accounting. I ran the inventory totals a dozen times and still couldn't reconcile the numbers. I cursed, tried one last time, then reached for the phone.

Jane Spencer is more than my friend, she's an investment broker and tax analyst to boot. Jane is a walking contradiction. She's a card-carrying member of Mensa but looks more like one of the Spice Girls. Posh Spice to be exact. Tall and willowy, with long, dark hair and chocolate-colored eyes. But beneath that never-misses-a-morning-workout, funky exterior is a certifiable geek. A geek who will free me from the shackles of accounting hell.

Her assistant put me right through.

"Patrick cancelled?" she asked.

"No, I'm really sorry about tonight. As I remember, you blew off lunch yesterday."

"For work. That doesn't count."

"But since you brought up work, I need help."

I heard Jane expel a breath. "It's tax season, Finley. I'm up to my eyeballs in ten-ninety-nines. Doesn't your fancy-schmancy law firm have accountants?"

"Not wonderful ones who I let borrow my very favorite pair of Jimmy Choo shoes."

"That was a year ago," Jane said on a small laugh. "I think I've more than worked off that footwear debt."

"It's not a big thing," I insisted. "I just need you to go over some figures for me."

There was a brief pause, then she said, "Okay. I can meet you for coffee . . ." Another pause, and I knew she was flipping through her ever present Week-at-a-Glance. "Monday."

I grimaced. "It's due to the clerk of court on Friday."

"Christ, Finley, nothing like waiting until the last possible second."

"I know, I know. Please don't make me file an extension. The heirs are expecting their money, and if they don't get it, they'll complain to my boss and then I'll get fired. I'll end up homeless, with nothing to eat but government-issue peanut butter and cheese."

"No, you won't."

I relaxed. "Because my dear friend is going to help me?"

"Because the government only gives peanut butter and cheese to WIC families."

"Please?"

"Actually, peanut butter and cheese would be an improvement over your normal diet."

"Are you going to help me?"

"Yes. Meet me tomorrow morning outside the gym. I should be finished by seven."

"A-freaking-M?"

"Do you want my help or not?"

"Of course, thank you. I'll be there. I'll be the one in the slippers and jammies."

"Suck it up," Jane joked. "See you in the morning. Say hi to Patrick for me."

It was nearing quitting time, so I started packing up the estate accounting for my predawn meeting with Jane. I needed to be out the door of the office at the stroke of five. Then I'd have plenty of time to shower, shave my legs, and glue a spare rhinestone on my cute new shoes before I went to Patrick's place.

At precisely 4:59, my phone rang. It was probably Stacy Evans, and I really debated the pros and cons of answering it. The biggest con of ignoring her was the very real possibility that she'd complain to Vain Dane and my ass would end up in a sling. I'd just have to shave fast.

"Finley Tanner."

"Hi."

The sound of Liam's deep, sensuous voice tickled my ear. "H-hello."

"I've got something for you."

His voice faded in and out, and I could make out the sounds of wind and traffic. He must be on a cell. "Great. We can meet—"

"I think you're going to want to see this."

"What is it?"

"Report on the car and a pretty—" the rest of his words were unintelligible.

"You're breaking up. Are you on your way to drop it off here?"

"I've got a thing," he said.

I stifled the urge to tell him to stick his thing in his ear.

"I'll drop it by your place—"

"I'm not going to be home this evening," I cut in. I didn't tell him I had a date, but for the life of me, I didn't know why I was keeping it a secret.

"First thing in the morning, then," he countered.

"I've got an early meeting."

"I've got the stuff with me now. I'll be at the Blue Martini from six until about nine. Can you stop by?"

He left me no choice, damn it. His "thing" was at one of the biggest pickup bars in City Place? So he's a player, eh? So much for the leisurely bath. I calculated time in my head. *If I leave now, I've got just enough time to get home, shower, dress, fix my shoe, swing by the Blue Martini, and still make it to Patrick's place before six thirty-one. Maybe. Hopefully.*

Traffic screwed me. I raced into my apartment, dress and shoes in hand. Dropping my shoes on the bed, I hung the dress over the hook on the back of my bathroom door and turned on the shower. The steam would smooth any wrinkles, and right then I was in serious need of multitasking.

I fumbled around on the top shelf of my closet, finally finding my box of treasures. Because of my forced foray into the world of factory damage, I keep a box of buttons, ribbons, stones, and other assorted items for emergency repairs. Luckily, I had a rhinestone that would work. It wasn't perfect—the stone had a slight pink cast to it—but it would have to do.

My trusty glue gun—the woman's duct tape—was under the sink. I plugged it in, then found a clip for my hair while the glue stick heated. So far, so good.

I secured the stone in place, then cursed when the glue oozed on to my thumb. That was going to leave a mark.

Wounded thumb and all, I managed to shower, dress, and run a flat-iron through my hair in record time. I should have been thinking about Patrick, but, honestly, Liam's sexy voice kept running through my head. No matter how fast I went, I was running behind. I hopped from foot to foot, tugging on my sandals while I hunted down my favorite Kate Spade Wristlet bag. I spent a few extra minutes I didn't really have applying my makeup, wondering just who the hell I was trying to impress. Then I transferred my license, money, cell phone, a credit card, and my lipstick into my purse. The Kate Spade was cute, but it didn't hold all that much. It was a fashion-over-function thing, but I was fine with that.

As I went to grab my keys off the counter, I saw the light on my home phone flashing. Tempted, but no time. I'd have to grab messages later.

It was almost six when I hit the entrance ramp for I-95. I was heading back into town, so traffic on the southbound lanes was light. I made the trip in under fifteen minutes, a personal best.

The line for valet parking was six-cars long, so I doubled back and found a spot about a block west of City Place. I'd been so rushed to get out the door that I'd left my pashmina at home. Now I felt every brush of the cool night air as it danced along my bared shoulders.

The Blue Martini is on the second floor, so I climbed the stairs at a brisk pace, hearing the click of my heels against the marble steps. The sound of music blended with the din of conversation as I reached the entrance. As always, it was crowded.

Liam was easy to spot. He was leaning sideways against the bar. I allowed myself a few seconds to admire his profile before I breezed past the bouncers. I weaved through the crowd completely aware of the fact that I was garnering my fair share of admiring glances. Nothing boosts confidence like a new dress.

When I got closer, I noticed two things about Liam. First, he was wearing a great-fitting pair of black slacks paired with a tight, torso-hugging black shirt. He looked perfect. Well, as perfect as any hot guy looks with a busty blonde hanging on his arm. By the way, she was the second "thing."

It was a battle to keep my expression bland, especially when I got a decent look at his date. She was pretty in a showy way. She had on a glittery, gold halter top that left her perfectly toned back bare. Her skirt was white, short, and belted low on her hips. If she had an ounce of fat, I certainly couldn't see it, and, believe me, I was looking. Her tan was fake but perfectly applied, as was her makeup.

She's prettier than I am. Definitely better built. Liam had never actually flirted with me, and now I knew why. God, compared to her, I was a real troll. My cheeks heated, but I blamed it on the crush of bodies. Liam turned then and saw me approaching. His smile slipped fractionally, and I knew that he thought I'd taken his call as an invitation. Which made me look like a *desperate* troll. Not good, especially when, for whatever reason, his nasty, lowlife, Barbie-dating opinion mattered.

Claiming a time-management issue is just a polite way of saying I'm late and I'm always late.

Five

I'm fine. I can do this. But just in case I couldn't drum up the calm, casual demeanor I needed, I shifted the handle of my purse into my right hand. It was a handshake-avoidance trick I'd learned from the master—my mother.

Three more steps and I'd be within perfume-sniffing distance of Liam and Drinking Beer from a Long Neck Bottle Barbie.

Liam flashed me a slightly crooked smile. His teeth seemed bright white set against his deeply tanned skin. To my surprise, Beer Barbie was just as friendly. I gave her some mental props. If the situation was reversed and I thought some other woman was poaching Patrick, I'd have tossed her a chillingly polite smile while quietly planning her death.

Liam provided the introductions. "Finley Tanner, this is Ashley."

She smiled and thrust out her hand. Since I didn't have any alternative, I slid the handle of my bag up on my wrist. "Nice to meet you."

Liam grabbed a manila envelope off the bar and handed it to me. "Looks Like Marcus's car is clean," he said, leaning in so that he didn't have to yell over the cacophony of a group of men gathered at the far end of the bar. A large television screen, volume off, was showing a baseball game, and based on their comments, it wasn't going very well for the Marlins.

Beer Barbie wriggled herself closer to Liam, her warm smile never faltering. Getting up on tiptoes, she whispered something to him, then hooked her arm possessively around his waist.

Whatever it was, Liam didn't react. At least not that I saw. He has one of those faces that's impossible to read. I have a feeling he could be giddy with happiness and no one would be the wiser.

These people had history, though, that was for sure. Beer Barbie's forefinger was making tiny circles on the fabric just above Liam's waistband. Personal history. Who am I kidding? History means past, and it didn't look to me as if anyone had put a period on this relationship.

Liam tapped his finger on the tip of Ashley's nose. "I'm making this quick."

"You'd better," she said. Her pretty smile morphed into an impressive pout. "This is *our* night, remember?"

"I'm supposed to be having one of those, too," I said, waving one hand in front of my fab new dress. I didn't really care if she approved of my clothing, I just felt a childish need to prove that I, too, had a man in my life.

Truth be told, I wasn't bent on proving it to her,

really. It would have been nice if Liam had given some hint that he'd noticed. I might not have surgically enhanced boobs spilling out of a flimsy top, but I looked pretty damned good in my own tailored, fitted way. Good enough to warrant a quick once-over by half the other guys in the bar.

Self-confidence semi-restored, I finally decided that Liam liked them slutty. So be it. Just another reason to add to my growing list of reasons why he was the wrong kind of man for me. Not that he'd been offered to me, but I like to think ahead of the curve.

Liam leaned closer to me, and I got a whiff of his cologne. The classic blend of bergamot, citrus, and honey, with just a hint of coriander, amber, and moss on a base of sandalwood, leather, and cedar was easily recognizable as Hugo. It suited him. As did the lock of hair that fell forward. The only thing completely wrong with this whole picture was my almost overwhelming urge to reach out and brush the midnight-colored strands back into place. Bad, bad idea.

I didn't want to make a scene and—oh, yeah—I had no doubt that Beer Barbie could take me. Time to cut this short.

"I've got someone waiting," I said as I tucked the bulky envelope beneath my arm. I glanced at the clock. Somewhat pissed since it was already twenty-five of seven.

"Read the report, and watch that tape," Liam said. "I'll come by your office in the morning."

Even though I knew there wasn't anything on my calendar, my reply was, "Call first, okay?"

"Sure."

"Wait," Beer Barbie insisted as she dug through her Dooney and Bourke knockoff. She handed me a small stack of business cards. The graphics were nice, and the stock was heavy with a gloss finish.

"Thanks," I said, still scanning the cards in the less than perfect lighting.

The soft purple print was hard to read until I got outside. Which, as it turned out, worked pretty well for me. "Eternal Beauty," I read as I started back to my car. "Full Service Day Spa. Ashley Mc-Garrity, Owner."

McGarrity? I remembered the touching and rubbing and decided there was no way in hell Beer Barbie was his sister. Not unless they were the biggest family of perverts in South Florida. Too much touchy-feely to be cousins, either. No matter how far removed. Someone—I couldn't remember who at that second—had said Liam was divorced.

"That's one friendly freaking divorce," I grumbled as I unlocked my BMW, tossed Liam's sacred envelope on the passenger's seat, and started the engine. He might be divorced, but from what I saw, he still had an ongoing relationship with her genitalia. I guess when you look like Liam, you get vaginal visitation rights.

Okay, I'm totally in favor of sexual equality, but my support waivers with the whole "friends with benefits" thing. If I want no-strings-attached sex, I want it with a complete stranger. Not someone who called me in the middle of the night to arrange for a quickie, then calls a week later to invite me to his place for a cookout. How uncomfortable is that? If I ever get that desperate, I'll buy a vibrator to go with my DVD of Dennis Quaid in *The Big Easy.* In my opinion, the hottest seduction ever put on film.

My cell phone rang just as I was turning south

on A-1-A. It was probably Patrick calling to ask if I actually knew how to tell time.

Flipping it open, I quickly said, "I'm on my way. I had a meeting that—"

"Miss Tanner."

Stacy Evans made my name sound like a childhood disease.

"I'm sorry. I thought you were my boy—next appointment."

"No, I'm your client. The one whose calls you've been avoiding all day."

Man, this woman had a guilt-o-meter that could give my mother's a run for her money. Speaking of which, I made a mental note to meet Ricardo for the orchid-replacement ceremony.

"I've been working on your case," I insisted. "In fact, I was just with the investigator, and he's uncovered a few things."

"Such as?"

How should I know? I haven't opened the envelope because I'm on my way to have dinner and some serious sex with my boyfriend. "I don't feel comfortable sharing any specifics until I have more information." My conversation with Trena flashed through my mind. Why did she tell me about the blood samples? "Would you be willing to sign a release for the medical examiner's office?"

"A release for what?"

Please, pleeease let me explain this right. "They keep biological samples for a period of time following autopsy. I'd like to have an independent forensic lab do a more elaborate tox screen on your husband's blood."

"He wasn't drunk when the car crashed." I could hear her annoyance level increase with each syllable.

"I know that. But other things can impair a person's driving. Was your husband on any medications?"

"Just cholesterol pills, but he's been on those for years and never had any ill effects."

"No drowsiness? Nothing like that?"

"No. What are you getting at, Miss Tanner?"

"What about cold medication? Something for allergies? Anything new or out of the ordinary?"

"Not a thing. Are you suggesting that my husband took some sort of drug?"

"I'm not suggesting anything. Just trying to cover all the bases." *Do I tell her about the other dead jurors?* I thought long and hard before I said, "I've uncovered a couple of other, um, irregularities, and I just want to make sure to follow up on all the possibilities."

"I'm expecting nothing less."

I had reached the entrance to Patrick's place. "I'll call you tomorrow."

"No," Stacy countered. "I'll call you at three. Make sure you're available."

The line went dead. Apparently I was dismissed. Which didn't put me in the best frame of mind for my Patrick reunion, which should have been great, but not after that verbal spanking from Stacy. And not when I was already feeling guilty for being late.

Those weren't the only things bothering me. Thing, actually. Even as I parked and started toward the elevator, I was still haunted by the image of Liam and his ex-wife. It was just abnormal. Divorce was, by my definition, supposed to be final. Hell, my mother's were so final that by the time the ink dried on the Dissolution of Marriage papers, the ex–Mr. Stepfathers were never heard from or spoken of again.

I fluffed my hair with my fingers and reapplied gloss before reaching Patrick's floor. I took one deep, calming breath and told myself to put the day's events behind me.

Turning left off the elevators, I went to the third door on the right and knocked softly. I could hear his approaching footsteps as well as the muffled sound of his stereo through the door.

Patrick greeted me with a broad grin, then an eager kiss. Any other guy would have ragged me for being late, but not Patrick. He wasn't big on recriminations, which was just one of his many good qualities. I felt a little pang of guilt as his tongue slipped inside my mouth. He was a great guy, and lately I'd been selling him short. Liam might have zing, but Patrick had everything else.

His palms slid from my face, down over my bare shoulders, my ribcage, and eventually came to rest on my hips. His pale blue eyes scanned my face, then moved lower. The corners of his mouth curved in an appreciative smile.

I was half-tempted to reach for the buttons of his slate-colored silk shirt but knew better. Dinner first, sex second. That was the way it worked. That was the plan. Never a deviation.

"I've missed you," he said as he draped one arm around my shoulder and fitted me against him.

"Sorry about the presents thing," I said, rubbing my cheek against his chest. "I had to pick something up for work, and it took longer than expected."

"You?" he asked. "The woman who prides herself on never working an instant past five?"

Not wanting to ruin our evening, I let that little dig pass. Besides, I still hadn't gotten my presents.

Patrick led me into the combination living

room–dining room. Like the rest of his one-bedroom, it was very male. I'm really in no position to criticize since decorating my own place is still on my to-do list. Much to the utter mortification of my neighbor, Sam Carter, I still have the same black leatherette sofa I bought as a transitional piece five years ago.

Patrick's tastes were narrow. Everything—lamps, art, pillows, rugs—all of it had some sort of aviation thing going on. Okay, "art" is a stretch. Framed posters, magazine covers, and news articles about Charles Lindbergh cover three of the four walls. The only reason the fourth wall isn't Lindberghed is because of the huge picture window.

The furniture is big, masculine, and all done in flight-jacket brown. Even his dining table is brown leather. The lamp bases are little bronze airplanes. Not my taste, but, then again, our relationship hasn't progressed to the one-drawer, one-shelf point. I'm not sure if that fact is good or bad. Normally after two years in a relationship I would have at least given him one drawer in my dresser and he'd have given me one in his. Same with the bathroom. I'd keep one of those cut-yourself-shaving sticks in my medicine cabinet for him, and he'd have some feminine hygiene products handy for me. But with us? Nope, we're keeping our respective drawers to ourselves.

"Even though you were late, you can still have your presents."

As if there was ever any doubt. I smiled. "Thanks."

"Thank that dress," he teased as his hand fell away from me when he stepped around his flight case to get to the bedroom. He returned a minute later with a medium-sized box and a smaller gift bag. Both were professionally wrapped, and I recognized the logo on the bag. My heart sped. It was from my favorite chocolatier in Switzerland. The box was black, tied with a gold satin bow.

"This one first," he said, dangling the bag from his forefinger.

I liked the way his pale blue eyes sparkled as he waited patiently for me to dig past the tissue paper. "Thank you," I said, my mouth watering now that I officially owned a one-pound box of my favorite assortment of truffles.

"Now this," he said, holding another, larger box between us, relinquishing it only after I gave him a quick kiss.

Inside was a silk nightgown in my favorite shade of pink. He might fail miserably at home furnishings, but he was a regular metrosexual when it came to choosing lingerie. Pinching it at the straps, I held it up and said, "You're amazing. It's beautiful. Thank you. Want to take it for a test drive?"

"Sounds like a plan," he said, but then, crushing my hopes, "We'll do it right after dinner."

While Patrick hunted down his keys, I folded the nightgown, put it in the box, and left the box on the edge of the bed. I know I shouldn't take it personally, but I did. Patrick's remark made me feel sexually undesirable. The fact that it had been weeks since we'd last been together, coupled with a sexy new nightgown, still wasn't enough to veer him off course.

I bet Liam wouldn't have passed up that kind of offer. Hell, I thought with a frown, Liam and Beer Barbie were probably already rolling around in the sack. My mind flashed some vivid, x-rated images of Liam in bed.

Now I wasn't sure if I was pissed at Patrick for not taking the hint, or pissed at Liam for violating my thoughts without permission, or pissed at myself for, well, for just feeling pissy.

I washed away my foul mood with two glasses of pinot grigio before our main course was served. Fendu is one of those intimate places with incredible service, soft piano music, and fabulous food made even better by artistic presentation.

We had a conversation dominated mostly by Patrick's retelling of his latest hops around the globe. He was animated and passionate when he talked about flying. But I was only half listening. My thoughts kept drifting between Patrick and work. God knew *that* had never happened before.

Maybe it was just my general disinterest in the changing Atlantic air currents and/or the long monologue on wind sheer. Still, I kept going back to the three dead jurors. I was literally shocked out of my thoughts when Patrick snapped his fingers. "You're like a million miles away."

Surprised, I reached across the table and patted his hand. "Sorry. I've got this thing"—I couldn't even think the word without hearing Liam's voice in my head—"at work. It's making me a little nuts."

"Math or greedy heirs?"

I smiled. "I've got a math problem, but Jane's going to help me with that in the morning. I got a new client this week." I paused to admire the attentive expression on his handsome face.

"And that's bad?"

I shrugged my shoulders and ran my fingernail up and down on the stem of the wineglass. "It's different. She doesn't believe her husband's death was an accident."

Patrick gave a little laugh. "What does she expect you to do about it?"

"Investigate," I said, feeling suddenly defensive.

"Isn't that what cops are for?"

"She tried that. They didn't find anything worth investigating."

"So I'm back to my original question. What are you supposed to do?"

"I'm kinda learning as I go along."

"You're taking her seriously?"

"She's Dane's friend. He passed her off to me."

Patrick nodded. "Now I get it. She's some sort of nutty widow, so the great Victor Dane handed her off to you."

"Maybe." I squirmed.

"There's a possibility she's right? Really?" He raked his fingers through his neatly cut blond hair. "How did it happen?"

"Car accident."

"Isn't that by definition an accident?"

"Unless someone tampered with the brakes."

"Did this dead guy have enemies?"

I shook my head.

"A mistress?"

"No."

"Gambler?"

Okay. Patrick's unbiased perspective was making me feel less enthusiastic. "No."

"Sounds like a hell of a case. Ought to keep you really busy. Speaking of that . . ." He hesitated. "I took a quick turnaround."

I met his level gaze. "How quick?"

"I leave tomorrow midday."

"Why?"

"It's a chance for me to bank some extra downtime. If I want to go on that hiking trip this summer, I need the extra days." He pressed my hand to his mouth and gave me a whisper of a kiss. "I know I should have run this by you first, but it was a last-minute opportunity and I just couldn't say no. Not when they offered me five comp days."

Was I angry? No . . . just a little disappointed. "It's fine, really. Besides, my mother comes back this weekend. Now you'll be saved from the post-vacation Sunday brunch."

"I hate to bail on you, especially when you have mother duty."

Not wanting to think about "duty" or "plans," I opted to grab the opportunity in front of me while it was available. Casually checking the slim Liz watch with the black alligator strap I'd picked up on my last trip to Vero, I saw that I had ten, maybe twelve hours, to stock up on hormonal bliss. I offered Patrick my most sultry smile, rubbed my finger up the stem of my wineglass, and exuded pheromones. "You can make it up to me."

Patrick's head whipped around searching for our server. "Check, please."

After a quick exit from the restaurant, we hurried back to his apartment. Patrick made the ride more interesting by stroking my thigh and making wonderful little circles against my skin with the pad of his thumb.

He was the picture of control in the elevator, while I was practically thrumming. Patrick's not a big fan of public displays of affection. But I knew the second his front door closed behind us he'd have me out of my designer dress in no time flat. My upper thighs ached, and my lower belly tensed. Sex with Patrick was always physically satisfying, and my expectant body was ready for the ride.

My fingers fumbled through the buttons on his shirt. I flattened my hands against his chest, enjoying the strong beat of his heart beneath my fingertips.

Reluctantly, Patrick loosened his grip on my hips, and I stepped back ever so slightly.

My eyes roamed boldly over the vast expanse of his broad shoulders, drinking in the sight of his impressive upper body. I openly admired his powerful thighs and washboard-perfect abs. My mouth watered. "My self-control is about to go right out the window," I said, liking the way his eyes darkened, really loving the anticipation building between us. My stomach fluttered.

Protected in the circle of his arms, I closed my eyes and allowed my cheek to rest against his chest. I could forget everything. Marcus Evans, Vain Dane, José Vasquez, Graham Keeler, and even Liam McGarrity for a few more hours. Forget everything but the comfort of being with him.

His fingers danced over the outline of my spine, leaving a trail of electrifying sensations in their wake. Passion flourished and blossomed from deep within me, filling me quickly with frenzied desire.

But I knew the rules. Patrick had a thing about specific, deliberate pacing. What I really wanted to do was bypass all the foreplay and get right to the good stuff.

Then he moved the tip of his finger across my taut nipple and for a split second I couldn't think anymore. Except maybe to consider begging when he stopped.

Patrick moved his hand in a series of slow, sensual circles until it rested against my ribcage, just under the swell of my breast. Tilting my head back, I wanted to see carnal passion in his eyes. They were certainly a darker shade of blue, but was that enough?

I'd bet my best La Perla panties that Liam McGarrity's eyes smoldered when he was in the throes of passion. God, I had to stop this. Comparing Patrick and Liam was like comparing a Jaguar to a Volvo. Both excellent cars, but only one had a proven reputation for dependability.

Patrick was trailing warm kisses along the side of my jaw. That brought me back to the present. His lips moved to cover mine. His mouth was warm and pressed urgently against me. My arms slid around his waist, pulling him closer.

He whispered my name as he reached out to trace the outline of my lips, then led me into his bedroom. The pink satin nightgown was still in the box. I'm sure he wanted me to slip into it, but I was feeling too impatient for a fashion show.

"Next time," I promised him as I pulled off my sandals. Then came the clothes, mine in a heap on the floor, Patrick's neatly folded over the edge of his desk chair.

Patrick yanked down the comforter and began showering my face and neck with kisses as soon as we hit the mattress. His mouth searched for that sensitive spot at the base of my throat. A pleasurable moan spilled from his mouth when I began running my palms over the tight muscles of his stomach.

Capturing both of my hands in one of his, Patrick gently held them above my head. The position makes my back arch and is a particular favorite of his.

"This isn't playing fair," I told him. "You should let me do it to you. Maybe we could buy some of those padded handcuffs or something?"

His answer was warm but dismissive.

"Believe me, it's better for both of us if I don't let you keep touching me," he said with a smile and a kiss.

I responded by lifting my body to him. The

rounded swell of one exposed breast brushed his arm. His fingers closed over the peaked fullness.

"My turn," I insisted.

"Not yet," he whispered as he ignored my futile struggle to release my hands as he dipped his head to kiss the raging pulse point at my throat.

I felt my skin growing hotter and hotter as he released my wrists and worked his mouth lower and lower. My fingers twined in his hair as my insides started to boil. I choked out a small gasp when his mouth found that magic little spot. It was only a matter of seconds before my body exploded in a million little shards of orgasmic bliss.

Patrick slid up my body and kissed my cheek as he reached into the nightstand and took out a condom. With that accomplished, he thrust inside me. I lifted my hips and bracketed my hands at his waist. He kept the rhythm of our lovemaking at a slow, deliberate pace. I nibbled the side of his neck until I felt his body convulse.

I've never been great at the postcoital chitchat thing. "Ohhh, baby, that was fabulous" just isn't me. Likewise, "Thanks, that was great" feels hookerish, like there should be a hundred waiting for me on the dresser.

I was toying with the soft hairs on Patrick's chest and listening to the even rhythm of his heartbeat. I should have been content, but I was feeling a little guilty. Was it cheating if you thought of another man before sex? During? It had been all Patrick, all me, just like always, but before . . .

My heart skipped, and I sat halfway up, propped on one elbow. "Hey, do you mind, uh, being an impartial party?"

I immediately saw concern in his eyes. "What's up?"

Guilt. I strangled it in favor of work, which I never realized was such a handy emotional scapegoat. "Just the juror thing, do you mind?" He shook his head no and got more comfortable while I ran through the sketchy details of the juror's deaths.

He was quiet for a minute, then asked, "You told the widow you'd run blood tests without knowing if there even is a blood test beyond what the medical examiner's office does?"

"Sure. Trena said they only check for alcohol levels and run-of-the-mill drugs. What if Marcus Evans was given some sort of 'exotic' potion that caused him to wreck his car?"

Patrick bit his lower lip and joked, "When did you turn into McGruff the Crime Dog?"

"I'm *just* doing my job," I said, rolling away from him before I gave in to the strong temptation to smother him with an embroidered airplane pillow.

"Hey, sweetie, this is obviously stressing you out. *'Your job'* is filing papers and distributing money to beneficiaries. Isn't solving crimes a little beyond your skill set?"

So much for the magical glow of spent passion, or sneaking in another session before he left again. I began snatching my clothes up off the floor. "I've got to go."

"Fin, honey, I'm sorry." He got out of bed and gently closed his hand over my wrist. "I didn't mean that the way it sounded. Stay. Spend the night. I promise I'll make it up to you."

My satiated body wasn't willing to give in. "I've got an early meeting," I said, placing a half-hearted kiss on his cheek.

His lips twitched, and amusement danced in his eyes. "In an old abandoned building where you knock three times, then say Leo sent you?"

I pulled my wrist free and got dressed, ignoring Patrick's volley of jokes and apologies. I couldn't exactly blame him. It wasn't like I'd ever taken my job particularly seriously before now.

Patrick and I parted on okay terms. Basically, I was okay with the fact that he'd been an asshole. He'd be gone for a week or so, and I knew from experience that I'd be over it by then. Besides, I had a month's worth of truffles to help me through it.

In fact, by the time I got home, I already had rescheduled the week ahead, minus my boyfriend. Normally, I would have tried on my new nightgown immediately, but instead, I changed into some comfy Victoria PJs and opened the envelope Liam had given me.

There were about twenty pages of Marcus Evans's financial statements. Bottom line, the family had several million dollars in assets. At least on paper. "Okay, Liam, if there's a clue here, it's lost on me. Don't you own a highlighter?"

Slipping the video out of the envelope, I took it over to the machine, inserted it, and hit PLAY.

It was black-and-white and really poor quality. Certainly not anything like the old *Friends* tapes I can't throw away. There was no sound, just a time-and-date stamp on the bottom corner. It took me several minutes before I realized what I was watching. It was some sort of surveillance video. My guess was that it was from an ATM. When it ended, I moved closer to the set, rewound the tape, and played it again.

Then it hit me. This footage was from the day Marcus Evans had died. Assuming the time stamp was right, it covered from 7:16 to 8:16 the morning of the accident. "What am I supposed to see?" I asked, growing frustrated. None of the faces of the people using the machine were even remotely familiar.

I watched the tape a third and fourth time, and still nothing. My eyes hurt, and I was really tired. Maybe a jolt of caffeine would help.

I pulled a bag of Starbucks coffee from the freezer and had my second ah-ha! moment. Jogging back into the living room, I rewound the tape and started it from the beginning. The ATM was in a parking lot, and its lens coned out for a wider view of the parking area.

Directly across from the bank was a Starbucks. Using the remote, I went frame by tedious frame through the tape until exactly 7:46. I froze the picture on the screen. Though it was small, I could easily see that the man seated alone at the front table sipping a coffee was Marcus Evans.

I quelled the urge to call Patrick to tell him to kiss my McGruff McAss. Instead, I continued my slow-motion film fest. Every now and then the view was obstructed by someone using the automated teller machine. Then I saw it. Kind of. Someone— tall, lean, baseball hat, T-shirt, and jeans—bumped Marcus's table. Coffee spilled. They appeared to be talking to one another, but I couldn't see what happened for a few minutes because some techno-challenged guy spent the better part of two minutes trying to withdraw cash. His image practically filled the screen, and by the time he walked away, Marcus was alone again, sipping coffee and un-folding a newspaper.

"Something is different," I mumbled as I re-wound the tape to the point just before the person bumped the table. I smiled and felt a surge of excitement. I'd found my first clue.

*Multitasking is the ability
to screw several things up at once.*

Six

Dragging ass didn't even begin to describe the way I felt as I leaned against the brick wall outside the gym waiting on Jane. The strap of my rarely used briefcase dug into my shoulder. Between the D'Auria estate stuff, the Evans financials, and the videotape, I felt—and probably looked—like a sherpa.

I sipped coffee from my travel mug, tapping my very cold foot. The temperature hovered in the low sixties—arctic, to my way of thinking. Shifting the briefcase to my other shoulder, I watched the sky beginning to lighten. Only fishermen and fitness junkies were up this early in the morning. Surely there was some sort of fish that slept in and the whole reason the gym stays open until midnight is so people don't have to start their workouts at o-dark-thirty.

My eyes felt scratchy from lack of sleep, and even though I'd showered, dressed, and applied full makeup, I desperately wanted to be back in my nice warm bed. This whole "taking my job seriously" thing wasn't working too well.

I checked my watch. "Damn," I grumbled. With all the Evans stuff, I'd forgotten to check on my eBay bid. The thought that I might be the high bidder on the Rolex box improved my mood considerably.

Glancing down, I admired the light reflecting off my Enzo peep-toe pumps. The bronze leather-and-suede wedgies were really comfortable, and I'd picked them up off the clearance table at Dillard's a few weekends earlier. My Carolina blue dupioni jacket and complementary print skirt with handkerchief hem—also outlet bargains—didn't offer much in the way of warmth.

Several cars pulled into the lot. Mostly men in them, mostly with necks the size of tree trunks. Almost to a one, they wore shorts and wife-beater T-shirts and carried huge nylon bags, big enough to stuff a dead body in. Shivering, I ignored them all, despite the appreciative glances sent my way. I wasn't there to make friends. In fact, if Jane didn't get her toned fanny out here soon, I'd have to consider crossing her off my friend list. Right after she fixed my accounting error.

"Hey," Jane greeted me energetically as she came around the corner. "Sorry. Lost track of time on the elliptical machine."

So why couldn't I just hate her and be done with it? Probably because I, being a fabulous friend, knew how much time she put into her gorgeous self. By the time she was done, the effort appeared effortless. Jane was beautifully dressed in a very short black skirt and very tight black blouse. A jeweled silver and turquoise drop belt cinched her slender hips, swaying with each deliberate step she took. Her steps had to be deliberate. The heels on her leather ankle boots were at least four inches high. A few strands of her chocolate brown hair was tousled like always, and like always, it suited her sex-kittenish look.

I rattled my empty travel mug at her. "Coffee. I need coffee."

Jane smiled. "When do you not need coffee? Let me get my purse out of my trunk, then we'll walk over to Bailey's and get your fix. You're a coffee junkie."

Her rev-up-and-go thing is exercise, while mine is Mocha Java. After all these years of friendship, we still make the same teasing jabs. I glanced at her hair. "For someone who worked out for the last hour, you don't look all skanky and sweaty. What do you really do in there? Get a facial?"

"Ha, ha." She smacked her thin thigh, which, of course, didn't dare jiggle. "This takes work."

Jane's naturally wavy hair was twisted into a loose ponytail. On anyone else, it would have looked like I'm-going-to-the-grocery-store-and-can't-be-bothered. But on her, it looks hot in a casual kind of way.

"You win. If I were to do that I could start an earthquake."

Laughing, Jane said, "Join me. I can get you a fifty-percent-off membership." She's not much taller than I am, maybe an inch or two, but her FM heels allowed her to tower over me.

"Never! God, last night didn't go well," I told her abruptly, going on to recap my less-than-perfect reunion with Patrick.

"At least you got some good sex out of it, right?"

I shrugged. We were getting close enough to

the coffee shop for the scent to quicken my pace. The smell of freshly brewed coffee was like a tractor beam, especially if I'm vertical before the sun has fully breached the horizon.

Jane got a fat-free, sugar-free, fun-free coffee while I opted for the deluxe, highest-possible-calorie-count latte with whipped cream. We took a table near the back, knowing the place would start to fill up as the morning progressed.

A good friend helps you with an estate accounting. A *great* friend simply does it for you. Jane was a great friend. What had taken me literally days and worn a small callus on my thumb without any success to show for my efforts took Jane just under fifteen minutes.

Tapping the tip of her red pen against the spreadsheet, she said, "You transposed the last two numbers for this account."

"I figured it was something simple and stupid."

Jane's brow furrowed. It could furrow now since it had been four months since her last Botox injection. "Don't beat yourself up. It was an easy thing to miss."

I stuffed the D'Auria papers back into my briefcase and debated whether or not to show Jane the Evans financials. Hell, why not. "What are these?"

Jane sipped her why-bother coffee as her dark eyes perused the documents Liam had stuffed in with the videotape. I went up for a refill and a couple of cranberry muffins, returning to the table to find Jane relaxing against her seatback.

Finally some answers, and a person who could explain them to me in a language I'd understand. "So, what does all that stuff mean?"

"Marcus and Stacy Evans are modestly loaded. Most of the big-ticket assets—primary residence in

Jersey, vacation home in Cape Cod, and the condo in Palm Beach—are joint. Marcus retained an interest in the jewelry store in New York and a trust for his grandchildren's educations. Checking, savings, and a few CDs at the Bank of South Florida."

A small bell went off in my head. My meager checking account was at BSF; maybe that's why it struck a chord.

Jane continued on, flipping through the pages. "In the last few years the generous bastard donated more than twenty percent of his retirement income to various charities. How come I never meet guys like him?"

I was a little disheartened. I guess part of me half hoped she'd find something sinister. Anything. "Basically you're telling me this stuff is useless?"

"Depends on what you're looking for. He wasn't cheating on his taxes, at least not based on these records. I'd need more information than these summary sheets to be sure. Why?"

"Three jurors who sat in on a malpractice trial have died in the last few months. Marcus Evans was one of them."

Jane's face registered interest. "You're working on a murder? Wow, how cool is that?"

"It would be cool, except that other than the Widow Evans, I'm the only one who thinks something is weird here. Even Patrick mocked me."

"Patrick the Great?" she asked, dramatically pressing the back of her hand to her head. "I'm stunned. Finley, he's a fantasy boyfriend. He's kind, never forgets a birthday or other special occasion, and the big plus—he's gone a lot. It's like you're single with a safety net. Too bad he doesn't have a clone."

Was it like being single? No, single was single. I was in a committed relationship. Well, semi-committed, at least.

She picked at the crusty top of the muffin. Everyone knows the top of the muffin is the only part worth eating, and Jane was no exception. "When did you switch gears?"

"From?"

"Estates to investigations?"

I shrugged. "Three dead jurors is a little coincidental, don't you think?"

"Statistically speaking, it's improbable." Jane stood and began clearing the table. "Of course, any statistical analysis would change based on variables such as how and when the individuals died."

"You are such a math geek," I said with a groan.

Jane smiled. "Which didn't bother you in the least a few minutes ago when you needed help with accounting."

"That's true. Thanks, Jane. I'll even forgive you for having better thighs than me."

I walked Jane back to the parking lot of her gym. I didn't have enough time to go home, so for the second time in a week, I was early for work. Earlier even than Margaret, a fact that should have given me great pleasure, but didn't. It felt strange, like maybe I was beginning a new bad habit. Like the time I'd tried soy lattes so I could be healthier. That only lasted a week.

My mind, usually free to be distracted, was totally preoccupied with the Evans matter. Jane was right, I needed something more concrete than jury duty, medically certified accidents, a grainy videotape, and a grieving widow. And a suspicious tingle in the pit of my stomach.

That meant I had to read the trial transcripts.

Where was Cami when I needed her? Since I was the first one in, I flipped on the light switches as I made my way to my office. I didn't feel particularly excited when I looked at the massive tower of white cardboard boxes. Still, I dove in bravely, knowing it was a necessary evil.

By ten o'clock, I'd consumed two pots of coffee and read the plaintiff's portion of the transcripts. Well, *"read"* was a bit of an overstatement. There was some definite skimming involved. And a few breaks just to rest my eyes and keep my brain from going completely numb. *Work* was definitely a four-letter word.

I'd flagged a few pages, things I needed to research or clarify, starting with the Internet. And, since I'd busted butt for hours already, I figured a small detour wouldn't hurt. Too much work and not enough time on eBay lost me the bid I'd had going on the Rolex box. Since I was already there, I searched for new listings and found another one, and while it was in good condition, it wasn't excellent, so I bid accordingly. I also found two more band links and bid on those as well.

Hell, while I was at it, I checked for any new Betsey Johnson designs and found an adorable, flirty blue chiffon vintage dress in my size. It was a little pricey, especially when I converted the Euros to dollars, and the shipping charges were a bitch, but it was a Betsey and it could be mine—assuming I didn't get outbid—in four days for about seventy bucks.

Shopping needs met, I decided to get some background on the medical witnesses who'd testified on Hall's behalf. I knew they had to be top-notch and expensive. Money always favors the defendant. Lots of money—the kind Hall had at his disposal—almost guarantees a favorable verdict. But that didn't mean he committed malpractice during or after the transplant. If he had done something wrong, he probably would have settled out of court. That was the smart move. The safe one.

The first witness was Dr. Carlton Peterman. His curriculum vitae was a zillion pages long, with enough commendations, awards, and certifications to qualify for sainthood. As Brad Whitley's primary cardiologist, his testimony was pretty persuasive. Especially the part about the infection being a known and foreseeable complication of the transplant that he had personally explained to Brad and his wife, Sara.

The other expert was from Johns Hopkins, the mecca of western medicine. While Dr. Zorner wasn't even present for the surgery, he was emphatic that Hall had done a stellar job. His credentials made the first guy look like a slacker.

Rubbing my forehead, I closed my eyes and reviewed what I knew to be true.

(A) Brad Whitley needed a heart transplant or he was going to die.

(B) The donor, Ivy Novak, had suffered massive head injuries as a result of a motorcycle accident, and once she'd been pronounced brain-dead by the neurologist on call, and Dr. Hall, her organs were harvested.

(C) Every expert, as well as the entire transplant team, testified that Hall performed the operation to perfection.

(D) The postop infection and not some surgical blunder caused Brad Whitley's death.

(E) Three of twelve jurors had died within
    weeks of one another. All of the deaths were
    ruled accidental by the M.E.

"The trial was three years ago," I mused aloud.
"Who would wait that long to seek revenge?" Assuming they really were murdered, and assuming the
motive really was revenge. "The only person with
motive is Sara Whitley."

I smelled Liam's cologne, and my eyes flew
open. He was standing in my doorway. God, he was
gorgeous.

"Morning." He walked in and sat across from
me. "I guess the tape I gave you pretty much puts
Stacy Evans's murder theory to bed."

*Speaking of that, did Beer Barbie put you to bed last
night?* How lame was I? "If that's what you think,
you're a pretty crappy investigator."

One corner of his mouth curved into a crooked
and incredibly sexy half-smile. "Seems to me that
tape proves Mr. Evans was just fine less than an
hour before the accident. *Accident* being the operative word."

"Fine *and* drinking coffee," I pointed out, wanting to win something—anything—to gain the
upper hand. "Who nods off at the wheel twenty
minutes after a caffeine hit?"

He looked bored instead of impressed. "Maybe
he had decaf."

I scoffed. "Drinking decaf in the morning is as
stupid as ordering a Virgin Mary at happy hour.
Besides, didn't you notice the coffee switch?"

"I noticed someone accidentally spilling his coffee. Then the view was obscured so, no, I don't
know that there was a switch."

"Then come with me," I said as I grabbed up the tape and headed for the elevator. "I take it you don't frequent Starbucks?"

"I'm more of a 7-Eleven kind of guy," he answered.

The elevator compartment seemed to shrink with him at my side. The scent of his cologne, the way he held his hands lightly fisted at his sides, all of it came together in a pretty impressive package. One that was guaranteed to blow up in my face. Gulping, I kept my eyes fixed on the number pad, truly afraid I might suffer a sexual psychotic break, yank the emergency STOP button, and jump him right there, before we ever reached the fourth-floor conference room. What *was* my problem?

The conference room was empty. It was also fully equipped, and normally reserved for depositions and other events the firm wanted to memorialize. I'd videotaped a few grumpy, bitter old women who wanted the satisfaction of telling their descendants from the grave that they weren't going to get a penny of their money. Bitter, I discovered as I observed the hearers' faces, could be an inherited trait. Then again, I'm not sure I'd take it well if I found out my relative was leaving several million to a foundation dedicated to saving some obscure swamp bird instead of bailing me out of debt.

I arranged two of the custom leather seats in front of the monitor, almost a foot apart so there would be no accidental touching, then went into the anteroom and inserted Liam's ATM tape into the machine.

He didn't bother to hide his opinion that this was a complete waste of time. I fast-forwarded through to the part with Marcus at the table.

"See?" I said, my enthusiasm building as I shined

the laser pointer toward the screen. "Marcus is there, minding his own business, drinking a grande." I redirected the pointer to track the grainy figure as it came into frame. "Here's mystery klutz. Then the table bump."

Liam sighed. "You do know I've watched this, right?"

Ignoring his question, I waited for the ATM-challenged guy to get out of the way, then I aimed my trusty pointer at the screen. "There! See it?"

"Sure, Marcus got more coffee."

"That," I said triumphantly, "is a venti."

"So?"

"In primo coffeeland, you don't change sizes in mid-beverage. You might—and that's a big might—go from a large to a medium or even a small. But I've never known anyone to do the opposite. What if the person intentionally knocked over his coffee, then replaced it with a cup that was spiked with—whatever you spike a drink with? It's possible, right?"

"On an episode of *CSI*, sure."

I glared at him. "There are things—drugs—that don't show up in a standard screen. I read a little bit about it on the Internet."

"A little information can be a dangerous thing."

Ignoring his cynicism, I clicked off my laser. "That," I said, "is where you come in. I got permission from Stac—"

Cami popped her head in. "Hi, Finley. Sorry to interrupt."

Though her comment was directed at me, Cami's eyes and attention were glued to the man next to me. I was fairly sure she wasn't the least bit sorry she'd interrupted us. She came in, extending her hand, using it like a Liam-directed divining rod. "I'm Cami Hunnicutt."

"Liam McGarrity."

"I, um, well," she stammered as if English was no longer her native language.

"Need something?" I was tempted to laser her right in the middle of her forehead.

She blinked twice and relinquished Liam's hand and reluctantly looked in my direction. "Yes. I need you to cc Mr. Dane on tomorrow's billing sheet. Margaret mentioned that you've been putting in some extra hours and—"

Keeping my voice coolly professional, I answered, "Not a problem."

"What's with the tape?" she asked.

Her interest in the video was such crap. It didn't take a genius IQ to know that Cami was doing a serious Liam scope-out. Or that I was jealous.

"Part of the Evans investigation," I said.

"Really?"

"No," Liam answered.

Thanks a lot, pal. I love feeling like a fool. "I meant the Evans estate," I corrected. "Is there anything else you need?" *Before you fall to his feet and beg to bear his children?*

"I'll tell Mr. Dane to expect your billing and expense sheets."

After she left, Liam asked, "Are they afraid you'll pad the bill because Mrs. Evans is loaded?"

Men. He had no clue he'd just been checked out and tagged as prime dating material. Well, considering his attitude, maybe he was so used to it, it just didn't faze him anymore. "Who knows. I'll need your charges to date. Can you fax them to me by tomorrow afternoon?"

"To date?" he asked. "Aren't we finished here?"

I shook my head. "I need you to get Marcus's blood sample from the M.E.'s office. Stacy will sign the release when she gets back from New Jersey. If I can swing it, I'll need the same thing on José Vasquez's blood sample." *Assuming I can get the widow to agree,* I thought, tapping the laser against my palm. "Maybe Graham Keller's bloodwork, too, though I'm not sure they did an autopsy on him, so I'll have to get back to you on that. I want everything tested by a reputable lab."

"You know you're wasting money and my time, right?"

"I'm only doing what the client instructed me to do." *And what my boss pretty much told me not to.* Who did I really work for? God, there was that word again!

"Your call." He checked his watch. "It's time for lunch."

Professionalism flew out the window, and my stomach tightened. I think I even forgot to breathe. *Ask me.*

He stood. "I'll talk to you after I get the test results."

Maybe I should ask him to lunch. Yeah, a casual "we both have to eat" kind of thing. An innocent business lunch. Who am I kidding? I haven't had an innocent thought about this guy since I first laid eyes on him.

"What about the car?" I asked, not wanting him to leave. "Any word from your expert?"

He shook his head. "It'll take him at least another week. He's got to take the car apart."

"What about this tape? Can it be enhanced?"

"Maybe," he hedged as we headed toward the door. "I think you're making too much of this."

He was probably right, but I wasn't ready to give up just yet. Liam followed me back to my office. I wanted to make a copy of the stuff Trena had faxed over from the M.E.'s office.

To my surprise and delight, two dozen pink roses were waiting for me. They also reminded me that I needed to meet Ricardo at my mother's place, for the orchid thing, after work.

Plucking the card from the tines nestled among the fragrant flowers, I read the simple message: *Thinking about you.* Romantic, but not. That was Patrick.

Behind me, Liam whistled softly. "You must've rocked someone's world last night."

I felt my cheeks get warm. I was half pissed at him for reading over my shoulder. The other half of me wanted to childishly stick out my tongue and say, "I got some too, buddy. And it was good."

"Well, if it isn't Oliver Stonette," Becky remarked when I ran into her at the vending machines around two-thirty.

"Screw you," I replied cheerily. "And what is that supposed to mean?"

"You met with the investigator again," she said as she pulled her Moon Pie from the bottom tray of the machine.

"So?"

"So," Becky said, her voice dropping to a near whisper as she pulled me into the vacant employee lounge. "The senior partners are freaking out."

"Why?"

"This firm is still on retainer to Dr. Hall. Between his personal and professional interests, he brings in big bucks."

"It's not like I'm working pro bono for Stacy Evans. She's a paying client, too."

"A probate client," Becky corrected. "Christ, Finley, the way I hear it, you're about to retry the malpractice case. A case Victor successfully defended, remember?"

"I'm not doing that." *Much.* "I've read most of the transcripts. There's no evidence that Hall committed malpractice. I'm starting to think that maybe Sara Whitley is exacting revenge on the jurors who exonerated the man she believes negligently caused her husband's death."

Becky sighed heavily. "After all this time? C'mon, no one has that kind of patience."

"I'll know Saturday."

"You? Working on a Saturday? Who are you, and what have you done with the real Finley?"

"I have a ten-thirty appointment with her."

"Who? Sara? To do what? Waltz into her house and ask her if she's a killer? That's your plan?"

"Actually, I do have a plan. A widow plan. I've arranged meetings tomorrow with Rosita Vasquez and Martha Keller."

Becky raked her fingers through her hair. "I don't have a good vibe about this."

"I don't have a choice," I insisted. "I need Mrs. Vasquez to sign a release so I can get José's blood sample from the M.E.'s office." I frowned, still unsure what to do about Keller. Maybe there was some blood drawn at the ER the night he died.

"I think you're getting in over your head," Becky warned.

"Any ideas on what it takes to exhume a body?"

"Yeah. A backhoe and a couple of beefy guys with shovels."

If you don't have anything nice to say . . . lie.

Seven

I was a little surprised that I didn't hear from
Patrick before his flight left. Technically I guess I
did hear from him, I decided, breathing in the fragrant scent of the roses adorning my desk. Suffering an attack of relationship paranoia, I wondered
if this was the beginnings of the dreaded Slow
Withdrawal. Could this possibly be phase one of
him dumping me? If so, I needed a plan. It's always better to be the dumper than the dumpee.
God, I hate this shit.

No, no, no. I was being silly. Patrick was too
sweet, too kind to break up with me without telling
me first. He was way too considerate to play mind
games. If he thought there were problems between us, he'd offer suggestions to fix it. Not send
me two dozen brace-yourself-bitch roses.

Luckily, Stacy Evans called, pulling me out of
my whole "dating sucks" downward spiral. To say
she was thrilled with my progress was an under-

statement. She gushed enthusiasm—as much as an elderly tight-ass is capable of gushing—while I went over my discoveries to date.

"I'll contact the authorities as soon as I get back tomorrow."

"I wouldn't advise that quite yet," I cautioned.

"Why not? The police should arrest Sara Whitley for my husband's murder." Almost as an after-thought, she added, "And killing those other people."

"Suspicions aren't probable cause for an arrest," I explained, impressed that I even remembered that tenet of criminal law. I'd only taken the one required course needed for my degree.

"Shouldn't she at least be questioned?"

This wasn't going well. "Yes. Of course. But first we need to establish that your husband's death was a murder."

"How much longer will that take?"

I tucked my hair behind my ear and leaned back in my chair, trying not to let the woman's impatience get to me. "First, I have to have the blood sample analyzed, and it will help if I can get the other two families on board."

"Shall I call them?"

"Let's just wait and see how my meetings go. Incidentally, did your husband go out for coffee often?"

"Every morning," Stacy said, her voice holding a hint of sadness. "It was part of his ritual."

Rut, I thought, but kept that to myself. A lot of older folks fall into patterned behavior. It seems to magnify with people post-retirement. Especially in Florida, the home of Ten-Percent-Tuesday. I envied the gray-heads who got an extra discount once a week from Dillards, even on sale merchandise. It wasn't fair. Most of them had enough disposable income to pay full retail. Hell, maybe I should get a wig and some orthopedic shoes and give it a try. Ten percent is ten percent.

"Finley!" Stacy yelled in my ear.

"Sorry," I mumbled. "Could you repeat that?"

"I *said*, I never understood why he went to Starbucks when we always had perfectly good coffee at home. A waste of time and money."

Glancing down at my trash can, I counted no fewer than four paper travel cups with the familiar green Coffee Haven logo. Then I did the math. Cripe, I had a twenty-, maybe thirty-dollar-a-day habit. At this rate, I'd need an intervention. Or a second job. Soon.

"So he went every day, at the same time?" I asked.

"You could set your watch by it."

Stacy spent the better part of the next thirty minutes grilling me about the questions I planned to ask the other widows before she gave me her return-flight information. To her credit, she also added a "job well done, Finley" before hanging up.

So, she was over calling me "Miss Tanner?" Were we bonding? No, she was just placated. For now.

Confirming Marcus's coffee habit was my second clue. I was almost giddy—which rarely happens— when I created a new document on my computer. Completely lacking imagination, I named the file *clues* and added the confirmed information.

Okay, time for another admission. I love *Court TV.* Not the trials; they're usually a big yawn. The forensics shows are a whole other thing. I'm particularly fond of *Body of Evidence.* Dayle Hinman. She's smart, attractive, and trained to profile the worst of the worst. She's also a local girl—kinda. She's in northern Florida, which, in my opinion, doesn't really count as Florida. They have winter. With frost and everything.

Anyway, her voice was in my head, reminding me that people with predictable schedules were easy targets. Whoever—The Widow Whitley, in all likelihood—killed Marcus—okay, I didn't have actual proof he was murdered, but I was going with it—must have followed him. Memorized his routine and came up with her plan.

A pretty good one, too. Follow him to Starbucks, accidentally knock over his drink, then replace it with another one containing . . . what? Hopefully, the blood panel would answer that question. I'm not exactly a walking encyclopedia on poisons.

Waiting's not my strong suit. Come to think of it, I'm not good with a lot of "w" verbs: walking, waiting, working. Though I was getting better at the working part. I was the one who'd noticed the error on the videotape. Not too shabby, considering this was my first real investigation. Maybe I should celebrate with another latte.

Liv called me just as I was about to leave for the day. She was pulling together a last-minute girls'-night-out in Delray. Becky and Jane were game, and I readily agreed. My newfound commitment to my job had ebbed after such a long day. An evening with my friends was just what I needed.

We agreed to meet around seven o'clock at our favorite bookstore, Murder on the Beach. It's an amazing shop, complete with big, comfy chairs and a fabulous staff. The owner, Joanne, hosts all sorts of events, reading groups, and fun-themed parties. Liv's working with her on a mystery weekend party, which means the girls and I get to hit Boston's, one of my absolute favorite restaurants.

Before I could detox, I had to meet Ricardo at

my mother's place. I did, using the photos stored on my cell phone to make sure each obscenely overpriced replacement orchid was in its proper place. If it wasn't, I'd hear about it at the Mandatory Mother Brunch on Sunday.

Mom insists we share brunch after she returns from every trip. It's not sharing so much as a debriefing and degrading session. I'd get a blow-by-blow of her travel exploits, followed by blows in general. "Finley, you're not living up to your potential." "Finley, why hasn't Patrick asked you to marry him yet?" "Finley, why can't you be more like your sister?" Just the thought of it made my stomach clench.

I went home and surveyed my closet, finally settling on a pair of soft pink capris and a Marc Jacobs wool polo in dark gray. Normally not one of my better colors, but thanks to a small—and easily repairable—snag in the open-lace stitching, I'd gotten it at a deep, deep discount. Well, deep for a Marc Jacobs. I'm still lusting over a pair of shoes from his spring collection, but I'll need to pay down some of my credit-card balances before that's even a remote possibility. I completed my ensemble with a gemstone belt and cork wedge sandals from Rack Room.

After switching back to my pink Chanel purse, I realized the message light on my phone was still flashing. A glance at the digital clock on the microwave told me I had a few minutes to check my voice mail. I grabbed the handset and punched in my passcode.

Two from my neighbor, Sam Carter. The first message asked me to call him because he had something important to ask me. Sam's definition of "important" and my definition of "important" are worlds apart. I could only guess at the pressing matter, but I was afraid it had something to do with my apartment. More specifically, my decor or lack thereof. Every time he enters my apartment, he cringes. He firmly believes my faux leather sofa is an abomination and claims he gets hives just looking at it.

What is it about gay men that makes them such good friends? The answer came to me instantly— unlike straight men, they actually listen. I can, and have, told Sam many of my secrets, cried on his shoulder, and huddled in a god-awful shelter with him during three hurricanes.

In his next message, "important" had morphed into "urgent." I made a mental note to return his call. We are pretty close, and I really do adore him.

Then, three hang-ups. Scrolling through Caller ID, I discovered the numbers were blocked, and I silently consigned all telemarketers to hell.

It takes just over a half hour to get from my place to Delray Beach. *If* you take I-95, which I didn't. The turnpike is a little out of the way but a much easier drive. I can bypass the never-ending construction delays and cruise at an average speed of seventy-five without worrying about a ticket. Plus, there's a Starbucks in the West Palm Beach Service Plaza. That fact alone is worth the price of a Sunpass.

Even though the sun had set, it was still warm enough for me to open the sunroof. I'd purposely done my hair half up and half down. Boston's sits right on the beach, so the mussed look was way more practical than battling the hair-flattening effects of ocean breezes.

I took the Atlantic Avenue exit and headed east, downing the last of my vanilla Frappuccino as I saw flashing red lights up ahead. I have really bad train karma. The red-and-white striped arm guarding the railroad tracks lowered just as I reached the crossing. Like all true Floridians, I shifted my car into PARK while I was forced to wait for the train to chug by. And, like every other native, I counted the freight cars as they passed just to kill the time.

One hundred sixteen mostly graffitied boxcars later, the bells stopped flashing and ringing and the caution arm raised. "About freaking time," I muttered as I put my car back into DRIVE.

I arrived at the shop a mere ten minutes late. Not bad. Becky and Jane were sitting in the reading area of Murder on the Beach. Liv was at the back of the store talking with the owner. Since I was a semi-regular, Joanne waved to me.

I took the vacant chair next to Jane. We exchanged hellos, then Jane said, "Liv needs to finish up. I'm starving."

"Me too." I hadn't had any real food all day. Unless you count peanut M&Ms. Which I frequently do.

Becky was flipping through an autographed copy of the latest Edna Buchanan novel. "I'll take this one, too," she decided, adding it to the small stack on the table next to her.

I chatted with Jane while Becky paid for her purchases and Liv finalized the details for the party. Ten minutes later we were walking down Pineapple Grove Way. The walking part was Jane's idea. I would have gone with the valet-parking option, but I got outvoted. With the exception of Liv, we all had pretty sedentary jobs, so the exercise, though forced, was probably a good idea.

It was a warm night, so we accepted a table on the upper deck open-air patio. My mouth watered at the yeasty scent of freshly baked rolls. Following Liv's lead, we weaved through the crowded first floor. I used the opportunity to peruse the selections of the other diners. The mahimahi presented on a bed of saffron orzo with steamed veggies was the hands-down winner. By the time we were seated, I had pretty much made up my mind.

For the sake of practicality, the chairs were teak. The tabletop was a mosaic of brightly painted tiles, decorated by a single flower and a trio of small votives. A gentle breeze swirled off the ocean, and I could hear the faint lapping of the waves and the sway of palm fronds. It was a relaxing setting, made more so when the waiter arrived with my Cosmo. Yes, I know, cliché, but in my defense, the citrusy tang cleanses my pallet before a meal. It's the alcohol version of taste-bud CPR.

Liv sipped a red wine while reading the menu. Defying nature, her pale brown hair was immune to the saltwater air, keeping its shape and fullness, giving me a serious case of hair envy.

Annoyingly healthy Jane drank water with a twist of lime. She rarely ordered a cocktail, mainly because she had the willpower to resist the call of the empty calories, and she claimed drinking made her sluggish during her morning workouts. Me? I'd bail on the workout. Then again, I consider a hangnail reason enough to avoid the gym.

Like me, Becky had a martini, but hers was neon green apple. Her menu sat unopened as she used a toothpick to fish the bottom of the glass for the cherry. Apparently she'd stayed late at work, since she was still wearing the same taupe silk blouse and rust skirt I'd seen at the office. I liked her as a redhead. It suited her coloring and her personality.

"Jean-Claude and I have a new client," Liv said as she put her menu down, running one perfectly manicured nail along the rim of her wineglass.

"Share," Jane said eagerly.

Liv turned her violet gaze on Becky. "Fantasy Dates."

"Sounds like an escort service," Becky remarked.

"An introduction service," Liv corrected. "Primo, of course. I'm signing you up."

Becky didn't even bother to control the groan that rumbled from her mouth. "Do it and I'll have you killed. Slowly."

"C'mon, Becky. It's perfect for you. It's like a dating service with income minimums. All the guys are prescreened professionals. The company runs rigorous background checks, financials—everything."

"Dorks with dollars?" Becky scoffed. "Pass. Besides, if it's such a great idea, why don't you kick Garage Boy to the curb and— No, wait! He doesn't have a curb. You'd have to kick him to his mommy's curb." She sighed dramatically. "Just doesn't have the same ring to it."

Jane and I shared an amused glance.

"You, too, Jane," Liv said. "It's going to be great. Once a woman picks a guy, I'll handle the details. Only the best restaurants, theater tickets, whatever. Choose a guy, name your fantasy date, and I make it happen."

"These guys would have to be real losers," Becky insisted. "They probably have lisps, hairlips, webbed toes—something. If they were normal, they wouldn't have to buy a date."

"What does it cost?" Jane asked. The question earned her a small elbow dig from Becky. "What? I'm curious."

"No, you're desperate," Becky said.

Ignoring Becky's open disdain, Liv replied, "The guy pays an annual membership fee of five grand. Plus the cost of the dates."

"Ouch." I grimaced. "You've got to have the social skills of a newt if you're willing to pay five thousand dollars for a date."

"Six months of introductions," Liv corrected. "It's a killer idea. I mean, the women have to meet certain, um, physical standards."

"Now it *really* sounds like an escort service," Becky grumbled.

"The guys can't be dogs," she defended. "The women have to be reasonably attractive and professionals. Cute guys hook up with cute girls. It's a win-win situation."

"Sure, if you aren't put off by a guy with an extra thumb or something."

"Where's your romantic soul?" Liv asked.

"I'm a lawyer. Our souls are surgically removed during the third year of law school."

I laughed. "I think the idea has potential."

"Thank you," Liv acknowledged, raising her glass to me. "I can sign you up, too."

"I'm probably off the market."

"Probably?" Liv asked, brows raised.

"Did something happen with Patrick last night?" The question came from Jane, but I had three sets of eyes trained on me.

I shrugged. "We had dinner and sex."

Liv leaned forward, wrapping her hands around her wineglass. "How does that turn your status into a 'probably'?"

I gave a vague recount of the date. "But he didn't call to say good-bye. He sent flowers."

"*Flower* flowers? Or the FTD Kiss-Off bouquet?" Jane asked.

"Roses," I answered.

Becky rolled her eyes. "Roses. A guy who's thinking about dumping you sends something lower on the flora food chain. Like carnations. Patrick is a lot of things, including predictable and considerate. He isn't going to bail on you without warning."

"She's right," Jane agreed. "Though I'm not so sure that wouldn't be a good thing."

"New topic," I said, raising my hands, palms out. The last thing I needed was a lecture on the pros and cons of my relationship with Patrick. No matter how well intended. Maybe he didn't rock my world, but maybe he wasn't supposed to. It was completely possible that we had simply reached that decreased-passion, totally-comfortable-with-you plateau.

The new topic turned out to be as depressing, if not more depressing, than my semi-elusive dating status. My friends were planning a leisurely weekend at the beach without me. They'd be lying on comfy lounge chairs while I was working and/or brunching with my mother.

I salved my mood by ordering the dessert sampler.

Friday is a great day. By midnight my paycheck will be direct-deposited into my account. So for six of the next seven days, I can hit the ATM without having to worry that the Account Overdrawn Goblin will eat my card. Again. Oh, yeah, and it's the unofficial start of my weekend. I try to sneak out of the office shortly after lunch, stealthily avoiding Margaret's ever vigilant eyes.

Today is a little different. A lot different, actually. I've got my meetings with the widows of the other two dead jurors.

Martha Keller arrived promptly at eleven. Escorted to my office by Cami the Intern. Cami was becoming a regular fixture, and alarm bells rang in my wrong-o-meter. Or was I just being paranoid? Since I couldn't be sure, I thanked her, then closed the door.

There was nothing remarkable about Martha Keller. Well, except for the heavy sadness haunting her dark eyes. She was very average—average height, average size. The kind of person who blends into the background, forgotten.

The scent of Clinique's Happy perfume filled my office. It was a huge contrast to the sense of deep loss fairly oozing from the poor woman.

I knew from reading the file that she was in her early fifties, though she looked younger. Maybe it was that her long hair was pulled into a no-fuss ponytail. She had virtually flawless skin. Well, flawless save for the dark circles under her slightly puffy eyes. If I had to guess, I'd say she'd cried every day of the three months since her husband's death. My heart squeezed in my chest. Normally I don't get this way, but something about Martha Keller's palpable grief touched me.

After she settled into her chair, I went through the usual offering of beverages. She asked for coffee, but after I poured it for her, she left it perched on the edge of my desk.

"I was surprised to hear from you," she began, her expression guarded as she clutched her small leather purse close to her chest. "My son said that because everything was joint with my husband, I didn't need a probate attorney."

"I'm not a lawyer, Mrs. Keller."

"But you said you were an estates person."

I'd been a little vague on the phone, mainly because I didn't think saying, "Hi, I'm Finley, and I think your husband was murdered," was the swiftest approach.

"This firm represents Stacy Evans." The name didn't seem to register, at least not in any way betrayed by her expression. "I'm handling her husband's estate."

"What does that have to do with me?" Her fingers tightened on her purse strap. "I don't know Mrs. Evans."

"Her husband served on the Hall jury with your husband."

She blinked. "That was years ago."

"Did your husband and Mr. Evans keep in touch after the trial?"

"Heavens, no," she answered, her slender shoulders relaxing just a bit. "Why?"

"I'm just gathering background."

She eyed me cautiously. "What aren't you telling me?"

"Mr. Evans died under, um, questionable circumstances. Much like your husband."

"My husband had a heart attack."

"But there was no autopsy, right?"

She cringed and swallowed audibly. "Of course not. The doctors didn't see the need, and, quite frankly, I find the whole idea of an autopsy disgusting."

Then I'm guessing you aren't going to want me digging up your husband. "Yes, ma'am, I completely understand. Do you know if any blood was drawn or any other tests were done?"

"What is this really about?" she asked. The question was filtered through the accusation in her eyes. She fidgeted nervously, crossing and uncrossing her legs.

"Are you aware of the fact that in addition to your husband and Mr. Evans, a third person from the Hall jury also died in the last three months?"

Tears welled in her eyes. "Oh, God. I told my son something was wrong when I found it."

It? What *it?*

Martha Keller was sobbing softly. "He keeps telling me I'm in denial because Graham died so suddenly." She grabbed up a tissue and dabbed at her eyes. "My husband was really stressed in the weeks before he died. I thought"—she paused to yank another tissue from the box to blow her nose—"it was work-related. He'd been distracted and distant, but I didn't think it would kill him.

"I mean, I know stress causes heart attacks, but Graham took such good care of himself, I didn't think he'd die. I swear, I didn't know."

Unable to contain myself any longer, I asked, "What did you find?"

She sniffled. "All that money."

*Life is about finding out what matters to you,
then doing it on purpose.*

Eight

"How much are we talking about?" I asked.

"What?"

"How much money? Where did you find it?"

"In our home safe," Mrs. Keller answered. "After Graham died, my son asked me to get all our important papers together. When my husband and I built the house, we had a fireproof safe installed inside the closet in the master bedroom."

Get to the frigging money, please.

"It was supposed to be for the deed to our house. Wills, stock certificates, that kind of thing."

Money. Focus on the money.

"I kept my good jewelry in there, too. Pieces from my family as well as the broach Graham's grandmother gave me on the day we got married."

I leaned against my chair back, afraid I'd have to listen to the complete history of the life and marriage of Graham and Martha Keller, and the provenance of every piece of "good" jewelry she owned. I didn't dare interrupt her. Until my question was answered, I had no choice but to let her ramble. A skill she excelled at, I decided as I watched the clock on my computer screen tick off the minutes.

Thirty minutes later I knew that 225 people had attended their wedding. I watched her smile as she told me that Graham, Jr., was born nine months to the day after their nuptials. *How Lisa Marie Presley is that?* She proudly reviewed her husband's professional accomplishments—she'd opted to be a stay-at-home mom to mini-Graham.

Bank of South Florida had hired Graham, Sr., as a teller. Through a series of well-deserved promotions, he'd ended up vice-president of the Private Banking Division.

"What's that?" I asked, not familiar with the job.

"Private banking is reserved for, um, important clients."

I doubted my tenuous account put me in that category. Hell, I couldn't even finagle a low-interest Visa card out of them.

She continued. "His office was in West Palm, just over the bridge at Flagler and Okeechobee."

I knew the area. It sat right on the Intracoastal, with stunning views of Palm Beach proper as well as easy access to the bridge separating the Have-Everythings from the Have-a-Lots. Several pricey condos share the street with tasteful, valet-parking-only office complexes and St. Mary's Hospital. Some of the best and most expensive specialists in Palm Beach County have their practices in the first few floors of the condo buildings. They even banded together to form a concierge medical coop. For the small sum of around two grand a year, participants never had to wait for appointments—the little people got rescheduled or had their appointments canceled flat-out—and for a thousand more, house calls were included as an option. Capitalism is a beautiful if unbalanced thing.

I thought for a minute, then said, "I don't remember a BSF on that corner."

"You wouldn't. That's the point. Private Banking wouldn't be very private if they had a sign, a drive-up window, and a night depository, now would it?"

"Guess not." I smiled. "What kinds of things did your husband do?"

"His division handled corporate and major personal portfolios."

"Handled?"

She shrugged. "A lot of it went over my head, but he invested money, and I know he was, well, like a business manager on some of the trust funds. Mostly those rich kids from the other side of the bridge."

"So he had access to personal fortunes?"

"Sure." Mrs. Graham must've finally realized how far off topic we'd gone, and her eyes narrowed. "Why? What does this have to do with his heart attack?"

Not sure, but I'm thinking a safe full of cash is suspicious. Money and murder often go hand in hand, at least they do on reruns of Murder, She Wrote. "As I said," which felt like a year ago, "my client, Mrs. Evans, is concerned that her husband's death wasn't an accident. It's my job to prove or disprove her suspicions. All I know at this point is that three jurors from the Hall trial have died in the last three months. So I'm hoping you'll give me permission to see if there are any blood tests that may have been run at the hospital on the night your husband died." Opening my desk drawer, I retrieved three blank copies of a standard, covers-everything-under-the-sun medical release form. "If you'll sign this, I'll take care of everything else."

She eyed the form suspiciously as I slipped it across my desk. "What will blood samples tell you? It was a heart attack. The paramedics and three doctors all said so."

"It's just routine, really."

"Not to me."

Sometimes the best tactical move is to make the other person feel like they're in the right. "I know this is an intrusion and an inconvenience. I wouldn't even ask except that, well, I have a feeling Mrs. Evans won't be able to accept the loss of her husband until she's completely sure there is nothing suspicious about his car accident."

Martha Keller visibly relaxed and plucked one of the pens from the cup on my desk. "Good luck to her," she said as she signed next to the X at the bottom of the pages she hadn't bothered to read. "Accident or not, it doesn't change the situation. I get up every morning and stare across an empty table." She passed me the papers, and her expression suddenly changed. Fear and uncertainty shone in her eyes.

I was afraid she'd had a change of heart and was going to grab the releases from me, tear them up, and toss the pieces into the trash. Crap, I'd be back to square one. "I really appreciate your cooperation," I promised her. "I'm sure Mrs. Evans will be grateful as well."

"What about the money?" she asked hesitantly. "My son told me not to breathe a word about it to anyone."

Well, tell Junior that ship already sailed. Assuming I could prove murder, someone was going to have to account for her husband's secret slush fund. It might have been the motive for his killing. "I'm not interested in your late husband's finances." *Yet.*

Mrs. Keller practically bolted out of the chair. "My son was right. I'm going to speak with him, then I'll get back to you about the hospital records."

She raced out of my office. I didn't follow her. I didn't have to. Martha Keller had left the fully executed releases on my desk. I glanced down at my Liz Claiborne watch with the bright pink band and rectangular face and knew I had plenty of time to get what I needed before the Widow Keller could stop me.

"Again with the pack-animal thing," I grumbled as I entered the elevator. My briefcase was full, mostly with the D'Auria estate accounting. Tucked in a side pocket, I also had the information I needed for my other side trips. My Palm Pilot was preloaded with Mapquest directions to Rosita Vasquez's home. It was going to be a busy afternoon.

And a warm one, so I thought I'd stop by the vending machines for a bottle of Diet Coke. Caffeine in its alternate form would have to suffice until I could find a coffee shop during my travels.

My timing couldn't have been more perfect. A young brunette was seated at Margaret's desk. She was the one who manned the phones while Margaret was at lunch. I tossed her a smile and felt a pang of guilt because I couldn't recall her name.

"Finley, I need—"

"Gimme a sec," I called over my shoulder, lifting my purse and the cutting strap of my briefcase as testimony. "I'm just getting a drink."

Ignoring her "but" and shoving some of the weight of my briefcase to the back of my hip, I rounded the corner into the alcove that led to the machines and the employee lounge.

As expected, the machine's electronic feeder copped an attitude, rejecting my first two dollars. They weren't pristine enough. Annoyed, I put my stuff down and reached into my wallet, selecting two crisp bills with the same care I'd use to pick just the right wine. Seemed like a lot of work for a freaking soda. But, the machine accepted my payment, which was the only thing that really mattered.

As the plastic bottle rumbled down toward the dispenser, I caught a few fragments of conversation coming from the employee lounge. I recognized Margaret's voice immediately. It had the same authoritative quality as—I don't know—the tone God must have used on Moses. I grabbed my drink and was going to leave when I heard my name mentioned.

Well, it wasn't my name.

"Fat is going to get herself fired," Margaret was telling someone.

Since I couldn't see inside the lounge, I couldn't identify the other person or persons she was sharing her gossip with. I could, however, feel my own annoyance and a pinch of fear pounding at my temples. Fired?

For the first time since the day I'd been hired, I was working. Not clock-watching, biding my time until five P.M., but honest-to-God investing myself in my case.

And that fact was almost as disturbing as knowing Margaret and her cronies were talking about me during their brown-bag lunch. When had I started bucking for employee-of-the-month?

". . . Mr. Dane wouldn't fire her," one of the other women insisted. "Fat was hired personally by Mr. Zarnowski."

"Whose name is only on the letterhead as a courtesy," Margaret replied in that all-knowing voice. "He's in his eighties. For all intents and purposes, Mr. Dane and Ms. Lieberman run this firm, and they don't approve of Fat's inability to follow instructions.

"I know her type," Margaret continued. "She doesn't think the rules apply to her. She does what she wants, when she wants to. That's why Mr. Dane has me logging all her calls and visitors."

What?! I stifled the urge to march into the lounge and tell Margaret and the Grumblers to kiss my actually working ass. It might provide some measure of instant gratification, but in the long run, it would blow up in my face.

I had to take countermeasures. Fired, crap! I can't get fired. I'm pretty sure Dillard's won't take the promise of my firstborn male child as a monthly payment. Neither would the five other revolving credit accounts I'd driven up to their limit. If I did get fired, how would I live on the measly thousand-dollar limit available on my new Visa until I found another job? Shit.

Think, think, think. I took two deep breaths and let them out slowly. Log my calls and appointments? I considered that information with complete frustration and a healthy dose of disdain. In all my years at Dane-Lieberman, no one had so much as questioned my coming and goings. So why now? When I really was doing my job? Well, mostly doing it. I'd only taken two personal detours this week—lunch with Becky and a quickie shopping trip. But I'd more than made up for that by coming in early and working through lunch. Twice.

Relief Receptionist was waiting for me as I returned to the lobby, soda bottle in hand. "What do you need?"

She slipped a clipboard across the polished surface and had the decency to look embarrassed. "I need you to sign in and out. Some kind of new policy."

Yeah, the Screw Finley Policy.

The form was divided into four columns. One for the employee's name, one each for departure and arrival, and the last one requested an explanation for out-of-office business. I noticed two other people had signed out ahead of me. Made sense. If the partners singled me out, they'd leave themselves open to a claim of creating a hostile workplace and/or wrongful termination. Smart bastards.

Placing my briefcase on the floor, I pulled a pen out of my purse and dutifully—if laced with attitude—scribbled the requested information. Through the fog of irritation, I caught the scent of lemon, cedar, musk, and pine . . . *Basile.* I knew the men's fragrance because I'd given it to Patrick on his last birthday.

It was quickly overshadowed by the heavy odor of Bal A Versailles. Not my favorite. It's my mother's perfume, and just one whiff is enough to send feelings of failure into my heart.

Sliding the clipboard off to the left, I allowed the couple behind me to speak to the receptionist. Under *Out-of-Office Business,* I wrote *D'Auria Estate and Evans Meeting.* Technically, I wasn't meeting Mrs. Evans, but rather Rosita Vasquez, but I justified

my omission by blaming it on the design of the
form. There wasn't enough room to write a lengthy
explanation, so I was comfortable with my answer.

I had just picked up the clipboard with the in-
tention of depositing it on the opposite side of the
desk when the man to my right said, "Dr. and Mrs.
Hall for Victor Dane."

The clipboard slipped from my hand, clattering
against the polished tile. The sound echoed through
the lobby as my head whipped around to get my
first up-close look at the doctor.

Kent Hall looked nothing like I'd imagined.
The grainy, simple news-clipping photos didn't do
him justice. He was short, no more than about five-
six. Never good—short men have crappy personal-
ities and dictatorial leanings. It's the whole
Napoleon thing. They compensate for their lack
of stature with huge egos.

Too bad, too, since Hall was really nice-looking,
for a short guy. He had soft, light brown eyes and—
since I knew from my research he was only forty-
nine—prematurely gray hair. If he'd been a few
inches taller, he'd have looked distinguished. Especially in that custom-made, gunmetal gray shirt
paired with a mauve and gray striped silk Hermès
tie. His suit pants were a darker shade, closer to
slate. His jacket was folded over his arm, which
made sense since the noon temperature had already climbed above eighty.

The woman at his side surprised me. I would
have pegged Hall as the type to require a Palm
Beach trophy wife. But nope, no blond, leggy
twenty-year-old for him.

They held hands, no easy feat given the size of
the rock adorning her left hand. I guessed it was

somewhere in the eight-carat range, a little big for a woman with such small hands. Meredith Hall was a petite woman with expertly styled and high-lighted brown hair. The cut flattered her heart-shaped face. She had great makeup, too.

In my experience, the more money a woman has, the darker her lip liner. The super rich usually pair chocolate brown with bright red. But not Meredith; she bucked that trend. She looked as polished and perfect as any model.

"Stunning watch," I remarked. She had the Rolex Jubilee Presidential diamond bevel, and it was everything I could do not to drool.

"Thank you," she replied graciously as the sound of sandals slapping across the floor pulled my attention away from the couple to the young woman joining them.

The daughter, I decided. She had Hall's light brown eyes and Meredith's small build.

"Zoe, did you remember to lock the car?" Meredith asked in that rhetorical mother tone.

"Of course."

Not "yeah," not "uh huh." This girl was polite and courteous. Probably a requirement in her school. I recognized the blue plaid jumper and crisp white shirt by the emblem embroidered on the breast pocket. Friends' Academy of Palm Beach. One year at the prestigious high school cost more than all four years of my college educa-tion combined.

Dr. Hall retrieved the clipboard I'd dropped and handed it to me with a gracious smile. "Here you go, Miss . . . ?"

Our eyes locked for a split second. "Tanner. Fin-ley Tanner. Thank you, Doctor."

The receptionist said, "Mr. Dane is ready to see you." She pointed to the elevator bank. "His office is on—"

"We know the way," Dr. Hall interrupted. "Thank you." He placed one hand at his wife's back and the other at his daughter's, then guided them across the lobby.

I waited until the doors closed on the compartment before gathering up my things. "I'll be back as soon as possible," I said, still pissed at having to get the employee version of a hall pass to leave the building.

I decided to drive to the courthouse for two reasons. It saved me the trouble of coming back for my car after filing the estate accounting, and I had some paranoid feelings that Margaret might be making notes on my activities.

My paranoia wasn't completely unfounded. "Logging my calls," I grumbled as I slipped behind the wheel. "Log this!" I scoffed as I pulled my phone out of my purse and dialed several numbers. I left messages for Liv, Becky, Jane, and Stacy Evans to call my cell until further notice.

I had to wait until I parked outside the courthouse to find Liam's number. After programming it into my cell's memory, I hit the SEND button and waited for his voice mail to answer.

"McGarrity."

I felt every one of those four syllables tingle through my bloodstream and felt instantly guilty. *I have a boyfriend. I have a boyfriend. He's boffing his ex-wife.* Equilibrium restored.

"This is McGarrity," he repeated, irritation creeping into his voice.

"Hi, it's Finley Tanner."

"Yeah?"

Obviously, he didn't attend the Friends' Academy. "First, I need you to call my cell phone from now on. Okay?"

"Why not? What's the number?"

I repeated it from memory, then said, "I've got a release from Mrs. Keller, and I should have one from Mrs. Vasquez in about two hours. Can we meet?"

"For what?"

It was my turn to be irritated. "So you can get an independent lab to see if any of them were drugged or poisoned or whatever. Remember?"

"I think you're wasting your time."

So what else was new? "Work with me here."

I heard him sigh. "On what? The prelim on the car was a bust. If you ask me, Marcus Evans died in a car accident. End of story. Tell the widow to put a period on it and move on."

"It's a little late for that," I said. "Stacy knows other jurors have died. I told her."

"Jesus, that was stupid."

That rankled, and I felt instantly defensive. Although my inclination was to tell him to go to hell, I needed him. "Well, I'm kind of new at this. Which is why I need you. I'll take care of getting the necessary releases, and you find me someone to run the tests. It's called the spirit of teamwork, like Starsky and Hutch, Cagney and Lacey—"

"Beavis and Butt-Head," Liam added, his tone laced with humor. "I'm Beavis, in case you were wondering."

"I'm not begging here. You're getting paid."

"Fine. I've got a—"

Don't say it!

"Thing tonight. You get whatever you have together and I'll swing by your place on my way home."

"Okay. My address is—"

"I'll find you."

I stared at the dead phone and thought of more than just a few ways I wanted to tell him to go screw himself. Then my thoughts immediately switched to assess my own shortcomings. Liam had mocked me, teased me, dismissed me, criticized me, and I was now more intrigued by him than ever. God, am I pathetic or what?

Snapping my phone closed with a little more pressure than necessary, I grabbed my stuff and my now tepid soda and headed toward the courthouse.

The midafternoon sun was strong, making the glass-over-street walkway connecting the building and the parking lot feel more like a greenhouse. Luckily, I'd opted for a simple, sleeveless cotton dress in one of my favorite shades of aqua, so I was immune to my brief foray into the sweltering enclosure.

After a successful thirty-minute meeting with one of the clerks in the Probate Department, I could officially consider the final D'Auria accounting a done deal. Nothing left to do but send out the checks to the heirs and wait for the expressions of gratitude to come rolling in. That was a huge perk to my job. People love getting money for nothing, and when they do, even legendary tightwads discover generosity. So far the best thing I've received from a beneficiary was an all-expenses-paid week at the Atlantis Hotel on Paradise Island. Most of the time, though, it's a nice fruit assortment or designer chocolates.

My next stop was Vital Records over on 45th

Street. In a brilliant—at least to my mind—CYA move, I called Margaret. I knew good and well that the switchboard Caller ID would verify my location. I had to wait for official copies of the death certificates for Vasquez and Keller, so I asked her to see if anyone else in the office needed anything. Of course they didn't, which I already knew, but it did give me the satisfaction of knowing I'd protected myself.

"I have a message for you," Margaret said just as I was about to hang up.

"Yes?"

"Sam Carter called and asked that you return his call as soon as possible." I heard the clicking of her fingernails against the keyboard. "I don't have him listed in our client base."

Bite me. "He's on the board of my renters' association," I explained. Technically true, but Sam knew better than to involve me in association business. He knows I couldn't give a flying fig about who is violating the assigned parking-spot rules, or who didn't double-bag their trash. "Anything else?"

"Yes, Mr. Dane would like to know when you think you'll be back in your office."

"An hour or so." *I hope.* "I have one more stop to make, and I'd like to grab something to eat. It is almost two, and I haven't had a thing all day." *I hope you feel guilty, you leftover-meatloaf-sandwich-eating witch.*

"I'll let him know."

"Thank you."

A few minutes later, I was back in my car, reading the death certificates as I started the engine. The only thing that popped was the fact that Graham Keller's body was taken to JFK Hospital off Congress Street—which, coincidentally, was right on my way to Rosita Vasquez's house. Since I had medical releases tucked into my briefcase, I figured I might as well grab a copy of Keller's medical records and put in a request for any blood or tissue samples.

Because I knew several of the records clerks, I was able to get the copies in under ten minutes. The lab request would take longer, though they promised they would respond to my request by Monday.

Now for the hard part, I thought with a sense of dread as I worked my way through a neighborhood of modest homes in West Palm. Once I found the address, I parked at the curb in front of the Spanish-style home. The ghost of beautiful landscaping was overgrown now, possibly neglected in the three months since José had died.

An older-model Volvo was parked in the driveway, surrounded by an assortment of bikes, skateboards, and toys. A cement statue of the Virgin Mary stood in the center of the small lawn, surrounded by a bed of white stones.

As I walked up to the front door, I heard children playing close by and soft, rhythmic salsa music coming from a nearby house. Mrs. Vasquez was waiting for me, holding open the screen door and greeting me with a cautious but warm smile. She had on shorts and a T-shirt from last year's SunFest. Long ebony hair fell well past her shoulders. Her eyes were black and, like Martha Keller's, permanently stained with grief. Her skin tone was somewhere between caramel and café au lait.

The interior of her home was awash with bright color and framed photographs. One in particular caught my eye. "You?" I asked, hoping to break the ice.

"My Quinceanera," she explained in heavily accented English. "My fifteenth birthday."

I smiled, moderately familiar with the celebration. "Your dress is stunning."

"My aunt and mother worked for months on it," she said.

Their efforts showed. Quinceanera dresses look a lot like wedding dresses—very white and very ornate. And in keeping with tradition, Rosita was posed in a formal portrait.

"Sit," she insisted, stopping to toss a stuffed toy onto the floor. "You are here about my José?"

I pretty much repeated what I had told Mrs. Keller. "I think— Excuse me," I interrupted as I grabbed my ringing cell phone out of my purse. "Hello?"

"Finley, this is Stacy Evans."

"I'm in a meeting," I said, offering my uneasy hostess an apologetic smile.

"I won't keep you. I just wanted to let you know that I've contacted the other jurors and told them to expect a call from you."

I grimaced. "That might have been a little premature."

"They could have information. Or be in danger themselves."

"Mrs. Evans, I—"

"I faxed their phone numbers to your office. Let me know when you've completed the interviews. I won't keep you any longer. Good-bye."

Shit, shit, and double shit. I flipped my phone closed and tried not to let my annoyance show. Margaret was logging my time, and Stacy was arranging my appointments. How had I managed to completely lose control of the situation?

Liam's words played in my mind. He was right.

As it had turned out, telling Stacy about the other jurors *had* been stupid.

I spent about twenty minutes with Rosita. I walked away with two things. A pair of signed releases and her insistence that José was not a careless man. While she seemed resigned that his death was an accident, she kept telling me over and over again that I should speak to Tomás Montoya. He was José's crew boss and was to have been there with him on the morning of the accident.

I returned to Dane-Lieberman with a bag of lukewarm French fries. I placed the sack on the clipboard while I signed in. I derived more than a little bit of childish pleasure when the grease drained through, staining the page.

The fax from Stacy was waiting on my desk, topped by a Post-it from Cami noting the time it had come through the machine. Again I felt the prickly sensation between my shoulder blades. Why was Cami suddenly cropping up all over the place? The logical answer was that she was bored. The "I'm freaked out" answer is that she's keeping tabs on me.

Was it really paranoia if everyone was, in fact, actually keeping tabs on me?

I spent a few minutes eating my fries while completing my timesheet. Then I e-mailed the spreadsheet of billable hours to the Accounting Department. Next I sifted through the boxes of transcripts and selected the ones I would take home for the weekend.

"I'm losing it," I grumbled as I condensed the relevant bound volumes into a single white box. I never take work home, yet here I go. Not only was I going to meet Liam tonight, I had the Widow Whitley on Saturday, and now I was adding hundreds of pages of transcripts. Oh, yeah, and I was having brunch with Mom on Sunday. My friends were going shopping and to the beach. Could this weekend get any worse?

Even though it was after five o'clock, I took the time to copy the D'Auria estate stuff, print out the disbursement checks, and write the cover letters to the heirs. Since I was on an employee-of-the-month roll, I managed to get everything signed and sealed in time for the last express mail pickup of the day.

By the time I started loading my car, Margaret had already left for the evening. "Slacker," I muttered on my second trip past her vacant desk.

Because of my late departure, the sun set before I reached my apartment. It wasn't until I pulled into my parking spot that I remembered I was supposed to call Sam. Knowing him, he'd be pretty miffed by now.

I was tired and not looking forward to dragging the heavy box of transcripts and my briefcase and the medical files from my car to my apartment. I really didn't want to add pissy attitude from Sam to my list of challenges.

I arrived at my door and forgot all about Sam. I forgot everything as I looked at the single sheet of paper nailed into place. My heart stopped as I read the words scrolled in bright red marker.

Do you want to die too?

Earning it is good, but having it
fall into your lap is so much easier.

Nine

One by one, like eyes blinking awake, lights came on in my apartment building. Then heads popped out of windows, making me feel like I was playing a giant version of the carney game Whack-A-Mole.

"You okay?" the unibrow guy in 4B called.

"What if she's not? What can you do, Herman?" I heard his wife whine. "Close the window before the bugs get in. You know I hate bugs."

After apparently hearing me scream, Sam Carter rushed to my side. The first thing out of his mouth when he saw the note was, "Geez, Finley. Who'd you piss off this time?"

"Today? Or just generally?" I asked, trying to make light of the situation even though my knees were still shaking.

Sam scooped up the contents of the box I'd dropped when I saw the note, shoving the binders inside while I struggled to insert my key into the lock. My hands were steady, but I kept looking around the parking lot, half expecting some hooded fiend to jump out and attack me. Then I remembered this wasn't a cheesy horror flick, and I began to relax. The bad guys had to be long gone.

Once the front door was open, Sam followed me inside, practically glued to my back as I went from room to room turning on every light possible.

"What's going on?" he asked. "Should you call the cops?"

I didn't question my reluctance to involve the police, I went with my gut. "Probably just a prank." *I hope.* "No one broke in."

"No wonder, especially if they looked in the window and saw your horrid furniture. Taking this crap"—he paused, his face pinched in disapproval—"would be considered junk hauling, not stealing."

My heart rate returned to normal. "Go grab my briefcase out of the back of my car," I instructed.

"Do I look like the flipping doorman?" he demanded. But he went. Taking instructions gracefully wasn't one of Sam's strengths. Which explained why he'd gone through jobs like I go through pantyhose. The difference was, Sam had saved, scrounged, and borrowed enough money to start up his own interior design company, knowing without doubt what he wanted. He might be a temperamental pain, but his work was amazing, so his business was growing quickly. Which meant he was extra-free with his opinions on my seriously-in-need-of-replacement furniture.

Sam played up his gayness. He thought it gave him that balance between sympathetic and sophisticated. People still assumed that his over-the-top flamboyance—in dress and gesture—came from having been forced to hide his "true" self in a prejudiced world in the past. In reality, Sam hailed from a large family in Philly that was completely accepting of his sexual orientation.

Yet, he really played it up. Like now. He was dressed in jeans and a cotton, button-down shirt—normal enough—but Sam added an ascot. Who, aside from the elderly members of the royal family, donned an ascot?

He was gone for thirty-one seconds. I timed him, staring at the door, waiting for him to return. Possibly a little more freaked out than I wanted to admit. After depositing my briefcase on the countertop with a loud thud, he ripped the note off the door and brought it inside.

I watched him smooth a hand over his perfectly coiffed hair. He used so much product, I was sure that when he died it would be from mousse poisoning. Or maybe inhaling too much hair spray. I wasn't sure, but it would definitely be the first haircare fatality on record.

Expertly styled hair aside, Sam was a really attractive guy. Tall, slim but not skinny, mid-twenties, blond, grayish-blue eyes, tanned, and intelligent. He loved shopping, had a great sense of color, and knew how to find a bargain. If it wasn't for the whole sexual-preference thing, he'd be a great life partner. Wasn't that how it always worked? The good ones were either gay or married. My mind flashed the image of Liam and his ex-wife in the throes of passion.

"What?" Sam asked, slipping onto one of two mismatched bar stools. "You look pale. Is it the note? Should we call the police, really?"

To report a non-divorce divorce? I thought, still fixated on my mental image of Liam and his ex-wife. *Don't think that's any more of a crime than the murders I can't prove.* I shook my head. "I'm sure it was just a piss-poor joke."

"Could be those little bastards in Three-C. I know they're the ones that spray-painted 'fag' on my door last month. Not that their mother gave a damn when I confronted her."

"You were crying when you knocked on her door," I reminded him. "She was freaked out by your meltdown, but as I recall, she sent a check to you to cover the cost of repainting."

Sam sighed, not completely willing to give up the pouty look just yet. "They were tears of frustration," he insisted, making each word sound as if he was delivering a Shakespearian soliloquy. "Because I am . . . unique, I've had to endure a great deal of teasing and taunting during my lifetime."

I rolled my eyes. "You're so full of crap. You were never shunned by your friends and family. Jeez, Sam, you were even voted homecoming queen at your very inclusive, very forward-thinking high school. I don't want to hear any 'poor gay me' stories. We both know you were only in tears because you hated the color of the spray paint they used."

"That, too," he admitted with an impish gleam in his eyes. His expression turned slightly more serious as he tapped his forefinger on the note. "What about this, Finley? It gives me the creeps. You've been threatened."

Raking my hands through my hair, I couldn't decide what, if anything, I should do. Taking no action at all seemed like the path of least resistance, and one that I was familiar with. "I'm sure it's nothing," I said, trying to instill a voice of reason into the situation. For both Sam and myself. My nerves were jumping, and my brain was going a mile a minute. I was scared. And, God help me, excited in a perverse way. Because if someone was threatening me, that meant my investigation was getting someone's attention.

Now I just had to figure out what my next step might be.

"It can't be 'nothing,' but it's your call," Sam said, like he was in charge. "What's all this stuff?" He waved his hand in an arc over the things I'd brought from the office.

"Work."

He blinked as if I'd just recited the atomic number of all the known elements in the universe. "You?" His brows drew together questioningly. "What gives, Finley? Your weekends are sacred to you. You must have really screwed up at work if they consigned you to a weekend in Paralegal Purgatory."

I smiled. "My choice. I need to do some research on a case."

"A case?" he parroted. "Your clients are all dead people."

I spent a few minutes bringing him up to speed. Sam sat in complete silence until I'd finished. Then he gave a low whistle. "So how come Sara Whitley would wait all this time before turning into a cold, calculating killer? And why go after the jurors?"

A question I'd been asking myself for days now.

"And," Sam continued, quite animatedly, "why not kill off the doctors and nurses who didn't treat the postop infection in time?"

I didn't have any real answers. Just gut feelings. "Maybe I'll be able to figure that out after I meet with her tomorrow."

"For the love of— Finley, you shouldn't go meet her. At least not alone."

I was touched by his concern. "Want to come with me?"

"I can't. Which is kinda why I've been trying to reach you the past couple of days."

"Sorry about that. I meant to return your calls."

"I need you to take care of Butch and Sundance this weekend." He must have read my mind because he added, "I've got to meet a new client. And it is only until Sunday night. Monday morning at the absolute latest."

Butch and Sundance were Sam's cats. They didn't need watching, since their whole lives consisted of eating, sleeping, and licking themselves. Oh, yeah, and the whole gross litter-box thing. I found that completely disgusting.

"You know I'll do it." Tired of transcripts, widows, and the thought of all the reading ahead of me, I asked, "New client?"

"Kind of," he hedged.

I grinned. "New man?"

"I'm not sure," Sam admitted, clearly perplexed. "He's totally hot, but I think he might be a switch-hitter. You know I'm not into the whole bisexual thing. Hell, how hard is it to pick a gender and stick to it?"

"What makes you think he's into women?"

"He has pictures in his office. *Family* pictures. Kids, dog, the whole suburban package."

I put on a pot of coffee. "Maybe he came out after he married. Or they could be nieces and nephews."

"Then they should be labeled as such. I mean, he totally checked me out during our first meeting. He's redoing an old cottage in the Upper Keys. Then he insists on personally taking me to said beach house for the weekend 'to get a feel for the place.' That all points toward him wanting me, right?"

"Sure. Or, just playing devil's advocate, he's a closeter who's whisking you out of town so there's no chance you'll run into his wife and kids."

"You are so not helping."

"I just agreed to police cat poop for you. How is that not supportive?"

"Why are men so complicated?"

"Gee, aren't you the one more qualified to answer that?" I didn't wait for my state-of-the-art machine to stop spitting and sputtering. I grabbed a mug for myself, then turned and asked Sam, "Coffee?"

"No." He slid off the barstool. "I'm going up to pack."

"Good luck with He-She Man. Let me know how it works out," I called as Sam disappeared down the hallway and out the door. I followed a few seconds later, turning the latch on the lock and sliding the safety chain into place.

I went into the bedroom, took off my dress, adding it to the pile I needed to drop off at the dry cleaners, then changed into a pair of satin boxers and a camisole. Twisting my hair into a makeshift knot at the nape of my neck, I grabbed a silk demirobe off the hook on the back of my door and returned to the kitchen.

Before I decided on my dinner options, I checked my wallet. Ten dollars was enough for a quart of Chicken Lo Mien plus tip. That along with the rest of the Lucky Charms would easily get me through the weekend. Especially if I humiliated my mother by asking for a doggy bag after brunch.

I called the Hunan Hideaway, placed my order, then sipped my coffee as I started reading the Vasquez medical reports I'd gotten on my way home. Maybe someone at the hospital had told someone else that I was asking around. Then that someone told whoever put that flipping note on my door. It was hard to concentrate on medical jargon when I was distracted by the reality that someone had taken the trouble to threaten me. Then again, it could be nothing more than a practical joke. Someone from work, maybe? Margaret had left before me. But I just couldn't picture her sneaking over to my apartment and tacking a threat to my door.

Back to the medical reports. This sort of stuff is the main reason my degree is in women's studies—nothing beyond the most remedial math and science required. I didn't know what a *cc* was because, aside from drug dealers, only the medical profession used the metric system.

If I excluded the weights and measures, the ER notes from the morning José died seemed pretty straightforward. There were some terms and abbreviations I didn't fully understand. Still, I got the gist of what killed him. He'd sustained a crushing blow to the chest caused by the trunk of a palm tree. He'd been hit with sufficient force for the impact to break his rib, which then punctured a major ventricle in his heart. Not that the reports said it in normal words, but the bottom line was, José had bled to death from the internal injury.

Moistening my fingertip, I flipped through the paperwork to the intake form. Tomás Montoya's signature was at the bottom of the admission sheet. His phone number was included, so I added that to my list of notes. Though I couldn't for the life of me figure out how Sara Whitley could make a tree fall on someone.

With my stomach growling as I waited for the delivery guy, I went and got my laptop. A few minutes later, I had a theory, if not an answer. Apparently, the variety and size of the Royal Palm José was planting was supposed to be "topped," meaning basically all the fronds are stripped off so all the weight is in the root ball.

However, when I compared it to the newspaper photo of the scene, taken just a few hours after José's body had been removed, the tree had a full canopy. Why would an experienced landscaper do something so risky?

Before I could even begin to guess, the doorbell chimed. I thought my stomach would clap with unbridled joy. Grabbing my wallet off the countertop, I went to the door, opening it only as far as the safety chain allowed.

Instantly, I realized two things. First, it wasn't the short Korean guy who delivered my food. It was Liam. After that fact solidified in my brain, I realized I was dressed all wrong. The Korean guy wouldn't have thought twice about catching me in my loungewear, but Liam was another story. He'd probably take it as a lame attempt at seduction or something.

"Hang on," I said, shutting the door, tossing my wallet on the counter as I ran into my bedroom.

With limited time and options, I removed the boxers and pulled on a pair of jeans, no time for panties, and, besides, I'd be the only one who knew I was commando. My camisole had a built-in bra, but just to be on the safe side, I grabbed a hoodie from my closet and hurriedly slipped it over my head. Body armor.

Sliding the chain free, I opened the door as I willed my breathing back to normal. Untangling my hair with my fingers, I stepped to one side to allow him to enter. "Sorry, I forgot you were coming by."

Liam was one of those guys who filled a space. I don't know if it's presence or sheer size, I just knew that I felt claustrophobic with him standing in the narrow hallway between my kitchen and my living room.

I also discovered something else. I couldn't identify his cologne. It was subtle and masculine and completely distracting. Okay, confession time: olfactory failure wasn't the only thing that had me carked. Liam's complete disinterest dinged my ego. Apparently, I didn't even rate so much as a passing once-over. I shouldn't care, but I did. And I hated myself for it.

He glanced around like an insurance adjuster doing an inventory. His expression was completely bland until his eyes landed on the note. Without asking, though I'm not sure there are rules of etiquette when dealing with a threatening note, he turned the page around with the tip of his forefinger, read the block printing, and immediately scowled.

"What's this?"

"Candygram?" I joked. I didn't want him to think I was a total chickenshit. Of course I was, but that was irrelevant.

His dark head turned, and I felt the full, intimidating force of his piercing gray-blue eyes. "Try again."

"It was pinned to my door," I said, glad my voice didn't convey any of the fear still lingering in my system.

"Did you call the police?"

"No. There's a few kids in the complex with pretty warped ideas about what's funny and what's not."

"The kind of kids that leave death threats on your door?"

"Boredom makes people do stupid things."

"Are you bored?" he asked.

"Me? No. Why?"

"Then what's your reason for *stupidly* not calling the cops?" He shook his head. "Never mind, I already know. You aren't sure it wasn't kids, and you'd rather die than look like a fool."

I lowered my gaze. "Something like that."

"Have you shown this to anyone?"

"Sam."

He laced his fingers and cracked his knuckles. I knew the timing was all wrong, but I couldn't help myself. I had a momentary and very vivid fantasy about his hands. Entwining in my hair, brushing down the sides of my body, slipping beneath my shirt and— *Stop!* "He's my neighbor."

"Any trouble between the two of you?"

"Trouble," I repeated slowly, like I was learning a new word.

"Is he the jealous type?"

"Totally."

I watched as curiosity lifted one of his dark eyebrows. "Enough to leave a nasty note?"

"Sure. But only if my name was Frank or Fred."

He replied with a pointed stare that told me he wasn't at all amused by me. "What about him?" he asked, crooking his thumb in the direction of the pictures of Patrick scattered around the living room.

"No. Besides, he's out of town. Probably even out of the country."

"You misplaced your boyfriend? You two must be really close."

"Kiss my—"

The doorbell chimed, and suddenly Liam had a gun in one hand and was using the other to shove me behind him. I grunted when my shoulder made contact with the wall, hard enough that my breath gushed from my body in a single whoosh.

Holding the gun behind his back, legs braced, feet firmly planted, Liam went to the door and yanked it open.

I watched his trigger finger twitch, then relax.

"Delivery for Miss Finley."

Recognizing Kim's voice, I grabbed the ten-dollar bill from my wallet and elbowed my way past Liam's rock-solid body. "Thanks," I said, exchanging the money for the brown paper bag.

"You need change?"

"No," I said quickly, flashing a smile before I closed the door. I'd just given Kim a forty-percent tip, so I glared up at Liam and asked, "What's with the gun? Is it real?"

"Yeah, they're more effective than the plastic kind."

"You could have hurt someone."

Using his thumbnail, he flicked what I guessed was the safety—I'd never been this close to a gun before, so I wasn't one hundred percent sure—and tucked the thing back into an ankle holster. "That's the general idea behind carrying a gun. It isn't like I'm not well trained. I wouldn't have shot the Chinese guy."

"Korean."

"What?"

"Kim is Korean, he just works at a Chinese restaurant."

"Well, hell," Liam teased, his mouth twitching at the corners, "if I'd have known that when I saw him standing there, that would have changed everything."

"Why do you feel the need to jerk my chain at every turn?"

He shrugged his broad shoulders. "Because it's so easy to get a rise out of you."

The scent of Lo Mien filled my apartment as Liam walked over to the sofa and sat down. Was I supposed to offer him some dinner? No. Definitely not. This was business.

"I've got the medical records and death certificates as well as a list of the contact numbers for the remaining jurors and—" I began.

"Do you always talk so fast?"

"Yes. Besides, I'm sure you have another *thing*." I made the last word sound as vile as possible.

Checking his watch, he leaned back, bracing his elbows on the back of the couch. "I've got time."

Before what? *Who* was more likely. I rubbed my temples, fighting off the beginnings of a lots-of-coffee-very-little-food headache.

"So what's your theory of the case?"

"Sara Whitley is getting even with the jurors because they refused to hold Dr. Hall responsible for her husband's death."

He gave me one of those looks a teacher gives a child when they're claiming the dog ate their homework. My blood pressure went up a few notches.

"It's a good theory," I insisted

"For a bad made-for-TV movie, maybe."

"Well, since you work for me, you're stuck with it."

"You're right. So, what's your plan?"

"The blood tests are crucial. The samples won't be available until Monday."

"I can get around that."

"How?"

"I have ways. Don't worry about it. What hospitals?" He pulled a small memo pad from the back pocket of his jeans. A golf pencil was tucked into the spiral binding. He took notes while I dictated.

Retrieving one of the volumes I'd brought home, I handed him the page with the trial witnesses listed. "I need current addresses for all these people. Phone numbers, too."

"Okay."

"Oh, and how would I trace the money in Graham Keller's safe?"

"How much money are we talking about?"

"I didn't ask."

He cast me a sidelong look. "A woman tells you she finds a secret stash of cash, and you don't bother to get details?"

"He was a banker. I wasn't sure it was connected."

"I take it you don't have a lot of interview experience."

My spine stiffened. "As a matter of fact, I worked for a newspaper for a year. I interviewed lots of people."

"Really?"

My ears turned the word into *liar.*

"What kinds of people?" he asked.

"Important people. I even interviewed the president once."

He cocked his head. "The president of what?"

Busted. "The, um, local kennel club."

"Well, well, you're a regular Erin Brockovich, aren't you? I'll sniff around the Keller slush fund."

I wanted him to leave before I made any bigger an ass of myself. "Good. Don't forget about the lab tests and the addresses."

"Got it. What's your plan?"

"I'm going to talk to Sara Whitley tomorrow."

"You think she's a killer, right?"

"Yes. Maybe. I don't know."

"But you're going to see her alone?"

"She has no reason to hurt me."

"Or to confide in you. I'll go with you," he said as he got to his feet. "What time?"

"Ten." He started past me, and I reached out and grabbed his arm. The muscles were as solid as granite. "That's really sweet of you." He was so close to me that I felt his warm, minty breath wash over my face. I could take one teensy, tiny step and my body would be pressed against his.

"Sweet?" he said with a chuckle. "Hardly, I'll bill you at my regular hourly rate."

He left me standing there, a quivering mass of alerted hormones, feeling like a total ass.

"Don't forget to lock the door behind me."

"I won't," I managed, my voice cracking slightly. *Then maybe I'll slit my wrists.*

Friends come and go—
enemies accumulate.

Ten

I spent the night having the kind of sensual-bordering-on-dirty dreams you don't normally admit to, even to your closest friend. The dreams all had a common thread, and that thread's name was Liam McGarrity. There was only one conclusion to be drawn: I was a subconscious cheater.

Which made absolutely no sense since Liam had, by word and deed, made it infinitely clear that he barely noticed I was a woman.

I'd heard Sam roll his suitcase out the door well before dawn. Easily done since he lived right above me. I pressed the heels of my palms against my eyes as I swung my feet to the floor and glanced over at the digital clock on my nightstand. I'd managed a solid, if x-rated, seven hours, so I needed to get going.

A pot of coffee and a hot shower later, I was standing in my closet feeling unusually indecisive. In spite of losing the multimillion-dollar judgment against Dr. Hall, Sara Whitley still had major bucks. I couldn't show up at her place looking too off-the-rack. On the other hand, I didn't want Liam to think I'd gone to any trouble on his account.

Putting off the decision, I pulled on a yoga outfit and went into the kitchen, simultaneously gulping mug four of coffeepot number two while feeling around in the junk drawer for my key to Sam's place. Though he'd only been gone a few hours, I had this neurotic compulsion to check on the cats. I knew if I didn't, I'd spend the day convinced that they'd knocked over their water dish and were lying on the floor, too weak from an electrolyte imbalance to save themselves by drinking from the toilet bowl.

Instead, when I went upstairs, I found the two of them curled together on one of a scrumptious, matched pair of Italian leather recliners. They were blue-point Siamese, whatever the hell that meant, and if I had to guess, I'd say they were gay, too. They were always touching each other like, well, like Brokeback Kitties. Butch or Sundance— they're interchangeable to me—lifted his head and tossed me a "keep it down, bitch," look.

A nice person would have scratched behind his ears. Me? I went into the kitchen and made sure there was fresh water and some food, then into the bathroom to check the status of the litter box. Under the sink, I found a box of disposable gloves, slipped on a pair, and went to work. I handled the situation like someone removing toxic waste. Quickly. This so isn't my thing.

Before I went back to my place, I dropped the odor-masking pet pickup bag into the trash shoot. As far as I was concerned, for the next twelve or so hours, Butch and Sundance were on their own.

Normally, I have pretty decent attire instincts,

but Liam seemed to have penetrated that aspect of my personality as well. So I called Liv for fashion advice.

"We've got to be quick, I'm supposed to meet Becky and Jane in twenty minutes. Sure you won't change your mind and join us? It's a beautiful day, perfect for the beach."

"I know," I practically whined as I glanced out the window and noted the turquoise sky, complete with the occasional wispy cloud floating by and big, beautiful sun. Had it really been over a week since my last lounge by the ocean? "Maybe next weekend." Then I explained my quandary.

"Easily fixed," Liv said cheerfully. "Wear that white garden eyelet dress with the bright fuchsia trim. It's Lilly, right? Can't make a mistake with Lilly."

Sure you can, I thought. *You can wait for someone to smear blush on it and then the shop has to sell it to me for one-third of retail.*

"Take along a shrug, and you're good to go. Casual yet sophisticated."

"Shoes?" I asked, balancing the phone between my cheek and shoulder as I plucked the assigned items from their hangers.

"So you want to go for style or comfort? Flat or—"

"Not flat." I knew that. Liam was really tall, and I didn't want to have to crane my neck all morning just to maintain eye contact.

"Go with the grosgrain wedges. The ones with the colorful ribbons."

I smiled, grabbing up those as well. "You're a genius. Thanks."

"This Liam guy sure has your number."

"Does not," I insisted. "I'm trying to impress Mrs. Whitley, not Liam."

My supposed-to-be-friend laughed and said, "Sure you are."

I could have denied it, but what was the point? "Okay," I relented. "I really don't like being made to feel like a jerk. Liam is a master at making me feel . . . invisible."

"Some guys just have that ability."

"I guess. Have fun at the beach."

"Sorry you won't be there."

Me too.

Liv's wardrobe guidance was spot-on. By the time I'd put it all together, I looked polished without looking like I'd dressed for a date. Miracle of miracles, I was also ready early. *Way* early. Since I had some extra time, I powered up my computer and clicked my way to eBay. I was still winning the Betsey Johnson dress, but bids on the Rolex band links had climbed well beyond my per-part budget. The auction on the signature red box didn't end for another seven hours. I muttered a curse, then searched for any new listings.

"Isn't anyone out there hard up for cash?" I asked the screen after finding nothing. What I needed was a down-on-her-luck divorcée in need of ready cash. Preferably one who'd been left to fend for herself with nothing but the Rolex DateJust on her wrist. No such luck.

I should have shut off the computer, but I didn't. Even though I knew I was about to do a pathetic female thing, I couldn't help myself. I switched to the Google search engine and typed in Liam's name. Knowledge is power, and I was definitely in need of some when it came to him. If I could learn just one little secret about the guy, maybe I wouldn't feel so lacking when I was with him.

"Officer placed on administrative duty following fatal shooting," I read, gently rolling the pad of my finger along the touchpad as I scanned the five-year-old article. Not much in the way of details. Liam and his partner responded to a burglary in progress, and the partner, James Roberts, ended up dead.

I found a couple of follow-ups, but they were brief and referenced closed hearings. The last one said that no charges would be filed in the death of Officer Roberts but Lt. Liam McGarrity would be resigning from the police force—effective immediately.

My curiosity spiked. "Why would he give up his pension if he was cleared of any wrongdoing?"

There's cleared, and then there's *cleared*. It wouldn't be the first time a police officer was given the option of early retirement to save the department some embarrassment.

I tapped the ESCAPE key, no longer interested in the life and times of Liam McGarrity. Well, still interested, but I didn't want to cross that line between interest and stalking. I know it's standard and safe practice to check someone out online, but I think that only applies to blind dates and potential employers.

With my computer shut down, I turned my attention back to Graham Keller's medical records. I'd read them last night until my vision blurred, and if there was anything suspicious about his death, I wasn't seeing it.

One major hole in my theory was an explanation as to how Sara Whitley could have caused a tree to fall on José. Now I had a second gaping ravine—the doctors, nurses, paramedics, and even the EKG machine all confirmed that Graham Keller died following a massive coronary.

I could practically recite Marcus Evans's medical history from memory at this point. And while it appeared as if he'd nodded off at the wheel, end of story, in *that* case I had the videotape.

The prickly feeling at the back of my neck insisted I was missing the obvious. I trusted that feeling. It told me Mike Mattioli was cheating on me weeks before I'd caught him screwing the busty bartender in our bed. I dumped him *and* bought a new bed. I never should have let that jerk move in with me. Words of warning I'd heard from every one of my friends, but stupidly ignored. That, I decided, was the problem. Men bring out the stupid in me.

Except for Patrick.

I felt a renewed surge of self-disgust for my Liam dreams. Squeezing my eyes shut briefly, I decided it wasn't necessary to take a soul-searching look into my subconscious. At least not this freaking early on a Saturday morning.

Back to an area I was comfortable with—dead people. I knew I should probably report the threatening note to the police. But I really wasn't ready to go through the whole explanation. There were practically no "who"s, definitely not enough "why"s, and they'd probably think I was overreacting.

Despite the guy thing, I'm not stupid. I'd be damn careful—I'd treat every excursion out of my apartment like a stealth mission through Macy's after Thanksgiving: elbows out, chin tucked, eyes wide open. I decided to keep the note in my kitchen drawer until I knew more.

I really, really wanted something tangible by Monday. A full confession by Sara Whitley would be great, but that was wishful thinking. I needed at least one concrete fact. It didn't have to be huge, just enough to protect myself. Especially if Margaret and her not-so-merry maids were right and I was on the precipice of getting canned. I wrapped the shrug tighter around my shoulders and focused on saving my ass.

Luckily, my coffee table is square rather than the traditional rectangle—much to Sam's chagrin. He claims the shape throws off the balance in the room. May be true, but it gives me space to spread out and organize, in my own special way, the various aspects of this case.

Stacy Evans had provided me with glossy reproductions of the police photographs from the scene of her husband's murder. "When did I definitely decide it was a murder?" I muttered, tapping the toe of my sandal and staring at the piles. *About five seconds after I found a threatening note pinned to my door.* If there was nothing to this, then there was no reason to try and scare me off.

I shivered but refused to be deterred.

I-95 is always under construction, so I looked past the orange-striped barrels scattered along the side of the road to find the car in the photograph. It was on its roof, front end partially submerged in a shallow canal. I looked at three more photographs showing basically the same thing, only from different angles and distance. My stomach lurched when I flipped to the next picture. It showed Marcus Evans, suspended in place by a seat belt. There was some blood but not a lot.

It felt, I don't know . . . intrusive, disrespectful, somehow wrong. Normal people aren't meant to look at dead people. Especially freshly dead ones. That's for doctors, nurses, morticians, and other people who've chosen ghoulish professions.

I've only seen one dead person up close. Stepfather Number Two had an open casket. Now, there's one disgusting practice. He was a decent guy, but seeing him like that, arms crossed, face covered with pancake makeup, ruined it for me. After that, whenever I thought of John Rossi, my mind instantly recreated that macabre memory from the funeral home. John, gray, pasty, and dead. It was really sad. And then there was the fly. All during the service a fly buzzed around the room, landing with frequency on the tip of John's nose. When I go, I want them hanging those toxic fly strips from the ceiling every six or so inches over my head.

Carefully, I laid the photographs on the table and stared at them, cataloging each element. I knew the southbound construction through the Jupiter interchange well. They were resurfacing and adding a wider exit ramp for easier access to the turnpike. At least that was the plan. Like most construction projects, this one was behind schedule. At the time of Marcus's accident, only the two left lanes were open. Barrels blocked off a long stretch of the right lane, which had been ground down for grading and resurfacing.

There wasn't enough detail, so I went back to my trusty junk drawer and found the plastic magnifying glass I'd been given as a free gift for applying for a home improvement store's credit card. It was denied, but I didn't take it personally—it isn't like I do a lot of shopping at stores with cement floors.

Like a well-dressed, female version of Sherlock Holmes, I sat hunched over the photographs, examining every inch and detail. I smiled slowly. Not because I'd found something, but because I hadn't.

I was still feeling euphoric when Liam arrived.

"Wouldn't have pegged you for a morning person," he remarked as he moved past me.

He smelled of soap, shampoo, and coffee, and

even though I shouldn't have, I took a deep breath and savored the clean, fresh scent of him. As usual, he had on well-worn jeans, this time paired with a Tommy Bahama cotton shirt I guessed was at least three seasons old. Not that it mattered. There was something decidedly sexy about the way it hung from his broad shoulders, then tapered flatteringly until it tucked into his waistband.

His black hair was still slightly damp and looked as if he'd opted to use his fingers rather than a comb as a styling tool. Even though his pinky toe was a hair's breadth away from peeking out of his weathered Docksiders, he looked good.

I looked bad. Very, very bad, at least in the privacy of my own conscious. I followed him into the living room, repeating a mantra in my head: *Patrickpatrickpatrick.*

"What's all this?" he asked, tapping my photo array before turning his gaze in my direction.

Those dammed eyes of his. They were like blue lasers capable of cutting me off at the knees.

Ignore him! "I think I found something," I said, unable to mask the excitement in my voice.

"What's this?" he asked, hooking his finger through the bright orange nylon strap attached to my pitiful magnifying glass.

I snatched it away from him. "I had to improvise." I stood next to him—minor mistake—and held the magnifier over the first photograph. "That's, like, what? A four-inch drop between the roadway and the lane under construction?"

"Roughly."

"Now this." I moved to the second, larger image. "See the ruts in the gravel? They line up in a perfect diagonal to where Marcus's car launched over the Jersey wall and into the canal."

Taking the magnifying glass from me, Liam did his own review of the photographs. "Son-of-a-bitch."

I felt . . . redeemed. "Even if he was asleep at the wheel, there's no way he would have stayed asleep after falling off the road. He'd have been jolted awake and reacted."

"But he didn't," Liam confirmed. "See the tire marks?"

I leaned in closer and nodded.

"They're even. If the guy was even marginally conscious, he'd have done something. Turn the wheel. Hit the brakes."

"So, he was drugged," I concluded. "Anything he might have done to prevent the accident would have made the tread marks . . . squiggly, right?"

He tossed me that amused half-smile that I still couldn't quite decipher. " 'Squiggly' works." He pulled his cell phone from the clip at his belt. "I did a little investigating into your coffee-switching theory."

I wanted to grab him and kiss him for taking my idea seriously. Who was I kidding? I just wanted to kiss him, period. "Did you find the switched cup Marcus drank from the morning he was killed?"

"No." He smacked his forehead. "Damn, why didn't I think of that? I should have gone combing through all the area landfills for a paper cup."

"No need for sarcasm." Maybe the cup was in the car. I made a mental note to check on that. I could have asked Liam to do it, but right now, I felt I'd rather gnaw off my own tongue than make the suggestion.

I was still glaring at him as he held his phone in my direction, switching it to camera mode. "I spent the morning conducting an unscientific experiment."

An image flashed on the small screen. It was obviously taken through the cracks of mini-blinds. The picture was of a bare-breasted brunette, riding crop in hand, whipping an old bald guy wearing nothing but a dog collar.

"Sorry, that's from an old case," he said, pressing a button.

"Quite the memento."

Liam ignored my barb, treating me to a slide show of people drinking coffee at the same Starbucks Marcus had visited the morning of his death. "You're right about the size thing."

"Imagine that."

"Twenty-six people hung around long enough to order a second drink. By the way, a fat-free, half-soy, sugar-free, no-whip, frappa-whatever would have to be made of gold for me to slap down that kind of money for a cup of coffee. Speaking of that—got any made?"

"Always." I went into the kitchen and filled a mug for him and topped mine off while I was at it.

"Not a single one of them," he continued, "went for the bigger size."

"Told you."

"They don't have security cameras, but there is a video feed from the drive-through. The manager said he'd have to get permission from corporate first, but he agreed to send you the tape if he gets the okay."

He downed the coffee in a few gulps. "Ready to roll?"

I'd emptied my briefcase save for a legal pad and a few pens. It weighed less than my purse, but, then again, so did most suitcases. You can never be too prepared.

I locked the door on my way out. "My car or yours?"

"You pick," he suggested, pointing to one of the visitor's spots.

"Car" was a generous description of the thing. "What is it?"

"A work in progress," he said unapologetically. "She's a sixty-four Mustang. I'm in the process of having her rebuilt."

"Out of Play-Doh?"

"That's putty," he corrected. "Don't rag on my car. It's only because I'm such a great customer that the mechanic at Charlie's Garage agreed to go over the Evans car."

"If you're such a great customer, how come he doesn't paint it?"

He shook his head slowly. "A car is restored from the inside out."

"Whatever," I said, tossing him the keys to my BMW.

He caught them easily, giving a little condescending grin when he saw the blue, white, and black logo. "I'm shocked to discover you drive a status-mobile?"

My car chirped and the headlights blinked when the alarm disengaged. "You're just jealous because mine has matching tires."

"I'm green with envy."

"No, you're not."

He slipped behind the wheel and flashed me a grin. "No, I'm not."

In my most professional voice, I said, "Sara Whitley lives—"

"At Whitehall House," he finished. "A pricey little gem—ten thousand square feet of house on its very own private acre on Palm Beach proper. Bet the taxes on that place are a bitch."

"I doubt she's hard up for money. Her husband built or brokered half the residential properties in City Place."

"She's come a long way from that trailer in Tupelo."

"What?"

"Sara Whitley comes from pretty humble beginnings."

"Wow."

Though I'd only seen her the one time at The Breakers the day before her wedding, she'd seemed poised, polished, and to the manor born. Damn, talk about marrying up.

"It probably helped that she's a former Miss Mississippi."

"Couldn't hurt," I agreed. "Forgive the broad generalization, but if Sara grew up in a trailer park, she might know people capable of murder. She doesn't have to be the actual killer to get the job done. Being an ex–beauty queen, she could probably charm a man into eating off his own foot. Convincing someone to kill for you wouldn't be much of a stretch."

He sent me that *look*. "Maybe you should meet the woman before you convict her?"

"I'm just running theories here." Damned good ones, if you ask me, which he didn't, so I sat quietly for the remainder of the drive, feeling invisible, even in Lilly.

Whitehall House lived up to its pretentious name. Well, pretty much any house with its own name is pretentious. The two-story home—correction, estate—was an oyster-shell gray with coral accents. A circular drive curved past impressive landscaping, widening near the arched front of the home. Sprinklers ticked as they spewed water on the shimmering green lawn. I could hear the faint hum of a speedboat passing by, drowned out momentarily by the shrill squawk of a gull.

A uniformed maid greeted us, her black eyes wary as she reluctantly ushered us inside the palatial space. The foyer soared up two stories, dominated by an abstract water sculpture flowing into a koi pond.

I glanced at the impressive collection adorning the walls. "Someone's a fan of cubist art," I whispered.

"Is that what you call the ugly shi—"

"Mrs. Whitley will see you now," the maid said.

We were led to a large, rectangular room at the back of the house. The far wall was floor-to-ceiling glass with a stunning view of pristine beach. Everything about the room was perfect. Everything except the woman standing off to one side, clutching a photograph in one hand and a highball glass in the other.

Even without the telltale glass, one look at Sara Whitley and I knew she was on the fast road to drunk. It didn't seem to matter that it was barely ten in the morning, nor did she seem particularly bothered by the fact that two complete strangers had caught her in the act.

"Mrs. Whitley, I'm Finley Tanner from the law firm of Dane-Lieberman." Okay, I expected that to get a reaction out of her. Hell, Victor Dane had successfully defended Dr. Hall.

Nothing. Nada, zero. Not even so much as a flicker of recognition in those bloodshot blue eyes.

She looked past me to the maid. "Maria, get Finley Tanner from the law firm of whatever and whatever something to drink." Her head moved jerkily toward Liam. "Who are you?"

Liam introduced himself. "Some coffee would be nice," he told the maid as he sat down on the edge of one of three ottomans.

"Sit," Sara told me, using her drinking hand to point in the general direction of a chair. Colorless liquid sloshed out of her glass, splashing on to the terra-cotta tile. It bled into the grout before she said, "Oops," with an inappropriate giggle.

"Maybe you should sit down," Liam said, rising to take the glass from her hand and steering her by the elbow to the closest chair.

They shared a little exchange before Liam handed her back the glass and she said, "Thank you."

Well, I knew how she'd spent a good portion of the last three years—inside a bottle of vodka. Tough to plan an intricate series of murders when you were killing off your brain cells one shot at a time.

Maria returned with an ornate silver coffee service, poured, then discreetly exited the room. "I appreciate you agreeing to see me," I said as I brought the porcelain cup to my lips.

"Did I?"

Great, this was like interviewing dryer lint. "Mrs. Whitley, are you aware that there have been some incidents with the jurors from the civil trial?"

She made a sound that was somewhere between a laugh and a grunt. "That wasn't a trial. It was a farce. The Almighty Dr. Hall wasn't responsible for Brad's death." She hugged the photograph more tightly. "Twelve people said so."

"You don't believe that, though, right?"

She shook her head and drained her glass. Looking at Liam, Sara rattled the cubes against the empty crystal. He responded by getting her a refill from a decanter on the bar. "The transplant was supposed to save him. Hall swore to me that nothing would go wrong."

"I don't think there are absolute certainties in medicine," I said gently.

"No, no, no," she said emphatically. "Hall said the donor was a perfect match. Told me nothing could go wrong."

Well, this was going nowhere fast.

"Ever think about getting even with the doctor?"

She stared at me, looking as confused as her pickled brain cells could manage. "How? I sued him. I lost."

"So you decided to crawl into a bottle?" Liam asked.

She looked shocked at his bald statement, but then shrugged. "Pretty much. I thought about suicide, tried a couple of times, but I can't seem to get the job done." Tears welled in her eyes. "I miss him." She looked down at the photograph as tears spilled unchecked down her cheeks.

A few minutes later, as we left Sara mired in her grief, even I was on the verge of tears. "She isn't a killer."

"Because she drinks and cries?" Liam countered.

"Because whoever orchestrated these murders put a lot of time and thought into them."

"Or they aren't murders."

I stopped suddenly and grabbed his arm, practically spinning him in a semicircle. "Do you honestly believe that?"

"No."

*Never put anything in your mouth you can't
cut with a knife and fork—namely, your foot.*

Eleven

There was another note waiting for me when I
returned from the Sara Whitley field trip. In
some ways, it was scarier than the first. It was from
my mother. Technically, it wasn't a note, but rather
a card tucked inside a FedEx envelope.

I could gauge my mother's level of displeasure
with me partly by her means of communication.
The fact that a formal invitation to brunch came
via FedEx did not bode well.

Here it was Sunday morning and I still had the
echo of Liam's derisive chuckle in my head. Dis-
playing a predictable amount of testosterone, he'd
snatched the envelope from me and ripped into it
over my fevered protests. To say that discovering the
calligraphied command from my own mother had
amused him was something of an understatement.
Not to mention that yet again, I'd ended up looking like an ass. He was probably still wondering—
and laughing at—the fact that my mother sent me

a written invitation for an already planned, agreed upon time-and-place, brunch.

I wished now I'd taken my yoga classes a little more seriously. Maybe then I'd actually know how to find my chakra. Any of the seven would do, so long as it relieved the knot of trepidation lodged in my stomach. But, no, I'd been more into the flattering way the Lycra outfit lifted my butt than actually learning ways to calm my inner being.

I'd read somewhere that a pet lowers your blood pressure, so I filled a travel mug with hot coffee and ventured upstairs for a morning visit with Butch and Sundance. They were less than enthused to see me. After taking care of the feeding, watering, and litter-boxing, I went to what Sam dubbed the "toy chest" and pulled out a couple of burlap mice.

The cats were on opposite ends of the sofa, as still as sentries. Only their shifty, almond-shaped eyes followed me as I sat on the floor and called, "Kitty, kitty?" Then I rolled the mice a few feet in front of me.

The one on the left glanced at the bright red mouse but didn't move. The other cat stood, arched his back, and started grooming his private parts. I tried again, still without success. I tried different toys, toys with bells, toys with springs, toys with fuzz, toys with feathers. Nothing seemed to interest the lazy balls of fur, so I grabbed my coffee and gave up. Maybe they just weren't morning kitties.

Before locking the door, I stuck my head back inside the apartment, smirked, and said, "You guys suck as companions. Have a nice day."

For reasons I didn't understand, I'd been up since six. Unlike yesterday, selecting today's outfit was a no-brainer. I could go one of two ways—classic Ann Taylorish, which would no doubt please my mother. Or trendy chic, which would annoy her on sight. It was tempting, but I went with the conservative: a navy cotton skirt, pale pink blouse, and seed-pearl choker. Uninventive, but definitely conflict-avoidance wear.

Since I was ready way, way early—this was turning into a nasty habit—is it possible that I might need to cut back on the caffeine? No! I went back to the Evans files, hoping another pass with fresh eyes might provide some answers. I was fortified knowing that Liam shared my suspicions, not that I needed his approval or anything. Why would I?

"Forget him," I grumbled, grabbing up the medical reports I could almost recite from memory.

Going with the theory that some sort of drug or poison had caused Marcus to crash his car, I figured Keller had suffered a similar fate. What, how, and why were still mysteries.

The notes from the paramedics who'd responded to the Kravis Center call only confirmed that Keller was in full cardiac arrest when they'd arrived. It had taken them seven minutes of CPR, oxygen, and IV meds to get him back. His heart rate was unstable during transport, but he'd arrived at the ER alive. Barely.

For the next thirty-six minutes every possible attempt had been made to revive him, but in the end, nothing worked. He was pronounced dead less than an hour after his public collapse at the Kravis Center.

Keller's brief, unsuccessful treatment had generated about thirty pages of notes and forms. Some only had single notations, but everything done to or for Keller was documented and initialed. Right down to the nurse's aide whose only job was cutting off Keller's tuxedo once he was on the exam table.

There were several pages labeled postmortem findings. Though the language was different on all of them, the conclusions were the same: Keller was dead. But, on the plus side, someone with the initials HC had ordered blood tests on the deceased, though no results were included in the records I had.

Weird. Keller's death was months ago. Surely the lab results would have made it into his file by now.

I went back through the treatment records and found several other entries by Helen Callahan, R.N., and even more places where she'd initialed various things. One sentence just before the notation of the time of death was scratched out and initialed by her. Holding it up to the stream of sunlight coming through my patio doors, I tried to read through the cross-out.

"IV, maybe?" I squinted and concentrated. More words I couldn't read, then *Cal*-something and the word *push*.

Firing up my laptop, I did a search for Helen Callahan. Unfortunately, there were eleven in Palm Beach County alone. But I knew it wouldn't be a problem, I could track her down at the hospital. I added her name and the hospital's address to my running list of people to interview. Just in case.

My e-mail dinged, and the inbox icon popped up on my screen. My mood improved when I read the notification from eBay that I had won the box for my not yet completed Rolex. Quickly, I clicked my way over to PayPal and completed the transaction. I shimmied my shoulders, thrilled to pieces.

It wasn't like me to blow off the end of an auction, but it really had slipped my mind.

There were a few dozen other e-mails, mostly offers to enlarge my nonexistent penis. One of these days I was going to learn how to block those ads, but today wasn't that day. I was about to shut down when an incoming IM arrived. Figuring it was a thank-you from the eBay seller, I clicked it open and read the comment:

Hi Finley.

The instant message was from someone named AfterAll. I smiled, thinking it was a pretty creative name for someone dealing in aftermarket items. Me? I'd gone with FATgirl, figuring it would keep the pervs from offering a cyber hookup. Wrong. Apparently there were a lot of guys—and a few women—into loving large.

"Thanks for the box," I spoke as I typed. "Looking forward to receiving it."

Don't be.

"No, no, no!" I typed furiously:

Why? I just paid you.

You won't live long enough to enjoy it.

The chilling comment was followed by an alert that AfterAll had logged off.

With my pulse pounding, delivering a healthy dose of fear to my entire body, I stared at my laptop. I didn't have to be a Mensa member to know that AfterAll was the same person who'd left the threatening note on my door. Great. He knew where I lived and my private screen name.

My hands were shaking. Hell, all of me was shaking, and it wasn't with the adrenaline from getting a Rolex part. I wished Sam was home—at least then I'd have someplace to run and hide. Under my bed wasn't feeling very safe. Under Patrick's

bed might be better, but I knew from experience
that tracking him down was virtually impossible.
Apparently a cell phone from Radio Shack was capable of disrupting the navigational system of a
DC-10.

So, by default, I dialed Becky's number. I cursed
colorfully when I got her voice mail. The same was
true when I tried Liv and Jane. What good are
friends when you can't even share a cryptic death
threat with them?

I was tempted to call Liam, but that just seemed
too damsel-in-distressish. Besides, he was probably
doing a . . . *thing*.

My mother was out. She wasn't exactly known
for her compassion and empathy where I was concerned, so I decided to go to the only safe haven
available—Dunkin' Donuts.

Normally, I would have hit Starbucks—personal
preference only—but there wasn't one on the way
to Ironhorse Country Club.

Again I considered calling the police. Prudent,
but what if I was wrong? What if this was just a sick
joke? Okay, too much of a coincidence, but still, I
didn't want to look like a moron. Not to the police, not to my boss, and definitely not to myself.

I'm no computer genius, so I figured the best
thing to do was to put the machine in HIBERNATE,
then maybe—and that was a big maybe—I could
take it to the computer geeks at Dane-Lieberman
and they could identify the sender. Then what? Simple. I'd have a name, and I could go to the police
and have AfterAll arrested. Then I'd file a civil suit
for harassment, collect a huge settlement. Maybe
even enough to buy a Rolex outright.

A little later, feeling foolish but justified, I taped
the 10X magnifying mirror normally reserved for

plucking the stray eyebrow hair between waxes to the end of a meat fork.

After checking outside for anyone or anything suspicious, I used the makeshift device to search the undercarriage of my car. I wasn't sure what I was looking for, TNT and a timer? Okay, maybe I was overreacting, but caution seemed appropriate considering I was scared shitless.

Holding my breath, I got into the car and started the engine, half expecting it to explode into a ball of fire. When it didn't, I admitted that perhaps I'd watched a few too many Mafia movies and needed to get a grip.

On the plus side, the most recent threat made my impending brunch date with my mother seem like a walk in the park. Of course, I didn't usually walk in parks, unless I was on my way to the beach.

Once at the busy Dunkin' Donuts, I downed three iced vanilla lattes while sitting with my back to the wall at one of the outdoor tables. The blend of caffeine and sugar calmed my nerves. Either that, or it was the fact that I was in a busy public place, insulated from AfterAll.

I'd brought along my legal pad, using the extra time before brunch to organize and formulate my thoughts on the Evans investigation. I had a pretty long list of people to interview, and at some point I was going to have to share my fears with the remaining jurors. Soon, too—since Stacy had already given them a premature heads-up. However, I'd feel better if I had a viable suspect to report.

The Evans thing had me in an awkward position. Dane-Lieberman was such a stodgy firm, they wouldn't welcome publicity. Particularly if I didn't have evidence to back up my assertions. I think someplace in the back of my mind that was one of the reasons I was so reluctant to go to the authorities about the note and the IM. Both could be easily explained away. Bored teenagers at the apartment complex took care of the note. Lord knew cyberjerks were a dime a dozen, and even I knew how to track bidders on eBay. It would have been quite simple for a geek to learn about my recent purchase and send an IM just to be a shit. I would have to *prove* these were not coincidences before I went begging for help.

Once I had proof, though, I'd use all my firm's available resources. I felt residual panic knot in my stomach and knew that dwelling on questions I couldn't yet answer wasn't the way to go.

Back to work. I scratched Sara Whitley off the list. If yesterday was at all illustrative of her drinking problem, she was way too far in the bottle to plan one murder, let alone three.

"Means, motive, and opportunity," I mumbled. I was leaning toward poison. It fit. However, I wouldn't know the truth until I got the lab results, and those would take at least another twenty-plus hours. And that was only if Liam got the blood early enough for an independent lab to run the tests on the same day. It might help if I could find the coffee cup Marcus had been drinking from that morning. Maybe there was some residue that could be tested. Given that the car had flipped onto its hood, I didn't hold out much hope. Still, it was worth a run by Charlie's Garage.

I had the address, er, addresses. There were two Charlie's Garages in the phone book, one in Riviera Beach and another down in Boca Raton. It made more sense for Liam to do business with someone up here rather than making a sixty-mile round trip. Especially when his piss-poor excuse for a car probably broke down on a set schedule.

Motive was easy—something about serving on that jury was costing them their lives. Or maybe it was just those three jurors? Maybe there was something the three of them did or said that made them targets. Belated targets, I reminded myself. Therein lay the rub. Three years was a long time to bide your time while holding a fatal grudge.

Opportunity seemed the result of planning. I knew Marcus kept a strict schedule. I added a note to my pad to check on the regular activities of Keller and Vasquez. If they also lived routine-driven lives, it was pretty easy to see how someone could find a way to get to them.

Just as they had gotten to me, I thought with a little shiver. Hell, in under a week, AfterAll knew enough about me to have me shaking in my navy linen BCBGirls, peek-a-boo sandals.

"Shit!" I managed through gritted teeth when I noticed the time. I swallowed the rest of my latte while grabbing up the legal pad and my purse. Dropping the cup in a battered green trash can, I hurried to my car. There was no way I'd make it to Ironhorse in time unless I completely ignored the speed limit.

I did, and was making great time until I heard the jolting sound of a siren, forcing me to glance in my rearview mirror. My prayer that it was an emergency vehicle signaling me to move out of the left lane was dashed instantly. The red and blue flashing lights atop the cruiser were all about me.

I pulled over, simultaneously pressing the button to open the window, unzipping my purse, and digging for my wallet. The officer, a pencil-necked, red-haired young guy, came up, pad clutched in his hand.

"Afternoon, ma'am," he greeted formally.

"Officer," I returned, handing him my license, registration, and insurance card.

The radio clipped at his shoulder crackled. "Do you know how fast you were going?"

Why lie? "Sixty-one, give or take."

He smiled beneath his polarized sunglasses. "The posted speed limit is forty-five."

I sighed, then looked directly up at him. Well, directly at my own reflection, but that didn't matter. "I had to go for it," I admitted. "My mother can be a real . . . challenge when I'm late, which I am, so could you write my ticket quickly?"

He shrugged, "Please remain in your vehicle." He clipped my license to his ticket book and walked to the back of my car. Drumming my fingers on the console, I kept one eye on the skinny cop. My stomach churned just thinking about the consequences of my actions. Not the ticket—I deserved that. But now I was not only going to *be* late for brunch, I'd probably get grilled into explaining *why*. If I was really unlucky, during the meal I'd be reminded of the time when she'd had to pay almost a thousand dollars in speeding fines on my behalf. The fact that I was sixteen at the time didn't seem to matter; apparently that particular childhood infraction didn't have an expiration date.

Officer Pencil Neck returned and recited my options. "If you wish to contest this ticket, as is your right under Florida statute—"

"I know," I interrupted. "Just let me sign and be on my way." One minute and seventy-eight dollars later, I had the ticket tucked in my purse and was back on my way.

Ironhorse is a manicured, gated golf community bracketed between I-95 and the turnpike. I waved to the guard, who passed me through on sight, then checked the clock on the dash. Twenty minutes late was a lifetime in mother-years.

Making a quick right, then a left, I weaved through the foliage-lined parking area and grabbed the first open spot. The minute I stepped out of the car, I smelled the scent of fresh-baked goods. Ironhorse had amazing desserts, and if I played my cards right, I'd be able to stick a few of their signature chocolate macaroons into my purse without my mother noticing. Maybe I could wrap them in my speeding ticket?

The country club is accessible by way of an awkward climb up a pretty steep, man-made walkway. It's worth it, though, because the food is fabulous and the views of the golf course with its lagoons and colorful landscaping are stunning.

The fact that my mother has an equity membership to an exclusive golf club is the very definition of irony. It was the spoils of her second divorce. While the food is great, and they do throw nice parties, the truth is, she only wanted it to punish her soon-to-be ex. That was the true spirit of divorce, not that *whatever* Liam had going on with Beer Barbie.

I stepped into the lobby, smiling as I passed through the bar area toward the hostess. A small group of people were watching some sporting event on the television mounted discreetly off to one side. One woman waved to me. I returned the gesture even though I didn't have the first clue who she was.

Peeking around the carving station, I saw my mother seated alone at the table, sipping a mimosa. To the uninitiated, she was the personification of pleasantry. She was, as always, beautiful. Her brown hair was pulled up in a perfect twist, save for a few soft tendrils left loose to soften the overall effect. Thanks to her years at the Met, my mother was an absolute artist when it came to cosmetics. She kept herself in good shape, too. She followed a strict exercise regime, never allowing her size to creep above a six.

Sadly, the only thing we had in common was eye color, pale blue. So, with a fortifying breath, I asked the hostess to show me to the table. It felt a lot like an inmate asking the warden to show him to the gas chamber.

"Finley!" my mother exclaimed, mostly for the benefit of our fellow diners. Half rising from her chair, she offered me her cheek, which I dutifully kissed. Heavy Bal A Versailles vapors nearly knocked me to my knees.

She sat, giving me a good once-over in the process. "I could have easily made a later reservation."

"Why?" I asked, thanking the waiter as he adjusted my seat.

"You would have had more time to do your hair."

She shoots, she scores! My hair looked fine, thank you, but I knew better than to trade barbs with the master. "I had some work to do this morning. A new case."

"A new case of what?" she asked, lifting the menu I knew damned good and well she had memorized by now.

Herpes. No, Finley, don't say it. It's not worth it. "A murder case."

Mom reacted as if she'd been slapped. "You? Involved in a murder?"

"The investigation part, Mom. It's not like I'm a suspect or anything."

"Are you qualified to do something like this? Doesn't one need some sort of education or training to investigate a serious crime?"

"I *have* an education." I twisted and got the attention of the waiter, mouthing the words *Bloody Mary, strong*, practically pleading with my eyes.

"I meant a real one. Like law school."

Under five minutes. Breaking the previous "Finley, you're wasting your life" taunt record by more than a minute. "Maybe someday," I hedged. It was easier than telling her it wasn't going to happen and then listening to her opinions.

"Who was murdered?"

"Three 'who's,'" I elaborated. I gave a vague rundown on the case, and to her credit and my surprise, my mother actually seemed mildly interested.

"I know Dr. Hall and his wife, Meredith. Lovely woman." My mother leaned across the table in a rare expression of consideration for others. "Though his practice must be struggling."

"Why?"

"Well." She paused while the waiter delivered my drink. "They're patrons. Have been for some time, and you know how desperately the Opera Society needs patrons? If you went to law school, you might earn enough money to make philanthropic donations just as Lisa does."

How did we get from the Halls to my lack of an advanced degree, to my sister's perceived superiority all in one sentence? Amazing. "Lisa and David are generous people." The fact that my sister's fiancé comes from a family with more money than a Saudi principality didn't hurt. The St. Johns could give ten grand away every day for the rest of their lives and never notice it. I was sure David IV was smart enough to add my mother's pet charities to his list. The Opera Society of Palm Beach was Mom's baby. Opera was the only thing I think she ever loved unconditionally.

"Why do you think Dr. Hall's practice is in trouble?"

"I didn't say trouble," Mom amended as the waiter arrived.

"Have we decided?"

"Yes," my mother answered. The fact that I hadn't even touched the menu was of no consequence.

"It's gotten so late, I think we'll order lunch, so I'll have the house salad, then red snapper, broiled, without the buerre blanc, please. Oh, and have the chef substitute steamed broccoli for the potato, and no rice."

"Very good, and for you, miss?"

Rebellion bubbled up inside me. "I'd like the Caesar salad, please. Filet mignon, rare, extra béarnaise on the side. May I have the twice-baked potato with extra sour cream?"

"Thank you, ladies."

"I'm glad you brought your appetite," my mother remarked, her tone completely negating the marginal compliment.

"About Dr. Hall?" I suggested.

"Their donations have fallen off the past few months."

"How many months?"

"Three, four maybe. The Society depends on the regular patrons. It's quite a hardship when someone cuts off funding without notice."

"Just like that? Out of the blue?" I asked.

Mom nodded, shifting as the waiter served our

salads. "You'd think people would be more considerate, wouldn't you?"

"Um, I guess," I mumbled, trying to fit this new piece into my puzzle.

"Is your back bothering you?"

I peered up and met my mother's gaze. "No, why?"

"The way you were slouching, I simply assumed you'd injured your back."

I straightened immediately. "Sorry. How was your cruise?"

"Lovely," she said. "Europeans, mostly."

"Any interesting people?"

Placing her fork on the edge of her plate, she reached into her purse and pulled out a small stack of photographs.

Though she'd spent nearly a month at sea—the Mediterranean, no less—the dozen pictures were all of men. "This is Philippe. He's Belgian. He owns some sort of manufacturing plant in Ghent."

I looked at Stepfather Candidate Number One. He was bald, with a snow-white beard and moustache. I'm not really into facial hair, so I subtracted a few points. He almost earned them back with his smile; it seemed genuine.

"This," my mother said, passing me another photograph, "is Peitro, Pepe for short. He breeds polo ponies in Argentina. I invited him to visit the next time he's in town. He's in the middle of a divorce."

Handsome, in a dark and swarthy way. A rebounder was never a good choice, though. Too unpredictable. Candidate Number Two wasn't doing it for me, either.

By the time we finished eating, I had met eleven men from three continents. Philippe, Pepe, Gino—

sounded way too much like names for poodles, if you asked me. Luckily, no one did.

I also got the update on Lisa and David IV's nuptials. They were still at the color-scheme-selection stage. My mother seemed quite excited that Lisa was leaning toward "bone and chalk." Sounded a lot like a crime-scene outline to me, but I kept that to myself. Surely it would be an improvement over the last theme—moss and pumpkin—which in my book was just a fancy way of saying green and orange.

We ended with an air kiss and my mother's offer to see if she could get me in to see her colorist, unless—her words—brassy highlights were currently the vogue.

And I'd forgotten to snag the good cookies. Crap.

Normally I rebound from a visit with my mother by restoring my sense of self-worth with a glass of wine and some online shopping. But thanks to AfterAll, I wasn't in any huge hurry to return to my apartment, or my laptop. A visit to The Gardens Mall seemed like a decent alternative.

I was flush, thanks to direct deposit, and I hadn't yet tested the new colors at MAC and Sephora. Sunday afternoon was a great time to visit the up-scale shopping mall, but April was a lousy sale month. As I handed my keys and a few dollars to the valet—yes, the mall has valet parking—I decided that between my mother and all the work I'd been doing, I'd earned the right to splurge.

The mall is anchored by Nordstrom's, Macy's, Lord & Taylor, Bloomingdale's, and Sears—though I wouldn't complain if they tossed Sears and welcomed Neiman's. I don't foresee a time when I'll need any Craftsman tools, but no one consulted me before selecting retailers.

The interior has an open, atrium feel to it—lots of skylights, fountains, and tiled planters. At Christmas they rig up a bubble machine, creating fake snow to float down on stunning holiday displays.

With Easter approaching, the decorations are all pastels, with pretty, delicate eggs hidden among the plants. As I meandered past small specialty shops, glancing at window displays, I was assaulted by a variety of odors—chocolate from the gourmet kitchen place, gardenia from the bath shop, and heavy colognes from the spritz Nazis patrolling the cosmetic counters of the department stores. I tend to take a detour through costume jewelry to avoid the unwelcomed spray-first, ask-second tactics employed by the perfume reps.

I was still purchaseless when I took the elevator up to the second floor. A first for me. Nothing was calling to me. Maybe I was coming down with something. The best I could muster was a trip over to Tiffany's to visit a ring I'd been coveting for some time. Whoever came up with the idea of calling some engagement rings "right-hand rings" should get a huge bonus. Yes, I know it's a sales tool, but it's effective. I don't feel like a complete loser lusting after a ring that doesn't require boyfriend validation to own.

The only thing standing between me and the right-hand ring is thirteen thousand dollars. Still, I enjoyed the ritual of having the sales associate lift it from the case, lay it on the black velvet cloth, then allow me to slip it on my finger.

Nothing sparkles like this 1.7 carat, FL-IF–clarity,

E-colored round diamond. Extending my arm, I admired the ring for several minutes, watching the reflected light prism little rainbows around the store. With a returning-to-reality sigh, I took it off and handed it back.

I'd earned the right to splurge, not completely ruin my already stretched credit. Needing to buy something, I went down to Victoria's Secret and found a darling pink polka-dot cami and boxer PJ set with matching robe. By paying full price, I got a free sample of their lip plumper, so my bargain needs were met.

I picked up a few new cosmetics, then checked my watch. The mall was due to close soon, but I wasn't ready to go home yet. I called Sam's number; he still wasn't back. While I wasn't particularly hungry, I decided I couldn't pass up the opportunity for some lettuce wraps at P.F. Chang's. Besides, if I dallied long enough, Sam might get back from the He-She trip, and then I could go to my apartment without the possibility of wetting myself if my fear bubbled back to the surface.

I ate the lettuce wraps, even nursed a martini, but more speed-dialed calls confirmed that Sam still wasn't home. It was dark out now, and unless I was going to offer to wash dishes, I needed to leave.

Since I'd occupied the table for the better part of two hours, I left the server a very generous tip. Between that, the jammies, the second tip to the valet, and the speeding ticket, it had been a pretty damned expensive Sunday.

I headed toward the mall exit, fully intending to buck up and face my fears. Reaching the intersection, I made an impromptu left turn from the right-hand lane—a move not appreciated by my fellow drivers. Every now and again I seem to forget that I have a triple-digit IQ. This was definitely one of those times. If Palm Beach County has a bad section, I suppose Riviera Beach would be it. Well, some parts of it. More specifically, the part where Charlie's Garage was located. Yes, this would have been better during the day.

Slowly, I turned down a rutted dead-end street, flicking on the high beams as I crept along in the dark. It was an industrial area, and even with the windows closed, I smelled the stench of rotting vegetation, overfilled Dumpsters, and motor oil.

Charlie's was at the end of the road. Through a six-foot, chain-link fence with KEEP OUT signs posted every few feet, I saw a three-bay garage connected to a corrugated aluminum building I guessed was the office.

Digging a penlight out of my purse, I cut the engine but left the headlights trained on the fence. The sound of a dog barking didn't do a lot for my fading bravery, but I wanted to know if the coffee cup was still in Marcus's car.

A smart person would have come back in the morning, but not me—not once I shined my little flashlight through the fencing and recognized the crushed Cadillac from the accident photos spread out on my coffee table. Which made me think of the laptop, which made me think of the note, which made me think of the boogeyman who knew just where I lived. Charlie's Garage had to be safer than my own home.

I walked around the edge of the fence, hunting for a gate. Found it. Padlocked. Looking up, I realized there was no razor wire on top of the fence and figured it was worth a try. I've done the rock-climbing wall at the gym; this wouldn't be so different. Hopefully, the harness thing wasn't a necessary element for scaling a wall, since it was one of the few items I didn't carry in my purse.

Slipping my foot into one of the metal openings, I hoisted myself off the ground. Carefully, I moved one hand, then the opposite foot, then the other hand, and kept going until I reached the top of the fence. Now came the tricky part.

Clenching the flashlight in my teeth, I hiked up my skirt and began my descent down the other side. When I was a little more than a foot off the ground, I jumped, then stumbled. Landing on four-and-a-half-inch-high sling-backs isn't all that easy.

Brushing off my hands and purposefully not thinking about the damage I'd done to my skirt and blouse, I moved through the rows of dead and dying cars to the Caddy and shone my flashlight inside. I cringed when I saw the crimson spot on the fabric seat. *Blood*. Perhaps this wasn't such a great idea. Too late now. Not finding anything, I walked around to the passenger side and felt a rush of excitement when the beam of my flashlight reflected off something white.

Getting to it was a whole other thing. The roof was crushed almost even with the car's body. While there was no glass left in the windows or where the windshield had been, shards littered the car. So much for safety glass.

Bending sideways, I wedged as much of myself into the narrow opening as possible. My fingers fell about an inch shy of the cup.

"Damn!" I shimmied out, removed one of my shoes, then, balancing on one leg, I tried again, this time using my shoe to coax the cup from under the seat.

"Success!" I cheered as I reclaimed my shoe and reached back to hook my pinkie inside the rim and retrieve the cup.

I did my best to scrape the dirt off my foot before slipping on my shoe. The fact that I'd tracked down an honest-to-goodness piece of evidence all on my own made me feel great. My pulse was racing, my heart was pounding, and—

The rattle of metal and a low growl brought me back to reality. Twenty feet away, a really big, really mean-looking dog stood there, teeth bared. Big teeth.

"N-nice doggie."

He barked. I yelped.

Whoever advised that you shouldn't make any sudden moves around a strange animal obviously never spent any time trapped behind a fence with a Cujo wannabe. I decided to make a run for it.

Not a good plan. I had scaled less than two feet of fence when the damned dog bit me in the ass.

Stupidity should be a federal offense.
But then we'd have to build a lot more prisons.

Twelve

"I'm not a thief!" I yelled to the dumb dog, hearing the distinctive sound of fabric ripping over the wail of rapidly approaching sirens. Next I felt a warm trickle of blood at the back of my leg, which freaked me out. I consoled myself by acknowledging that at least I still *had* my leg. Amazing, given that I was being eaten alive by the Hound of the Baskervilles. I was completely convinced that the slobbering, growling guard dog was hell-bent on chomping me up like his new favorite chew-toy before spitting me out.

There was a quick, sharp whistle, then the dog gave me one last scowl before turning and jogging back to its master.

The dog's handler wasn't much of an improvement over the mangy—yet effective—animal. I recognized some German shepherd, some Doberman, and a few other breeds in the animal. Not exactly a former AKC champion. The man standing beside it.

I remained clinging for dear life to the chain-link fence as, one after another, three patrol cars skidded to a halt in a spray of gravel and shrieking sirens. They surrounded my car, then blinded me with white-hot spotlights.

"Thank God you're here!" I called in desperation to the silhouette of an approaching officer. "This freaking dog is mauling me!"

"Hey, Charlie!" one of the officers called. "Hook up that dog so the lady can get down."

Charlie? The garage owner is pals with the cops? There was no way this was going to work in my favor.

"C'mon, Boo-Boo."

I cringed. I'd been bitten in the butt by a dog named Boo-Boo? This was going from bad to worse to shit really fast.

After Charlie put the dog somewhere out of sight, he opened the padlock and let three sheriff's deputies inside the lot. My fingers had gone numb. I was still dangling off the fence like a bloody cobweb.

"You can get down now," the officer instructed. "Do you need help?" He pressed a button on the mike clipped at his shoulder. "We've got an injury incident at Charlie's Garage. Four seventeen Perry Court."

Injury incident? What is it about cops that they can't talk like the rest of us? A car is a *vehicle,* a woman is a *female,* going into a building is *entering a dwelling.* Geez, these guys could overcomplicate anything.

"I'm fine," I lied, trying to hold on to my last shred of dignity. I was far from fine. My butt burned, and my worn-twice skirt had jagged rips even my miracle dry cleaner wouldn't be able to fix. Oh, yeah, and I was probably in serious trouble.

A half-second before joining me and the cops, I got a whiff of Charlie. Stale beer and even staler cigar smoke. He was every negative stereotype possible. His hair—and I'm using that term generously—was a dark, slick, greasy comb-over, that even the stiff gusts of wind whipping through the garage lot couldn't budge. He was a big, beefy guy with no neck and arms the size of telephone poles. Said arms were adorned with tattoos ranging from elaborate dragons to bare-breasted, winged women. Then there was the poignant one—a bright red heart with *Mom* printed in crooked script high up on his hairy shoulder.

His chin sported a few days' worth of stubble. His fingernails had an even longer history of crud trapped in a black line. At some point in time, his torn and ratty T-shirt might have been white. Now it was a dingy shade of gray with as many stains as holes. Charlie was glaring at me, even as he checked out my boobs.

"You shouldn't have put the dog on her," the officer said.

Charlie shrugged and tucked the stub of an unlit cigar in the stained corner of his mouth. It fit perfectly, since Charlie was missing a few teeth on that side.

"She was trespassing."

"Ma'am, want to explain what you're doing here?"

Nerves sometimes make me say inappropriate things. I just can't seem to find that filter between my brain and my mouth. I didn't want to lie, but stretching the truth seemed a better alternative than admitting I was a nosy paralegal trying to prove something to myself. "Liam sent me."

"McGarrity?" Charlie asked, suspicion dripping off each syllable.

"Yes. We're working on a case together."

"McGarrity sent you here?" Charlie challenged. "To climb my fence? Bullshit."

"He didn't actually send me, it's kind of along the lines of me taking some initiative." I could feel blood running down the back of my leg and considered fainting, but vetoed the idea. I'd still have to explain myself when I "regained consciousness." Might as well get this over with. Of course, if I bled to death standing here, that would be a whole other problem.

Charlie addressed the officer. "Looked more like she was taking stuff out of that car." He pointed to the smashed Caddy. "I'm responsible for the vehicles and the contents." He turned back to me, his foul breath filling the foot or so separating us. "I'm not getting sued again, so hand over whatever you stole, lady."

Shit! The cup! I'd dropped it during my failed attempt to escape the jaws of death. Rubbing my hands over my face, I tried to think of a way to explain my actions that wouldn't get me committed to the closest mental health facility. "I'm Finley Tanner, and I work for Dane, Lieberman and Zarnowski." I felt a touch of relief when the name seemed to register with the semicircle of men.

"You the broad who needs that car checked for tampering?" Charlie asked.

"Yes," I practically wept. "I'm not a broad, though—" I stopped myself. This wasn't a time for a lecture on appropriate word choices, and, besides, I didn't think Charlie was the type to conform his vocabulary to political correctness. Hell, he probably couldn't spell *correctness*. Or *political*. *Car* might even be a stretch. "Anyway, there was a paper cup in the car that I needed to retrieve. I didn't think you were here, so I climbed the fence."

"I live here," Charlie grunted, as if it was normal to curl up next to barrels of used motor oil.

One of the officers received some sort of coded message over his radio, then pulled the other two aside in a huddle. I looked around, desperate to find the cup. Letting out a breath I didn't know I'd been holding, I spotted it next to a pile of rusty parts and old tires. Then I groaned. It was half-submerged in a puddle of God only knew what. I had a sinking feeling that wasn't good for something I hoped to use as evidence.

The officers returned, crowding me while asking Charlie to check out my story with Liam. Grumbling all the way, Charlie went back inside the garage. Opening and closing the door quickly enough that Boo-Boo only had a chance to growl and attempt to lunge off the hopefully strong leash.

"We ran your plates."

Glancing at the officer's name tag—WILEY was printed in all capital letters—I asked, "Why?"

"Standard procedure when a suspect's vehicle is found at the scene. You failed to mention that you received a citation and a summons today."

"For exceeding the speed limit! I was late for brunch," I explained. "Is that considered a major crime?"

"Sometimes. Can you account for your where-abouts today?" he asked, pulling the same kind of pad and pencil from his shirt pocket that Liam had used the night before. Where was the ambulance? And I wanted proof that Boo-Boo's shots were current, too.

I struggled to coax the question out of my mouth. "Are you serious?"

"Miss Tanner, I don't think you appreciate the gravity of the situation. Charlie would be completely in his rights to have you arrested right now. You'd better hope McGarrity backs up your story. Now, back to how you spent your day?"

Time to pull a few sympathy strings. "I got up early and did my usual workout." So? He didn't know my exercise was reaching for a coffee filter and standing on my toes to pour water in the reservoir of my coffee machine. "Then I went upstairs to feed my neighbor's cats. Did some work from home. Got a death threat over the Internet that closely matched the death threat taped to my door the other night. Went to Dunkin' Donuts for a latte—"

"Back up. You've been getting death threats?"

"Two. One was handwritten. The other was an instant message."

"What was the name of the officer who took those reports?"

"I didn't report them." One look at his moderately handsome face and I knew what he was thinking. I explained my reasoning, but that only seemed to make it worse. "Officer Wiley, I'm between a rock and a hard place here. The client insists her husband was murdered. My boss wants me to pat her on the head and let it drop."

"Your whereabouts?" I could see his black, polished shoe impatiently tapping the gravel.

"I got the ticket on my way to brunch," I gave him the address of the country club as well as the names of at least three people who would verify my story. "I hit The Gardens Mall, shopped for a bit, then had some lettuce wraps at Chang's."

"So . . ." He thumbed back through his notes. "You claim you received a threatening communication; stopped for coffee; went to brunch; did some shopping; had a light meal and then, what? Pulling your first B & E seemed like a good way to round out the evening?"

My shoulders sank along with my spirits. "Sounds pretty stupid when you say it like that, but yes." I looked up into his brown eyes, hoping to find at least a hint of compassion. No such luck. "I'm in trouble?"

"There are usually repercussions to breaking the law."

"I'm sure Liam will smooth things over with Charlie. I was referring to the threats. And my job. I can't afford to get fired."

"Because you were threatened?"

"No," I didn't think he wanted to hear my song and dance about Dane's edict that I blow Stacy Evans's concerns out the window. Or that I was already on the top of the employee shit list. Or that I was so far in debt that losing my job would be a complete disaster, not to mention a résumé killer, if it came to that. "Isn't it obvious? Someone doesn't want me looking into the murders of the jurors."

"Perhaps it's one of your coworkers?" he suggested. "Maybe they're just trying to keep you out of trouble."

I immediately thought of Cami. But, while she was nosy, she didn't seem like the type to send threatening notes.

Charlie came sauntering back, his expression as

sour as my mood. "Got his voice mail. He must be doing a thing."

"Can't I just take the cup and leave?" I pleaded with Wiley. "I swear, this was a one-time thing. You'll never see me again."

"The last time I gave some punk a pass, he and his buddies were back the next day. Little bastards tagged half the cars on the lot. So, no."

"Do I look like a closet graffiti artist?" I practically shouted at the unyielding jerk.

"You have great legs, but I'm still filing charges. If and when I hear from Liam, I might change my mind."

I let my head fall forward as rage and a strong urge to cry jockeyed for position. The ambulance arrived, as did a few neighborhood gawkers alerted by the commotion. I heard their snickers, but I was well past the point of humiliation.

"Since this stupid charge is going to be dismissed," I said to the officer, "would you at least do me the favor of bagging that cup and putting it back in the car so my investigator can collect it in the morning?"

His lips twitched with amusement. "Bag it? Big *CSI* fan, are you?"

Two EMS attendants flanked the gurney they were rolling my way. They transported me to the ambulance, then examined and cleaned my wound. "I don't think you'll need stitches," the younger of the two pronounced before stepping outside.

The female tech began to apply sterile strips, then leaned close to my ear and whispered, "You may not need stitches, but you'll definitely have to replace your thong. Sorry, honey."

It felt like a lifetime since I'd been in Tiffany's

trying on rings and silver bracelets. *Be careful what you wish for,* the little voice in my head mocked as one of the officers eased my hands behind my back and slapped handcuffs on my wrists.

Just like on TV, he placed his hand on my head, protecting it as he placed me in the backseat of the cruiser. As he clicked my lap belt into place, I asked, "What about my purse? And my car?" *And my life?*

He stood and yelled, "Hey, Tidwell, grab her purse and lock up the Beamer."

"You're leaving it here?" I asked, horrified. If the locals didn't strip it, I was pretty sure Charlie would take revenge by sugaring the gas tank or something equally macho.

"Of course not," he assured me.

At least that was something.

"It'll be towed to the impound yard. You can claim it if and when you make bail."

Bail. *Bail?* We'd driven maybe three feet when I asked, "How long does that take?"

He shrugged on the other side of the protective wire mesh. "You have to go through Intake. Then if there's a judge still sitting night court, you could be released tonight. More than likely, it will be some-time tomorrow."

A night in jail? The thought of it made me shiver. "I want to call my lawyer immediately."

"Now I *know* you watch too much television."

"What does that mean?" I asked, feeling like I was starring in a revival of *The Twilight Zone.*

"The Supreme Court says you get to call your at-torney. But they don't say when. So long as no one interrogates you, Miranda doesn't apply."

Not the best time to find out all the things I'd learned on *NYPD Blue* were crap. "Please?" Now I was begging. "You could make the call. Her name's Rebecca Jameson. I really don't want to spend the night in jail."

"In my twelve years on the force, I've never met anyone who did."

My fingertips were black, and my French manicure was completely ruined. Because my skirt was in such shreds, I'd been given a white jumpsuit with DOC stamped in big letters on the back. The nice desk sergeant did allow me to keep my pearls, but only because they weren't visible beneath the ill-fitting ensemble.

I also had to relinquish my peek-a-boo sandals and was forced to wear rubber shower shoes that, even though they smelled heavily of disinfectant, creeped me out. They were the inmate version of rental bowling shoes—I had no idea where they'd been, and I cringed just thinking about it.

It was eleven minutes before midnight, and I learned from Big Ethel that night court stopped accepting bail motions at the stroke of twelve.

Pacing in the six-feet-by-three-feet cage, I felt a surge of something new. Something unrelated to the fact that I was in police custody and dressed like the Pillsbury Dough Girl. In the past, this kind of adversity would send me straight to an all-day spa to bury my embarrassed head in a facial wrap. Maybe flashing my ass to Charlie had put things in perspective. I was getting close to thirty and what did I have? Credit-card debt.

But now, for the first time ever, I had a Cause, with a capital C. I would crack the Evans case, keep my job, and restore my dignity.

Problem was, I didn't have a clue how to go about doing those things.

But wait! I was smart, resourceful, and more determined than Boo-Boo when he'd sunk his gnarly teeth into my flesh to see this through. I was done with doubts, regardless of who thought I was or wasn't capable. Screw Dane, screw Liam, and anyone else who got in my way.

I felt inspired after my mental pep talk, but I also wanted the hell out of jail. As if on command, I heard Becky's voice in the other room. I had four minutes to make a motion for release. If not, I was supposed to do rock, paper, scissors with Big Ethel to see who got dibs on the lower bunk.

"You cut it a bit close," I snapped at Becky as we exited the courthouse and I sucked in deep breaths of fresh air. "Freedom is a wonderful thing."

"You were only locked up for three hours."

"In this," I groused, yanking on the front of my jumpsuit. My clothes—or what was left of them—were in a plastic drawstring bag hanging from my wrist.

"Well, I'd say you bit off more than you could chew, but the way I hear it, you weren't the one doing the biting."

I couldn't help but grin. "It was a good plan. Only the execution sucked."

"Ya think?"

Becky drove me back to my apartment, listening intently as I filled her in on the information I'd gathered thus far. By the time we were at my front door, she seemed almost as spooked as me.

"Why don't you pack a bag and stay with me?" she suggested.

"I was thinking about that while I was in the pen."

"It was county lockup, and you were in a holding cell, not solitary."

"I think AfterAll is trying to scare me off."

"And doing a fine job of it," Becky remarked.

I glanced over to find her studying the note from my drawer. "Cripe, Finley, you need to give this to the cops."

"In the works," I assured her. "Don't touch that. A detective is going to call me first thing tomorrow to make arrangements to pick up the note and my computer."

Becky's head whipped up. "You can't do that."

"Sure I can. I spoke to a nice sergeant, and he—"

"I mean you are barred by the Canon of Ethics from turning over your laptop."

"But it's mine," I reasoned. "I have the twenty-two-percent finance charge agreement to prove it."

"You've used it for work, though, right?"

I nodded. "A few times. A lot in the last week."

"Then the data contained on that machine is attorney-client work product and can't be turned over to anyone without prior written consent and waiver by the client."

"The police said their tech people could track down whoever sent me the IM. They also agreed to test the note for fingerprints and other bio-something-or-another stuff. They told me it would probably only take a matter of hours for them to know who sent this to me."

"You can't do it," Becky stated flatly.

Tossing my hands in the air, I let them fall to my sides with a frustrated smack. "I'm not a lawyer, I'm the victim, so those canons shouldn't apply."

"They always apply. We'll have the firm's tech people go over your laptop, and I'm sure that totally hot investigator, Liam, can find someone capable of lifting prints and/or DNA from the note."

I flopped down on my sofa and cautiously curled my legs beneath me, not wanting to irritate my already sore tush, as I hugged a pillow to my chest. "This isn't fair."

"C'mon, Finley"—Becky glanced down at her watch—"pack a bag and come to my place. In the meantime, I'll call the police and explain why you can't turn over your computer or the note."

I shook my head, dismayed by the surrealness of it all. "Toss me the phone. I'll call Sam and see if he's home."

He was, and after a tiny bit of coaxing, he agreed to spend the night so long as he could bring his own bedsheets—he doesn't do anything under one thousand thread count—and the cats.

Becky hung around until Sam showed. It took him two trips.

"Be careful, and watch out for her," she warned Sam.

"I'm your girl," Sam insisted with a dramatic salute.

While I showered and changed into my PJs, Sam first covered the sofa with a body pillow, then created a makeshift bed that looked as comfy as the one in my room. Butch and Sundance were stalking around the kitchen, getting the lay of the land. Either that or they were looking for someplace discreet to pee.

Sam had changed, too, into a pair of silk pajamas with bright red, green, and gold stripes. He looked a lot like a clown, sans red nose and wig, but since he was kind enough to hang out with me, I didn't dare share that thought.

"How was your weekend?" I asked, pulling one of the chairs off the patio to join him.

One look at his deflated expression and I had my answer. "He's redoing the beach house as an anniversary surprise for his wife. I got the impression she'd be more surprised if she found out what we did in the hot tub, but what's a guy to do?"

"Sorry."

"Not as sorry as I am." He sighed. "He's an interesting man. I think, under different circumstances, we could build a life together."

"Sure, if it wasn't for the fact that he bats for both teams."

I got up, wincing at the stiffness in my thigh, and scrounged around in the kitchen. I was really tired—getting arrested can be exhausting. "Want something to drink?"

"Nope."

I looked over and saw him studying the medical reports and photos. "Sure?"

"Uh huh."

Grabbing the last bottle of Diet Coke from the vegetable bin, I twisted the cap and checked to see if I was a winner in their latest game. I wasn't.

Sam's legs were stretched out and crossed at the ankles. One of the cats was curled into a ball by his feet; the other was nowhere to be seen. "What does 'probable injection site' mean?" he asked.

"Sometimes the paramedics or nurses can't get an IV positioned, so they try another location, like the hand or sometimes the wrist. Why?"

"This Keller guy had one."

I took a long sip of my soda. "He had a lot of stuff, Sam. They were trying to save his life."

"Before they got to him?"

"What?"

He sat up, leaning over to highlight the notation with his fingernail. "See? Right here. The paramedics noted a suspected injection site on his neck when they found him on the floor of the Kravis Center."

I'd been so focused on the hospital findings that I'd pretty much glossed over the EMS reports. "You are brilliant," I said, kissing him full on the lips. Then, "Where are the postmortem photographs?" I asked rhetorically as I started sifting through the piles on the table. "Success." Taking the cheap magnifying glass, I went over every centimeter of the picture until I found it. A small, reddish pinprick about two inches below Keller's right ear. "Someone injected him with something. I've got to call my mother."

"I know the two of you have your problems, but do you honestly believe your mother gave Keller some sort of injection?"

I shook my head and smiled. "No, she only kills her young."

"So why call her?"

"Give me a minute," I insisted, as I tugged the cordless free from the base and pressed the assigned speed-dial number.

"Hello?"

"Mom?" I breathed excitedly, relieved that she answered the phone. She has a habit of turning off the ringers and forgetting to turn them back on again.

"It's well after midnight, Finley."

And we both know you never go to sleep before two.

"I'm sorry, but I need to ask you a question about the opening night of *Figaro*."

"An exceptional performance," she proclaimed. "I did offer to get you a ticket, but as I recall, you had made other plans. I'm not sure what they were, as you were rather evasive when I—"

I'll stand still for the verbal spanking later. "A guy had a heart attack that night."

"It was quite distressing."

"You were there?"

"Do I ever miss an opening night?"

"Right. Of course you were there. What do you remember?"

"It was intermission, people were mingling, and then I saw him crumble right there. Practically at my feet. You have no idea how that affected me."

It didn't work out too well for Graham Keller, either. "Was anyone with him or around him before he collapsed?"

"Talk about a blessing," my mom gushed. "As it happened, Dr. Hall and his family were right there. The doctor insisted someone call nine-one-one while he started CPR."

"Dr. Hall?" I repeated, a chill settling in the pit of my stomach.

"He's a renowned cardiologist, Finley. What else would he do under those circumstances?"

If Hall was all involved in treating Keller at the scene, why wasn't that listed anywhere in the medical records? "You're sure? Absolutely sure?"

"Yes," she answered testily. "He followed the ambulance that took Mr. Keller to the hospital. Which didn't seem to sit well with his wife." Another thing omitted from the hospital records.

"Mrs. Hall?"

"She wouldn't be Mrs. Hall if she wasn't his wife,"

Mom shot back brusquely. "Finley, what is all this about?"

"Were the Halls and the Kellers close?"

"I believe I saw them at some of the same functions, but, no, I never got the impression they socialized, just passed one another at the occasional charity event."

"Okay. Thanks." I was about to hang up the phone when I remembered that would be a huge mistake. Quickly, I added, "Thanks again for brunch. I enjoyed seeing you. Bye."

I shared my new information with Sam, watching his eyes widen as I spoke.

"So you think Dr. Hall injected Keller with something that killed him?"

I paced between the entertainment center and the coffee table, nibbling the tip of my chipped thumbnail while my mind spun possibilities. "Hall's financials show regular donations to the Opera Society, only, according to my mother, the Society wasn't getting the cash. Keller died with a safe full of unknown-origin cash."

"So Keller was blackmailing Hall, so Hall killed him?"

I took a theatrical bow. "I believe I have cracked the case. Thank you very much."

"Well done, Agatha Christie, but aren't you forgetting about the other two dead guys?"

I straightened, scowling. "There's that. Maybe Hall killed them to cover up the fact that he murdered Keller."

"But until you, no one thought Keller's death was a murder."

"Stop shooting holes in my theories."

"I'm being a sounding board," Sam corrected,

turning onto his side and bracing his head against
his palm. "The landscaper?"

"José Vasquez?"

"Yeah, he was the first to die, right?"

"Yes."

"Then Keller, then Marcus Evans. But Keller was
the one with the Hall's money squirreled away?
Presumably because he'd been blackmailing the
good doctor."

My feelings of jubilee were draining quickly.
"Vasquez might have been Hall's first target because a lowly gardener would be an obvious suspect in a blackmail scheme. I didn't see anything
at the Vasquez home to indicate José left behind
any secret rolls of cash.

"Hall must have figured out that Keller was the
blackmailer. But once he killed Keller, there was
no reason to kill Marcus."

"Unless they were in on it together. Maybe
Keller and Marcus and Vasquez, or some combination of the three, were all involved in the blackmail."

That had possibilities. "It would help if I knew
why, or maybe *what* they had on Dr. Hall." I went
back to pacing.

"An important detail," Sam agreed. "Maybe the
other jurors know?"

"You're right," I agreed. "I've been too focused
on proving the jurors were killed. What I really
need to know is *why*."

I assume full responsibility for my actions, except the ones that I think are someone else's fault.

Thirteen

"**G**ood God, Finley, your phone's been ringing nonstop."

Sam was exaggerating, as usual. I'd received only three calls: Liv and Jane offered sympathy after hearing about my injury and arrest. Becky checked in as well, making sure I was okay and reminding me that I needed to bring my laptop and the note into work. I promised to hand over the computer if she'd work on finding out who I had to suck up to at the police department in order to get my car out of the impound lot.

Sam remained prone on the sofa, one arm flung over his eyes as I zipped around my apartment, trying to get everything together since I'd already called for a cab.

"I need money," I told him. It was already after eight so I didn't have a lot of time for pleasantries.

"Don't we all," he said without moving a muscle.

"I need it now," I clarified. "I've got seven dollars, a few coins, and six Tic Tacs to my name. I'll hit an ATM during lunch and give it back to you tonight."

"Right front pocket of my pants," he said. "Take what you need."

"Thanks." I took a twenty, then kissed his forehead. Slinging my briefcase onto my shoulder, I started for the door when the bell chimed.

"Have a nice day, honey," Sam teased.

When I opened the door, the word "hello" lodged in my throat. I didn't think Liam moonlighted as a cabbie or had a paper route, yet here he was.

"Good morning," he said, stepping over my laptop carrier and the white file box I had stacked and at-the-ready.

"Yes, it is," I heard Sam say. Apparently, my friend was suddenly fully awake and no doubt fantasizing about the tall, dark man sauntering into the living room. How was it possible for him to have such bad gay-dar?

"Sam, this is Liam. Liam, Sam."

"You've been busy," Liam said, looking at me and drumming the rolled newspaper on the edge of the coffee table.

"If this is about the whole thing at Charlie's Garage—"

"I took care of it," he cut in. "Charlie's going down to drop the charges later today."

I felt relief roll through me. "Thanks."

"I heard his dog took a bite out of your . . . crime."

"Very funny." I still gripped the knob on the open door. "I've got to get to work."

"I figured as much," Liam said, digging into the pocket of his really well-fitted jeans, then taunting me by dangling my key between his thumb and forefinger.

Closing the door, I went for the key like a desperate bridesmaid during the bouquet toss. "I thought it was impounded."

He shrugged, and I inhaled, savoring the scent of his soap in the space between us. Reaching for my key, I felt the cool metal against my palm and the searing heat where his fingertips touched my skin. Our eyes locked, and I allowed myself to enjoy the liquid warmth spreading through me. It was one of those electric, tingly moments that don't happen too often. At least not to me.

"Hello? Gay man sleeping here?"

The moment was over, I practically jumped away from Liam. "Um, thank you. I really appreciate you taking care of it. It was really . . . I thought there'd be forms . . ." I let my voice trail off. Rambling isn't one of the things I do best.

"I still have a few friends on the force." Unfolding my paper, he spread one of the inside pages open. "But you don't."

Looking down, I read the two-inch piece in the morning police blotter: LOCAL PARALEGAL HELD IN BURGLARY. The crime reporter cited Dane-Lieberman as my employer—in bold type, no less. And hinted that the crime I allegedly committed was linked to a new investigation of a prominent Palm Beach cardiologist who'd previously been involved in a notorious malpractice trial.

That was wrong. I'd never made that claim to the officers. I guess I should be grateful they hadn't printed Dr. Hall's name. Oh, and they got my age wrong. I heard myself say, indignantly of course, "I'm twenty-nine, not thirty."

Liam chuckled. "Talk about your absolute journalistic disregard for the truth." I ignored the tsk-tsk sounds he was making between loud, dramatic sighs. That warm, fuzzy feeling I'd so enjoyed was totally gone, replaced by utter panic. "Vain Dane will have a cow when he reads this. A herd of cows."

"A herd would be cattle," Liam corrected, very clearly amused.

I snarled at him, sorely tempted to smack the mocking grin off his too-handsome face.

"Maybe he won't notice," Sam offered sympathetically. "Really, Finley, who reads the *Crime Blotter?*"

"Lawyers." *Damn, damn, and triple damn.* "I've got to get to work. Maybe I can sneak into my office before anyone else is at their desk." I turned to Liam. "You can help me cart that stuff to my car on your way out."

"Why not? Happy to help." He stood, leaving the newspaper behind, then tossed a "Nice to meet you" to Sam.

"My pleasure," he practically purred. "I'll lock up, Finley. Feel free to call me later."

Translation: Sam wanted to be among the first to know when the proverbial shit hit the fan. Oh, and he probably wanted to know if Liam had an identical, gay twin.

"I have the cup from the car and the blood samples from the hospital," Liam mentioned as he lifted the box into the trunk of my car.

"Already?"

"I'm efficient. I should know something in a few hours."

"Call my cell," I told him, reciting the number again.

"Will do." He held out a bright orange card, smiled, and walked toward his car.

How had he managed to get both cars here at once? I would have asked, but then I looked down at the card he'd given me. It was the GET OUT OF JAIL FREE card from a Monopoly game. Turning it over, I read his bold, block hand-printing:

Impound Fine—$150.00; Towing—$70.00;
Bite in the Ass—Priceless.

"Jackass," I grumbled, though I was smiling as I said it.

I made it to the office before nine but not before Margaret. One look at her pinched face and I knew she'd read about my weekend exploits. Knowing her, she'd probably scanned the clipping and e-mailed it as an attachment to every Dane-Lieberman employee, up to and including the janitor.

Even though I was balancing the box, my briefcase, my laptop carrier, and my purse, she insisted I sign the penance clipboard.

I piled my things on her desk, knowing full well she hated it when people disturbed her space. It was the only thing I could do since I wasn't exactly in a position of power. My job was dangling precariously by a thread, and I didn't dare do anything overtly confrontational.

A covert moment, however, was a whole different thing. While she was distracted by an incoming call, I looked at the message on top of one of her neatly, alphabetically-arranged-by-recipient piles. Even upside down it caught my attention. Jason Quinn, Esquire, wanted Vain Dane to return his call ASAP. In the reference line, Margaret had written *Graham Keller, Jr.*

I knew Jason Quinn by reputation. He was a big-time Miami attorney who handled a lot of high-profile trials and made regular appearances on national television. He had serious clout.

Margaret waited—on purpose, I'm sure—until my hands were full before she offered me my messages. Tucking them between my chin and chest, I went to the elevator, pressed the button with my knuckle and almost wept with joy when I stepped inside and the doors closed behind me.

Only one member of the administrative staff was at her desk, and she didn't even look up as I shuffled my way down the hall to my office. With the exceptions of my laptop and my purse, I dumped everything onto one of the chairs, then pulled the messages out from under my chin.

As I sorted through them, I turned on my coffee-pot. Seven of the nine surviving jurors from the Hall trial had called. Why hadn't they left me a voice mail?

Because, I discovered a few minutes later when I went in to record my daily message, someone had blocked my voice mail box. Someone inside the firm. Not one of the partners personally—they didn't do mundane things like that. More likely it was one of their minions. I imagined Margaret downstairs doing a Snoopy dance now that all my incoming calls were routed through her pudgy, power-hungry hands.

Nine A.M. and all's Hell, I announced in the privacy of my own mind. Someone—I couldn't remember who—once said the best defense is a strong offense, so I decided it was time for me to be as offensive as possible.

I started with Stacy Evans. She seemed genuinely horrified that I'd been mauled while gathering evidence. Okay, so maybe I overstated the extent of my injury, but I needed to make sure she was still my ally. She was.

"Is your job in jeopardy because of the incident at the garage?" she asked.

Big time. "I don't know yet."

"I'd be happy to talk to Victor. He called while I was in the shower, so I'll be speaking with him anyway. I'm quite pleased with the dedication you've demonstrated thus far. Victor needs to know what a valuable asset you are to the firm."

"Please don't say anything," I said quickly. "At least not yet. Once I have the lab results, I'll be in a better position to brief Mr. Dane, and I'm sure all this will blow over."

"I know he'll be impressed, Finley. And to think he wanted to reassign this to his niece."

"Excuse me?"

"His niece. Carly. Candy, something like that."

"Cami?" I asked.

"Yes. That one. Pleasant enough, but I told Victor I wasn't interested in having an intern, even one related to him by marriage, take over the case."

Well, well. I now understood why Cami had been shadowing me all last week. *Poacher. Screw her.*

After I hung up, I poured some coffee while I mulled over my options. A slow smile formed as I again reached for the phone. Stacy's revelation had answered a nagging question for me.

"Cami Hunnicutt."

"I'm so glad you're in." *You back-stabbing, interoffice spy.* "I need someone I can trust." *Which so isn't you.*

"Yes?" Her interest was palpable. "What can I do for you?"

"Could you come to my office? I'm not comfortable discussing this on the phone."

"Sure. Ten minutes?"

"Great."

Using that time to my benefit, I put the phone messages from the jurors through the scanner on my desk and made copies. Folded them in quarters, then tucked them into my purse. Next I downloaded all my notes on the Evans investigation to a memory stick and slipped that inside one of the zippered compartments in my purse. Which left me just enough time to hit the copy room and load the medical files into the machine. It could do the work while I picked Cami's brain.

When Cami arrived, I was seated behind my desk, Friday night's threatening note in plain view on my desk, sealed in a plastic zipper bag. I carefully gauged her reaction when her eyes dropped to the page.

"Holy crud, Finley. What is this? When did you get it?"

I briefly explained the circumstances. "The same person sent me an e-mail expressing a similar sentiment."

"What do you think it means?"

"I was hoping you could tell me."

"Me?"

I took a slow, deliberate sip of my coffee, never breaking eye contact with Cami. "Stacy Evans outed you."

Color stained her cheeks. To give her credit, once she realized I knew, she didn't try to lie. "It wasn't my idea. Uncle Victor told me to keep tabs on you. What was I supposed to do? Say no?"

"You could have given me a heads-up."

"In fairness to me, Finley, he did warn you not to make a big deal over Mrs. Evans's unsubstantiated suspicions. You chose not to let it go."

"Was it his idea to try and scare me off or yours?"

Her brows drew together as her mouth dropped open. "That's crazy. Uncle Victor wouldn't threaten you, and neither would I."

"No one else knew what I was doing."

"Apparently someone does," Cami insisted.

I'm pretty good at reading people, and I was convinced that neither Cami nor Vain Dane were AfterAll. "Why was Dr. Hall here last week?"

"You know I can't tell you."

"You owe me. It was pretty crappy of you to skulk around and report my comings and goings to Va—Mr. Dane. I don't care if he is your uncle."

Cami sighed, then relented. "It was a nothing meeting. The daughter, Zoe, turned eighteen a few months ago so they were just updating beneficiary information and changing their wills since the kid's now of legal age."

"Nothing about Marcus Evans?"

"I was in the room," Cami said. "The subject of the trial came up once. Dr. Hall said something to the effect that he hoped the matter would remain closed. The wife and the daughter both asked if Mrs. Whitley could file a second malpractice lawsuit, and Uncle Victor told them it wasn't allowed under the law."

"What about Graham Keller or José Vasquez? Either of those names come up?"

She shook her head. "The only thing slightly out of the ordinary happened as the Halls were leaving."

My pulse skipped. "What?"

"Dr. Hall forgot to sign one of the forms, so he came back upstairs alone. I was outside Uncle Victor's office, but the door was ajar. I couldn't hear the conversation, just a name. Helen Callahan."

My pulse went from skipping to racing. "Thanks."

"Don't thank me. The partners are upstairs right now discussing your future here."

"I figured as much. Guess they weren't too impressed to learn I'm facing a B & E charge."

"You might be okay. Becky Jameson talked Lieberman into letting her plead your case. Becky was waiting outside the executive conference room when I came down."

It was nice to know my friend had my back. But even better to know I had a new lead and a new theory. Even if both elements had a few holes.

As soon as Cami left, I considered another pressing problem. Putting my notes on a flash drive and copying a few dozen pages of medical and accident reports was one thing. Glancing over at the huge stack of trial transcripts, I knew there was no way in hell I'd be able to sneak those out of the office.

Hopefully, I wouldn't get fired, but I couldn't be sure. Becky would fall on her sword for me, but it was the partners who'd make the ultimate decision. I needed this job, and there was a very real possibility that solving the murders was the only way I'd get to keep it. Or, in the event they fired me, get it back. Uncovering a triple murderer was the only card I had in my deck.

The partner pow-wow couldn't last forever, so I had to act fast. Retrieving my copies, I sealed them in an overnight envelope addressed to Liv. Then, just in case anyone was watching the outgoing mail from my floor, I went up one level, waited until the coast was clear, and added my package to the middle of the outgoing stack of mail.

Back in my office, I put the hospital-supplied originals safely back with the other Evans materials. Speaking of hospitals, I called JFK, pretended to be a florist, and asked for the best time to bring a delivery to Nurse Callahan. She was working the three-to-eleven shift, but the supervisor suggested I bring them right over, offering to hold them in the employee lounge until the nurse arrived. I thanked her and claimed I'd have to check with the owner.

I'd wait until her shift ended, then confront her. "With what?" I mumbled, frustrated beyond belief.

Staying with blackmail as the motive for the jury murders, I tried to think of possible scenarios that could include the nurse and explain why Dr. Hall had mentioned her to Vain Dane outside the presence of his family.

Attorney-client privilege pretty much gave the doctor carte blanche to tell Dane anything without worrying about the consequences. Perhaps he'd used the opportunity to admit he'd injected Keller with something that brought on the heart attack at the Kravis Center. The nurse possibly figured that out, altered the medical records, and was holding the postmortem test results over his head in order to collect blackmail.

Except Keller was the one with a safe full of cash. I sighed loudly. No part of that scenario explained why Marcus or the gardener were killed. I was missing something.

I spent the next thirty minutes returning calls and making appointments with most of the remaining jurors. They were all pretty annoyed when I wouldn't discuss the matter with them over the phone, but too bad. This was still my case, and I was making the rules. In the end, I managed to set up appointments with them, but it would take the next few days for me to meet them all.

Juror Number Twelve was one of the two who hadn't contacted me. Her name was Paula Yardley, and she answered her phone on the second ring.

I introduced myself, then said, "I'd like a few minutes of your time."

"I'm very busy, Miss Tanner. Besides, as I told Mrs. Evans, I haven't spoken to any of the other jurors since the trial ended. It isn't like we hold reunions or anything."

My cell phone rang. It was Stacy calling. I didn't dare risk offending Mrs. Yardley, so I pressed one button and muted the ring. "I understand, and I promise I'll be as brief as possible."

"Oh, okay. Can you meet me at Dance-A-Lot at three-thirty?"

Was she suggesting some sort of clandestine location? "Excuse me?"

"My daughters have ballet this afternoon. We can talk during their class."

Not very clandestine. Mrs. Yardley gave me the address, and I wrote it down. I was about to call Dave Rice, Juror Number Five, when the intercom on my desk phone buzzed. My heart stopped. It was probably the executive assistant summoning me upstairs so I could hear my fate. No, I decided as the intercom buzzed again, I still hadn't heard from Becky, and she wouldn't leave me dangling if a decision had been made.

"Yes?"

"Patrick Lachey on line seven," Margaret announced curtly.

"Thank you," I said, disconnecting her and switching to the incoming call. "Hi."

"Hi back," his voice was a little off.

"Is everything okay? Where are you?"

"PBI terminal. Landed a little while ago."

That was a fast trip. "Welcome home." I thought about how good it would feel to be held in his arms. "I missed you."

"Really?" The "off" in his tone now sounded a lot more like annoyance. I had a ridiculous thought that Patrick had somehow telepathically learned of my dirty dreams featuring a gloriously naked Liam. Intellectually I knew that was impossible, but I still felt a slap of guilt. "Of course I missed you! Why would you ask me that?"

"I'm holding the morning paper, Fin. Tell me this is some sort of misprint and you didn't get arrested."

"The charges are being dropped. It was just a simple misunderstanding."

"People don't get arrested over a misunderstanding."

Guilt disappeared. Now it was my turn to be miffed. "I was working my case."

"What case?"

Miffed? Make that full-blown pissed. "The one I told you about the other night? Remember?"

"Not really," he said. Patrick was nothing if not honest. "Tell me again."

"Jurors being murdered? Ring any bells?"

"Oh, right. How did that get you arrested?"

I didn't feel much like explaining myself to him. I was filtering his comments through my trepidation and tenuous job status. Not fair, and Patrick deserved better than being on the short end of my bad mood. "It doesn't matter. Thank you for the roses, by the way. They were lovely."

"So are you," he said in a soft, low voice. He was back to Sweet, Understanding Patrick. "Are you free tonight?"

"I've got some appointments, but we can have drinks."

"I was thinking of something a little more, um, up close and personal than a drink. I have a present for you."

I found myself smiling. "Just one?"

"It was a quick trip, remember?" he teased back.

"Care to give me a hint?"

"Your hands will never be the same."

I vacillated between excitement and abject terror. When a guy you've been in a relationship says the word "hand," a ring is definitely one of the options. A good one. Right? I could build a nice, stable life with Patrick. I should want that.

"Fin?"

I snapped out of my fog. "Well, um, I can meet you late. Around midnight?" That worked on two levels. It gave me time to ambush the nurse after her shift, and staying at Patrick's was way better than asking Sam to spend another night on my couch.

"Fine, but why so late?"

"I told you, I've got some meetings." I'd tell him about the threats when we were together. I didn't want him to freak out. Not that he'd ever done that before, but this was a new situation, and I had no idea how he'd take it.

"I'll see you then. Take care."

Take care? That whole ring option suddenly wasn't looking real good.

I tried Dave Rice's number. A frail female voice answered. I did my introduction thing, then said, "Is there any possibility I could meet with your husband?"

"He works until seven," she explained, each syllable sounding like it was being pulled from her throat with pliers. "You can try him back then."

"Thank you." I made a note for myself and programmed his number into my cell phone. He was at work? I grabbed the juror questionnaires and pulled his from the stack. At the time of the Hall trial, Dave Rice had listed himself as unemployed. But that was three years ago, so it made perfect sense that he'd found a job by now.

It was after ten and I still hadn't gotten any official word from on high. I had hope. I also had to meet Juror Number Four, Wanda Babbish, before the lunch shift started at the café where she waitressed. Luckily, Café Normandy was only a few blocks from the office.

I reapplied lip gloss and checked my makeup. I'd pulled my hair back in a ponytail this morning—it just seemed to work with the BCBG theme I'd chosen for the day. Also, the black slim-flare pants hid the ugly scratch marks where Boo-Boo's teeth had missed their mark. My butt was in a sling, and it hurt, literally adding insult to injury. My BCBG embroidered tulle top was lacy and feminine, so the ponytail gave me a little bit of workplace-appropriate balance.

The ensemble truly represented one of my greatest bargain days ever. Since one trouser leg was shorter than the other—not a problem for me as I had to have them hemmed anyway—they'd been marked down to a mere forty bucks. The vellum-colored shirt was only thirty-eight dollars because one of the button-and-loop closures had been ripped by some careless shopper and the button was missing. However, I was able to discreetly rip a matching button off another top in a different size, so problem solved. No, I'm not a clothing criminal—the second top was missing two buttons already and had a big snag in the embroidery, so I considered it a salvage operation more than out-and-out theft.

My purse was black canvas from the Liz Claiborne outlet. Fourteen bucks. Matching watch—another thirty. I was getting really good at this whole bargain-hunting thing. Well, except for the shoes. They were Betsey Johnson Rosy peep-toe pumps, and the small flowers added just the perfect splash of color to complement my ensemble. I'd gotten them at auction on eBay, so after shipping and handling charges, I think I only knocked about forty dollars off the regular retail of nearly two hundred.

Speaking of eBay and Betsey Johnson, I quickly wiggled the mouse on my computer so I could check the status of my auction bids. It wouldn't let me log on. I tried again, thinking maybe I had keyed a typo into my password, but, no. Still nothing but that annoying yellow triangle with the big exclamation point.

I got a sinking feeling in the pit of my stomach. I tried logging on to one of my other favorite sites, perfumebay.com, and it rejected me, too. Someone had changed the firewall settings on my computer, restricting my Internet access. Okay, tracking my comings and goings was one thing—screwing with my online shopping was just . . . mean!

I doubted complaining would do me much good. Nor, I was fairly sure, would the EEOC consider limited Internet access part and parcel of an actionable claim of a hostile work environment.

As if being banished back to catalog shopping wasn't bad enough, Margaret called to let me know Mr. Dane wanted me in his office immediately. I hadn't heard her sound that cheerful in all my years at the firm. Forget a Snoopy dance, she was probably up on her desk shaking her fifty-five-year-old groove thing.

I put my purse back in the drawer and wondered if I should take a notepad or something. I wasn't sure if there was some sort of protocol for this situation. The last time I'd been fired I was sixteen. Eight days of smelling like a French fry had left me more than happy to turn in my burger-joint uniform and matching visor.

Stomach clenched and empty-handed, I took the elevator to the top floor with a funeral dirge playing in my head. Unlike my last visit, the sentry took one look at me and said, "Go right in."

Straightening my spine and mustering all my dignity, I went to Dane's closed door, knocked twice, then entered.

He was leaning back in his chair, scowling, his eyes narrow and irate as he wordlessly watched me take the long walk to his desk.

He angrily tossed his pen on the blotter. "Jesus Christ, Finley. Do you know who called me this morning?"

Since you just used the Lord's name in vain, I'm guessing it wasn't the pope. "No sir."

"Jason Quinn. *The* Jason Quinn."

"I've seen him on TV."

"Sit down," he growled. "You've put this firm, and me personally, in an untenable position. All you were supposed to do was handle a simple estate matter."

"I'm doing that."

"By getting arrested at the behest of one client, then accusing another client of threatening you? Dr. Hall could file a defamation suit against you—and, since you're an employee, the firm."

"For what?"

"You claimed Dr. Hall was threatening you, without so much as a shred of proof."

"That isn't what I said. I told them I was looking into the deaths of three jurors who'd served on his civil trial and that I had been threatened as a result of my investigation."

"We'll get to the alleged threats in a minute."

"Due respect, sir. There was nothing alleged about the note pinned to my door. I have it downstairs. I can show it to you."

"I'm not all that interested in seeing it. Not only does Dr. Hall have a legitimate cause of action because of your baseless accusations, Jason Quinn represents the Keller family. He threatened to file a complaint against me with the bar association because you grilled his wife about the money."

I felt my own temper flare. Tightly, I said, "She brought up the money, Mr. Dane. Not me. Until then, I didn't know anything about it."

"Her son doesn't believe that. And, frankly, I'm not sure I do, either. That issue is being handled for the Kellers by Mr. Quinn and a representative of the Bank of South Florida. Approaching Mrs. Keller could be construed as an attempt by this firm to interfere in the attorney-client relationship."

"It's money Mr. Keller extorted from Dr. H
though, right?"

Dane looked like he wanted to jump across his desk and wrap his spray-tanned hands around my throat. "Where would you get an idiotic idea like that?"

"Mr. Keller was murdered. His safe was full of cash. It's the most logical explanation."

"For the love of—" his voice trailed off as he glanced at the ceiling. "The money was inappropriately in the possession of Mr. Keller, but it did not come from Dr. Hall."

"You're sure of that because?"

"Because Jason Quinn is a top-notch attorney, and while I won't divulge details to you, I'm satisfied that the matter is unrelated and being handled accordingly. It's not our concern. Keller was not murdered, Finley. He had a heart attack in front of a couple of hundred witnesses. All you've done is impugn Dr. Hall's reputation, interfere with pending negotiations between one of this state's premiere attorneys, and get Stacy Evans all worked up over nothing."

"I don't think it's nothing. There's a third juror who also died under mysterious circumstances."

"Wrong. I spoke to Sharon Ellis. She runs the Environmental Studies Center. There isn't a scintilla of evidence to support your theory that his death was anything other than a tragic accident."

"I have a videotape of—"

Dane held up his hand to silence me. "Cami told me about the videotape. It shows Marcus having a cup of coffee. Period. But that does get us around to your activities over the weekend. I can't believe you were impulsive enough to break into a garage to retrieve some phantom coffee cup from Marcus's car?"

Okay, I'd give him the "impulsive" part. I was

about to argue that it wasn't a phantom cup and that I was having it tested even as we spoke, but I didn't think he'd be too thrilled with that update.

"You knowingly committed a crime, Finley."

"Only after I was threatened. Maybe my actions were a little . . . rash, but I felt there were exigent circumstances."

"Want to know what I think?"

Not so much. "Of course."

"I think the note on your door was nothing but a neighborhood prank. I understand from the officer handling the B & E charges that there have been other incidents at your apartment complex?"

I nodded.

"As for the e-mail, we'll have the technical department attempt to identify the sender. According to Ms. Jameson, you spend a good deal of time online."

"I think 'good deal' is a stretch." *Way to have my back, Becky!*

"Regardless, the technical department assured me that any middle-schooler with enough time, the desire, and a modem could easily track you down and send an e-mail. Threatening or otherwise."

"Okay. Is that all?"

"Not by a long shot. I don't think you grasp the seriousness of what you've done."

Yeah, well, I don't think you *grasp the fact that I've been threatened and bitten in the ass, so I guess we're even.* "I felt an obligation to Mrs. Evans. She is our client."

"Not anymore," Dane informed me. "Another firm will handle the probate." He passed a slip of paper across his desk. "Messenger everything to them by the end of business today."

"Yes sir."

"Everything else you have pending should be turned over to Cami Hunnicutt."

"So, I'm fired?"

"No."

I was confused. "I'm not fired, but I'm farming all my work out to your niece?"

"Former niece," he said, as if I gave a flaming fig. "Cami's mother is my ex-wife's sister."

Which ex-wife? I longed to ask but didn't dare. Dane had gone through three already. Each new bride got successively younger and younger. Apparently his idea of recapturing his youth included sleeping with one.

"You're not fired. You're suspended. Starting tomorrow."

"For how long?"

"A month. Without pay."

"A month? Without pay? I have rent. Utilities. Groceries." *Manicures, pedicures, and I'm due for highlights in two weeks!*

"Thank your friend Rebecca then, because I argued strongly in favor of letting you go. And there's one more thing you'll be required to do or the suspension will become a termination."

"Which is?"

"You will personally go to the Halls' home and apologize to the doctor. They're expecting you tomorrow at two."

*I will not suffer in silence when
I can still moan, whimper, and complain.*

Fourteen

"I'm sorry," Becky said. Her tone reinforced the sentiment. "I tried to call you, but you'd already gone upstairs."

I was walking down Olive Street, on my way to see Wanda Babbish, when Becky rang my cell phone. "Thanks for speaking up for me," I told her sincerely. "I'm sure that cost you."

"What are friends for?"

"Ratting out my shopping habits, apparently." I didn't check the mild irritation still lingering from Dane's revelation on that point.

"They asked. I had to answer."

"I know. The geek squad has to keep my computer overnight. Since my shunning begins tomorrow, would you mind bringing it to me after work?"

"Consider it done. Need anything else?"

"Food, clothing, shelter."

"I can float you—"

"I'll call the Bank of Lisa," I interrupted. I didn't mind owing money to nameless, faceless financial institutions, but I didn't want to borrow that kind of money from my friends. Lisa was my younger sister, so she fell into a different category. She had David IV's money at her disposal and was pretty good about bailing me out the few humiliating times I'd been forced to ask. Besides, if my mother was right and I was expected to wear bone or chalk taffeta for the wedding, Lisa could pony up a few dollars to tide me over and I'd promise not to complain—to her.

We spent a few more minutes Dane-bashing. I told her I'd probably spend the night at Patrick's place. Becky seemed to think that was a smart move in light of recent events. She was still worried about the threatening notes, while I was moving on to more immediate things, like rent. I thought about telling her I had sent copies of everything to Liv but decided against it. It wasn't that I didn't trust her; I just figured it was better not to put her in a position of having to take any heat should anything go wrong.

Just as I ended that call, my phone rang again. It was Stacy Evans. She wasn't happy.

"I want you back on the case."

"I am." *Sort of.*

"But Victor said the firm couldn't represent me anymore, and that you were taking a medical leave. Are you ill?"

"They can't, and I will be off for the next month, but I'm not ill."

"What aren't you telling me, Finley?"

What the hell. "They suspended me without pay for thirty days."

"Why?"

"Getting arrested doesn't reflect well on the firm."

"How can I help?"

"Have you met with your new lawyer yet?"

"No."

"Would you mind holding off for a few days?"

"Why?"

"I have a few more ideas I want to explore, but I can't do that once another attorney is involved."

"Consider it done. Anything else?"

I thought for a minute, then asked, "Do you mind paying the investigator directly? He has a lot of useful contacts, but he doesn't work for free."

"Easily done."

My fingers closed around the smooth brass handle on one of Café Normandy's double doors. *I wonder if she'd give me a month's wages? Nah.* "I'll be in touch."

"Thank you, Finley," Stacy said, genuinely appreciative. "I know you'll get to the bottom of this."

Glad one of us is that confident. "I'll do my best. Bye."

The café specialized in country French cuisine. The smell of fresh sage, garlic, and butter filled the empty room. It was a long, narrow space with tables running along both walls, separated by an aisle. I stood at the vacant hostess stand, watching the three staff members setting tables, checking condiments, and doing all the prep work required in anticipation of the lunch crowd.

I had no idea what Wanda Babbish looked like, but I excluded one of the people immediately. I was sure *he* wasn't Wanda. The other two looked about the same age—late twenties. One was a pretty, petite redhead; the other an attractive blonde with a killer tan.

The guy glanced in my direction and called out, "We don't start serving for another forty minutes."

That's when the redhead noticed me. She whispered something to the blonde, then walked over to me. "Finley Tanner?"

I nodded.

"Let's step outside," she said, leading me out of the restaurant and around the corner of the building. Pulling a pack of generic-brand cigarettes from her mini-apron, she flicked a lighter and inhaled deeply.

The action caused her chest to swell. I only noticed because of her outfit. The tight, short, revealing getup was a cross between a sex-shop French maid's costume and medieval wench. Luckily, I'd never had to wait tables, but apparently there was a direct correlation between cleavage reveal and tip collection.

"So what's the deal? And make it quick, would you?" she asked, puffing on the cigarette. "I missed two days last week because my daughter was sick. Boss isn't happy, and shit goes downhill."

Classy girl. "Are you aware that three of your fellow jurors have died in the last few months?" I asked as I pulled a pad and pen from my purse.

"Mrs. Evans said that when she called, but I don't know what it has to do with me."

"Has anything out of the ordinary happened the last few months? Calls, notes, strangers hanging around?"

She shook her head. "Nope."

"Has Dr. Hall or anyone connected to him contacted you in any way?"

"Me? Other than Mrs. Evans and you, no."

"Does the name Helen Callahan mean anything to you?"

"No? Should it?"

"She was a witness at the trial."

"There were a lot of witnesses. They all said the same thing. Even the ones that testified for Mrs. Whitley said the infection was something that just happens sometimes."

"What else can you tell me about the trial?"

She shrugged. "It cost me three weeks of tips. I mean, I'm sorry that Whitley guy died, but we all agreed it wasn't the doctor's fault."

"No problems during deliberations?"

She took a final drag, then flicked the cigarette into the street. "Nina Fahey was a pain in the ass. She thought the widow's tears were all for show and didn't see any reason to award money to Mrs. Whitley since she was already rich. She moaned and groaned when Dr. Wong insisted we deliberate anyway."

"Did Dr. Wong think there was malpractice?"

"Hell, no," Wanda scoffed. "He just got all psychologist on us. He went on and on about the stages of grief and on and on and on. Personally, I tuned him out after a while. Keller was the one who finally got him to shut up and move on."

"Graham Keller?"

"He was the foreman. It took him a while to find the balls to take control of the discussions, but he was an okay guy."

"What about Marcus Evans?"

Wanda smiled. "He was a sweet old man. Didn't say much. Pretty old-fashioned. He pulled chairs out for all us women. Even stood up when one of us would come back from a bathroom break or something."

"José Vasquez?"

She had to think for a minute. "I don't remem-

ber him even opening his mouth during deliberations. Some of the other jurors said some pretty
mean things about him behind his back."

"Like?"

"Like he didn't say anything because he didn't
speak any English. That kind of stuff. That wasn't
true, though. His English was fine. I heard him talking to Keller during one of the breaks. Something
about a small business loan or line of credit—I
can't really remember. It was three years ago." She
checked her watch. "I've gotta get back inside."

"Thank you," I said, handing her one of my business cards with my cell number on the back. "Please
call me if anything weird happens." I went back to
scribbling notes on my small pad.

She started to walk away, then turned and said,
"Do you really think someone might try to hurt us?
I mean, I'm a single mom. Should I be afraid?
Take precautions or something?"

"To be honest with you, I don't know." I knew
she was taking night classes for her GED as well as
working double shifts to support herself and her
seven-year-old. Being a single mother strapped for
cash was stressful enough. I didn't want to add "be
very afraid" to her list of stuff to worry about, but I
wasn't going to put her life in danger, either.

"Just be careful, okay?" I told her. She pressed
for details, but I didn't have any solid information
to share.

Walking back to the office, I was pretty impressed with myself. It was official: I had my very
first interview under my belt. I'd asked the right
kinds of questions, and I was confident that Wanda
had been honest with me. In spite of the fact that
I'd temporarily lost my job and my laptop, possibly
had rabies from the Boo-Boo attack, had uncon-

sciously cheated on my really great boyfriend, been arrested, and had a creepy stalker, I gave myself mental props in the interrogation department.

Damn, I'm good!

My phone rang, and I instantly recognized the number. *Damn, I'm screwed.* "Hello."

"How could you do this to me?" my mother railed loudly. This continued for a good three minutes. Obviously, she felt my arrest—listed in the paper for all to see, no less—was an intentional act to besmirch *her* reputation. One designed specifically to embarrass her in front of the Opera Society, the DAR, her condo association, and the local chapter of the Junior League.

"I'm sorry," I said for the umpteenth time. I *was* sorry—sorry I'd answered my cell. I'd been dodging her calls all morning, and I should have stayed with that plan. "It's all taken care of. The charges are being dismissed today."

"Will that be in the paper?"

"I doubt it. It's not that big a deal."

"I'm speechless."

If only that were true.

"Honestly, Finley, 'arrested' not being a big deal? And for robbery, no less. For heaven's sake, my friends will think you're some sort of klepto-maniac. That reflects terribly on me."

"It was burglary, not robbery."

"That makes a difference?"

"Technically, yes. Burglary is the unlawful break-ing and entering of the premises of another with the intent to commit a felony. Robbery is the tak-ing of anything of value from the care or custody of a person by threat of force." *Stick that in your ear and twist.*

"Don't take that tone with me."

"Gee, I'm sorry, Mom." Total lie. "I was just distracted by the fact that you haven't so much as bothered to ask if I was okay."

"You committed a crime! That alone tells me you aren't okay. I refuse to talk to you when you're like this."

She hung up on me. From experience, I knew that eventually my mother would understand that her egocentric response to hearing about my troubles might not have been the best reaction. Because, when it came right down to it, she wasn't evil, she was just flawed. Like everyone else. Myself included. Of course she was a lot more flawed than most.

Her occasional flare for the dramatic and my sometimes volatile temper were major hurdles that kept cropping up in our tempestuous relationship. Ironically, we both wanted a version of the same thing. I wanted her to be a different kind of mother, and she wanted me to be a different kind of daughter.

It dawned on me that I wanted something else, too. Something I couldn't get on eBay or in any store. I wanted to find the killer. Okay, I hadn't gone completely off the deep end. I still wanted the rest of the parts for my Rolex, but unmasking the murderer had been temporarily moved to the top of my To-Do list. Not only would it vindicate me in the eyes of Vain Dane, it would be one hell of an accomplishment. My accomplishment.

Christ, I was starting to sound as sappy as the dialogue written for Judy Garland in one of those old *Andy Hardy* films. I walked into the lobby of my office building feeling more than just a little foolish.

Margaret's caustic glare brought me back to reality.

"Where's the clipboard?" I asked when she didn't shove it over the desk at me.

"That policy has been suspended."

It was probably killing her not to add "*just like you.*" With a saccharine smile on my mouth, I asked, "May I have my messages, please?"

"You don't have any."

Fine by me. I had a lot to get done and a very limited window of time. I exited the elevator and went toward my office. About a foot from the door, I smelled woodsy soap and felt a flutter of excitement in my stomach.

Taking a fortifying breath and thinking *Patrick-patrickpatrick,* I plastered a nonchalant look on my face and walked in as if I had no idea Liam was there.

Not only was Liam there, he was in my chair with his size-thirteen feet propped up on my desk, thumbing through the latest copy of *In Style.*

"Is there anything I can get for you, or are you comfy?"

"I'm good, thanks." He swung his legs down, placed the magazine back on the credenza behind my desk, and slowly walked around close to where I was standing.

Moving a few files to the floor, he switched to one of the guest seats while I reclaimed mine. Well, mine for another five hours, give or take. "The receptionist doesn't like you."

"Really?" I asked, feigning a gasp.

"She likes me."

"I'm happy for you."

"She said you got blasted by the big bosses."

"How impolitic of her to tell tales out of school."

"She likes me," he repeated, smiling.

I wasn't sure if he was mocking me or feeling

sorry for me. Neither option seemed too appealing. His eyes were a whole other thing. Very appealing. Seriously appealing. The way those dark lashes set off the brilliant gray flecks against the more dominant blue color . . .

He waved a hand in front of my face as if I was one of those guards at Buckingham Palace that tourists loved to test for signs of life. "Hello?"

"Sorry."

"How bad is it?" he asked, glancing around at the various piles I'd semi-organized.

"A one-month slap on the wrist. No biggie."

Shifting his weight to his hands, he used the armrests to leverage himself out of the chair. "Okay, we can pick this up again when you get back."

"Wait!" Yelling was overkill, but I couldn't seem to contain myself. Every drop of panic inside me came out in that single word. "What do you mean, 'pick this up again'?"

"As soon as you're back at work on the Evans case, I will be, too."

I nearly tripped as I rushed to close the door before he could leave. I was careful to keep my voice barely above a whisper. "I'm still on the Evans case, and so are you."

Cocking his head to one side, Liam asked, "The bosses are letting you moonlight?"

"Not exactly," I hedged. "You and I both know something hinky is going on here. I need to prove it to everyone else."

"And I need to get paid. I don't work for free."

"I already took care of that. Mrs. Evans is happy to pay you directly."

"And when the people here find out about it, they'll never use me again. Do you have any idea how much business I get from this firm?"

"I won't tell if you don't. C'mon, Liam, be a nice guy and help me out here."

He shook his head. "When did I ever give you the impression that I was a nice guy?"

I began clicking things off on my finger. "You got Charlie to drop the charges against me. You brought me my car."

"Which reminds me, you still owe me two hundred and twenty dollars for that."

I held his gaze. "I know you believe that Marcus and the others were murdered. You know I'm right."

" 'Right' is often overrated."

"Stacy Evans is willing to cover all expenses," I said again, just in case, like me, he was worried about paying the rent. "Besides, you can't leave me hanging in the breeze. It shouldn't take much longer to find out what really happened. I must be getting close or the killer wouldn't be trying and almost succeeding to scare me off. Wouldn't you feel horrible if you walked away now and something terrible happened to the other jurors?" *Or me?*

He sucked in a breath, then blew it out slowly in the direction of his forehead. His ever present wayward lock of hair momentarily moved back into place. "I don't like being guilted into things."

"Then avoid my mother at all costs."

I held my breath as I watched the indecision play out on his face. "I know I'm going to regret this."

"No, you won't."

"The lab results are ready. I need fifteen hundred bucks before I can pick them up. And, since this isn't Dane-Lieberman–authorized, they'll want cash or a money order."

I made a quick call to Stacy. She agreed to messenger the money to Liam immediately. "Where should she send it?"

"I'll need a retainer, too."

"How much?"

"Three grand."

I covered the mouthpiece with my hand. "Three thousand dollars plus the lab fees? Don't you think you're getting a little greedy? Her husband was just murdered. Do you really think now is a good time to take advantage of her?"

"I've already put time into this case. I've got obligations, too. Or, if she doesn't like the price, I can bag the whole thing."

I narrowed my eyes, glaring at him, while I broke the news to Stacy. She wasn't exactly thrilled but accepted the terms. A messenger would deliver the money to Liam in the parking lot of the lab no later than three.

As I was hanging up the phone, Liam pulled a slightly mangled manila envelope from his back pocket and gave it to me. "Dr. Hall's bank statements for the last six months."

I tested its weight in my hand but didn't open it immediately. "How'd you get confidential bank records?"

"Do you really want me to answer that?"

I shook my head. "I want you to take this note to somebody and have it dusted for fingerprints."

"You put it in a baggie?" The amused smirk was back, and seeing it really yanked on my last good nerve.

"I was preserving any potential evidence," I stated in my most clipped, professional voice. "And what about the background information on the jurors?"

"Still waiting on a few things. I'll bring you what

I've got after I pick up the lab results. Should be able to be here by four."

"Make it a little later. I'm meeting Paula Yardley at three. I should be back here by four-thirty."

He made a "T" with his hands. "You're meeting one of the jurors?"

I nodded. "All of them, actually."

"Does the word 'dangerous' mean anything to you?"

"She's a suburban soccer mom with three kids. I think I can take her."

Liam had much the same "I'd like to strangle you" look that Dane had shown me a little earlier. "Do you have a gun?"

"Of course not."

"A knife? Some self-defense training? Anything?"

My patience was practically nonexistent at this point. "I've got a nail file and a bad attitude. Those will have to suffice for now. If there's nothing else"— I paused to open the door—"I'll call you when I'm on my way back from seeing Mrs. Yardley."

"I'll be waiting by the phone."

I doubted that, but my brain blanked on a snappy retort so I fell back on my nonverbal communication skills and flipped him off. His back was to me so he didn't see it, but I still considered myself as having gotten in the last word.

A couple of guys from the fileroom showed up just after Liam left. They carted away the trial transcripts, and before they could load the last box, I was informed that a courier was on her way up to take the Evans files over to replacement counsel.

It was like watching a swarm of ants carry things off one by one as my office was cleared of everything even remotely associated with the death of Marcus Evans.

All except for the things I'd secreted away in my purse. Including the bank statements. As much as I wanted to tear into them, I didn't. I figured it was probably best to wait until I was no longer on Dane-Lieberman's payroll. I had no doubt Vain Dane would can me on the spot if he knew I was continuing the investigation on my own.

I prepared an extensive, color-coded memo for Cami and slapped sticky notes in corresponding colors on a few files. I printed a copy of the memo for myself and took a picture of the files stacked neatly in the center of my desk. Covering my wounded ass seemed like the prudent thing to do in the current climate. Solving the jury murders should earn back my rightful place at the firm— and possibly a hefty bonus—but on the off chance that I couldn't find the killer, I wanted to make sure I could prove my competence.

With the clipboard system abandoned, I felt completely free to waltz out of the lobby without offering an explanation to Margaret beyond letting her know I could be reached on my cell. She didn't look too pleased, but, really, what could she do? Insist they double-suspend me?

As soon as I was out on the road, I dialed my sister's number and hit the SPEAKER button on the keypad.

Thankfully, she answered. "Dr. Tanner."

"Hey, Lisa."

"If it isn't my sister the parolee," she teased.

"Very amusing." Obviously she'd gotten a Mom-o-gram, so I didn't need to fill her in on much. "Is this a bad time?"

"Nope, I'm sitting here going blind reviewing charts."

"I need to borrow some money."

"How much?" she asked without hesitation.

I made seven hundred sixty-nine pretax dollars a week. If I went on complete shopping restriction and "accidentally" forgot to sign a few checks when I paid my credit-card bills so they'd have to return them without banging me with late fees, I could get by on roughly three quarters of my normal income. After doing the math in my head, I quoted her a figure.

"And that will put you how far behind with your creditors?"

"I'll catch up," I insisted. "Can you not tell Mom? She's already furious with me."

"I know. Are you okay? Getting arrested must have been a pretty scary thing."

"Paled in comparison to the dog thing," I admitted. "I really, really appreciate this, Lisa."

"I know you do. I can go to Western Union on my break and send you the money by six."

"It doesn't have to be this instant. I just got paid."

"Yeah, well, what if you get arrested again and need bail money?"

"I was released on my own recognizance," I said proudly. "The judge said she was impressed by my character and demeanor."

"Mom always stressed that first impressions are the only ones that truly count."

Lisa brought me up to speed on the wedding. It was my first time as a maid of honor, and I was still trying to figure out where the "honor" part figured into the equation. Every time we talked, she shared another little detail that was part of the job description. When she started giving me possible dates for the bridal shower I was hosting—in Atlanta—I no longer felt guilty about asking her for the loan.

"Is there something you can inject into a person that would cause a heart attack but not show up in normal testing?" I asked.

"You're that pissed at Mom?"

I grinned. "It's the other way around. No, this is just background."

I heard a tapping sound and knew what it was. Lisa had a habit of drumming a pen or a pencil whenever she was deep in thought.

"Nicotine."

"Like cigarettes?" I immediately thought about Wanda Babbish's habit.

"No, a purer form."

"Is that something you can get at a local drug-store?"

"No. It's strictly controlled. Potassium chloride might do it."

"Easy to get?"

"Easier," Lisa said. "Insulin would do it, too, though you'd have to dose appropriately or the person might just slip into a coma. Hang on a sec." She was gone for maybe a minute. "Florida doesn't require a 'script for insulin."

"Really?"

"Yeah. Stupid, but not all that uncommon. It's an unregulated drug in a lot of states. If I wanted to kill someone and make it look like a massive coronary, insulin would be the easiest way to go."

"Thanks."

I was about to hang up when Lisa said, "Fin?"

"Yes?"

"I'm sorry you're having a lousy time right now."

"Me too." Only the strange part was, I didn't feel lousy. I felt . . . inspired, and it was scaring the shit out of me.

When it rains, it pours . . .
then your umbrella turns inside out.

Fifteen

Even from a distance, I noticed Paula Yardley had a tan line where her wedding ring had once been. She was a tall, slender blonde with pretty green eyes. I watched from my car as she herded two little girls dressed in matching pink leotards inside the dance studio. A boy, toddler-sized, was balanced on her narrow hip.

No woman should look that thin after pushing three humans out of her body. It was . . . unnatural.

A few seconds later, she came out and sat down at a picnic table adjacent to the studio. I figured that was my signal, so I opened my car door and started digging for my trusty notepad. I had one foot on the pavement when a stern-looking woman with dark hair pulled back into a severe bun came out and went over to where Mrs. Yardley was sitting.

Bun Lady seemed annoyed, or maybe her hair was just too tightly pinned. At any rate, she resembled one of those Palm Beach matrons whose facelifts were so extreme they looked like they were standing behind a jet engine at full throttle.

Not that I was deliberately eavesdropping, but I caught the last half of the first sentence. ". . . if not, your girls cannot continue to dance here."

"I'll have the money next week," Mrs. Yardley promised, clearly embarrassed. Particularly when she saw me out of the corner of her eye.

"You'll have to cover the bounced-check charges as well."

"I will. I'm really sorry. It won't happen again."

"See that it doesn't." With that, the B-52 woman pivoted and walked gracefully back into the studio.

"Mrs. Yardley?" I asked, doing my best to pretend I hadn't overheard the discussion.

"Yes." She reached into a dated designer bag and pulled out a couple of toy trucks. Handing them to the little boy, she said, "Stay where Mommy can see you."

The kid squealed, then waddled off to a small pile of dirt mounded against the wall.

"Thank you for meeting me," I began as I joined her at the table.

"I'm not sure why you think I can help."

"Mrs. Evans believes that her husband's death wasn't an accident."

"She told me that, and about José and Graham. After I spoke with her, my husband insisted I call the police. They assured me all three men died accidental deaths."

If the husband was still in the picture, where was her wedding ring? Maybe she was like Liam, semi-divorced. Divorced with privileges. I had to stop obsessing over Liam and his not-so-ex-wife. It wasn't healthy, and it wasn't any of my business. It was, however, capable of making me more than just a little nuts.

"First, have you received any strange communications—letters, e-mails, strangers hanging around?"

"Of course not," she answered. "I'm sure you mean well, but if the police don't think there's anything suspicious going on, I trust them."

"Your call. Though I do think you should take extra precautions." I didn't think it necessary to remind her that she had three kids.

"Our house has a long driveway and an alarm system. Anyway, I just can't believe some lunatic has suddenly decided to kill people over a trial that ended more than three years ago."

I told her about the note and e-mail I'd received, but she dismissed them just as Vain Dane had done. Obviously this woman didn't want to hear what I had to say. Time to change topics. "Was there anything about the deliberations that now, looking back, seemed strange to you?"

"Not re— John, honey! Please don't eat the dirt. Sorry," she said. "Boys are a . . . challenge."

"And they don't get any easier even after they're all grown up, do they?"

She smiled at me. "I guess not. Look," she continued, tucking her hair behind her ears, "we were twelve strangers who just happened to be unlucky enough to be selected for that trial. It was tedious. A parade of medical experts and a ton of exhibits we were supposed to scrutinize."

"You didn't?"

"We did the best we could. One of the jurors was a flaky college freshman. Kayla was her name. By the third day of the trial, I wanted to put her in a time-out."

"Why?"

"She whined and complained about missing some audition. I think she was a drama major at FAU. I don't think she paid much attention to the witnesses, and I know for a fact she didn't touch the medical records when we were in the deliberation room. If you ask me, they shouldn't let people that young serve on a jury."

"Did anyone scrutinize the medical records?"

She nodded. "Dr. Wong translated some of the stuff for us. I mean, he wasn't an M.D., but he understood all that stuff about apnea tests and corneal reflexes."

I wasn't following. "Were they the initial signs of the infection that killed Brad Whitley? Signs that maybe Dr. Hall should have started treatment sooner?"

She shook her head. "I wish. That was all stuff about the transplant itself. The lawyers spent almost three days telling us all the steps that led up to the surgery before they even got to the postop complication.

"The details of it sailed over my head, but I got the main gist. Dr. Hall did the apnea tests and corneal reflex tests and something else that had to do with CO-two levels before they pronounced Ivy Novak brain dead. Then they harvested the heart and did the transplant. It still makes me queasy when I think about those disgusting diagrams they showed us."

"And all the jurors agreed that there was no malpractice, right?"

" 'Agreed' is relative," she said, adding a mirthless chuckle for punctuation. "A few people on the jury felt sorry for Mrs. Whitley and wanted to give her something just because they could."

"Were you one of them?"

She vehemently shook her head. "No, that was the drama student, Kayla, and Dave Rice and Harold Greene. They all fixated on the out-of-pocket costs Mrs. Whitley had to pay after her husband was dead."

"The Whitleys didn't have medical insurance?"

"Sure, but her husband was self-employed, like mine. We carry insurance. The premiums are high, and the coverage is low. If I remember right, she had to pay twenty percent of the total costs. The transplant was over two hundred thousand, and then there were other associated bills—radiology, pharmacy charges, that sort of stuff."

"If there was division among the group, what brought you all together?"

"The truth. No one, not even Mrs. Whitley's medical experts, could state"—she paused and made air quotes—"*to a reasonable degree of medical certainty* that Dr. Hall was negligent in any way, shape, or form."

We continued to talk for a few more minutes, then Paula Yardley claimed she wanted to go in and catch the last half hour of her daughter's dance class. Me? I'd rather join John eating dirt than watch uncoordinated mini-ballerinas dance out of sync.

Something about my conversation with Paula Yardley was bothering me. Why wouldn't she be scared of the possibility that someone might want her dead? Made no sense. Unless, I reasoned as I made a sudden U-turn, she had other things on her mind. It would have to be something huge.

Since her address was on the jury questionnaire, I found my way to her home with relative ease. It was inland, west of Wellington, where high-density housing gives way to sprawling nothingness. Her long driveway was crushed gravel, flanked on either side by in-need-of-repair fencing. Not post-hurricane repairs—more like simple neglect.

I parked in front of the large two-story and side-stepped bikes, trikes, bats, and balls as I climbed the two brick steps to the front door. Of course it had to have frosted glass, I thought disgustedly. I would have pressed my nose against it, but I remembered Paula's comment about the alarm. And, quite frankly, I didn't want to leave an incriminating nose print on the glass. One arrest per decade was plenty for me.

Maybe I should go around back, I thought, and started there until I saw the mail stuffed in the box hanging just to the left of the door. I was pretty sure tampering with mail was a federal offense, but I didn't know the actual definition of *tampering.* After a brief hesitation, I decided looking wasn't tampering, so I took the newly delivered stack out of the box.

More than half of the envelopes had *Past Due* stamped in bright red. Cable, phone, Florida Power and Light, all delinquent. Visa, MasterCard, and Discover weren't real happy with the Yardleys, either. I stuffed everything back where I'd found it.

Around back, I found the swimming pool drained. A pool was expensive to maintain. A pattern was becoming clear to me. It was reinforced when I went up to the sliding glass doors and peeked inside. I knew decorator touches when I saw them. But like Paula's purse and shoes, everything was a good two seasons' old. There was a huge collage of the Yardley family hanging above the gas fireplace. Squinting, I focused on the wedding picture. "Damn," I whispered. Clear as day, she was sporting an impressive ring. I counted ten half-carat diamonds channel-set in a platinum band.

There was a possibility that the ring was someplace inside the house and she'd simply forgotten to put it on her finger. But it seemed much more plausible, based on the evidence I'd seen, that the Yardleys had fallen on hard financial times. The dance-lesson check had bounced; creditors were sending them demands for payment; no functioning pool; neglected repairs—Paula must have hocked the ring to keep the family afloat.

"So, what? She decided to blackmail Dr. Hall?" I murmured. That didn't make much sense, either. If she'd blackmailed him, she wouldn't be up to her unwaxed brows in debt.

I rubbed my hands together as I walked back to my car. I was still missing something. If there was no malpractice, what *else* could have come out during the trial? Something incriminating enough that, if revealed, would make the doctor pay a blackmailer. Maybe it wasn't something they'd heard. Maybe it was something they'd seen. But what? Well, I couldn't dally at Paula's and risk getting caught snooping around her place, so I headed back to the office.

Highway 441, like all other roads in and around Palm Beach County, was under construction delays, so there was no way I'd make it back in time to meet Liam at 4:30. With my stomach in a knot, I called him and hit the hands-free option on my phone as the prayer, *Please God? Please God?* looped in my head. "Please let the lab results prove Marcus and the others were murdered," I said aloud.

"McGarrity?" he snapped, clearly irritated. Probably because he was cooling his heels at Dane-Lieberman waiting on my tardy butt.

"It's me. Sorry, I'm running late. So what's the verdict?"

"I've got good news and bad news. How do you want it?"

"Good news first."

"Keller's postmortem blood sample showed high levels of potassium and calcium."

"Yes!" I whispered, a rush of excitement surging through me. "According to my sister the doctor, that proves he was murdered."

"According to the director of the lab, it's inconclusive."

"What?" That couldn't be.

"Keller was hooked up to IVs while they tried to revive him. IV solutions contain potassium. Since he died, his blood might not have had time to absorb the potassium, resulting in a false positive on the test."

"Well . . . shit. How is that good news?"

"The calcium finding is suspicious."

"Because?"

"Calcium is the indicated treatment for an overdose of potassium."

An image of Keller's hospital chart flashed in my mind. "Helen Callahan made a note in Keller's file, then crossed it out. I could make out three of the letters, c-a-l. Assuming the potassium came from the injection in Keller's neck and not an IV, someone in that hospital room knew why Keller's heart was attacking him and tried to counter the effects. How do I prove that? Can they run more tests?"

"Nope. That's part of the bad news."

My heart sank. "Part? There's more?"

"Yeah. The machine they use—a centri-something—is on the fritz. They can't finish the tests on Marcus's sample until it's back up and running."

"When will that happen?"

"Maybe tonight. Tomorrow midday at the latest."

"That sucks. Can you take it to another lab?"

"The sample has already been partially processed."

"I am not happy."

"Stuff happens, Finley."

Like the tingle that danced along my spine when you said my name? "You're right. I guess I can wait another day." How Scarlett O'Hara did I sound?

"You didn't let me finish the good-news part."

I held my breath.

"Vasquez's blood showed a high level of oxycodone."

"Which is?"

"A Schedule II pain reliever. It's a commonly abused drug, but I checked with all the local pharmacies and his wife. José wasn't taking oxycodone. At least not legally."

"Is that what killed him?"

"Not enough in his blood to be fatal, but enough to make him seriously high."

"So, basically, we still can't prove anything conclusively."

"We're making progress. Patience isn't your thing, is it?"

Ignoring the question, I filled him in on my meeting with Paula and what I'd found at her house.

He laughed. "You trespassed again?"

Crap, I hadn't thought of that. "I . . . visited."

"In the future, try calling me first. I could have told you that two years ago her husband started an Internet consulting company. It's circling the drain as we speak. The Yardleys are about to file bankruptcy."

"Or try blackmail."

"She'd have to stand in line."

"Why?"

"Almost every one of the people on the Hall jury is in some sort of financial bind."

"That isn't very helpful information." I sighed, completely exasperated.

"Don't get your scrunchie in a twist. We just have to rethink the approach."

"As in?"

"The only common thread we're sure of is the Hall trial. We go back to the beginning to see what we missed."

I hung up feeling utterly frustrated. Trying to solve a crime was like riding a stationary bike. A shitload of work to end up right back where you started.

I was crawling along in the traffic when a sign caught my eye. "Environmental Studies Center," I read, then quickly flipped on my blinker. If José was high when he'd planted the attack palm, maybe Sharon Ellis had noticed. Hell, it was worth a shot.

After asking several overly cheerful people, I found Sharon in a small office off the Center's gift shop. She was an older lady with short gray hair. A bright green T-shirt with a silk-screened image of a sea turtle was tucked into the elastic waist of her pull-on jeans.

We exchanged the usual pleasantries. I gave her the quickie version of my mission, then asked, "Did you ever know José to have a drug problem?"

She vehemently shook her head. "Never. He was a good man, rest his soul. Cut his normal fees in half on account of us being a nonprofit and all."

"So you didn't notice anything out of the ordinary the day of the accident?"

"He didn't like the palm tree, but once I explained that it had been donated, he agreed to plant it."

"Donated? By whom?"

"Anonymously," she said. "We were so grateful. We lost almost all of our big palms during the last hurricane season."

I shivered, remembering all too well my sixteen days without power. Though, on the plus side, I had built character and learned a new skill—not gagging on instant coffee.

"I was a little surprised when his crew left him here alone," Sharon said. "They were called to some emergency. I think it had to do with a sprinkler-system malfunction. Anyway, José waited a while, sitting on the back of his truck, drinking water from the insulated jug he always kept there. It was an unusually hot day for January. Must have been in the upper eighties with high humidity."

Enough already with the weather updates.

"I didn't personally see him go back to work, but a couple of our volunteers did. They said he looked a little tired, but as I said, it was a hot day, and he does very physical work.

"He started pushing the tree into position and then it started to fall, and I guess he just didn't have time to get out of the way."

I stood, shook her hand, and left quickly. My first thought? Someone had spiked José's water with oxycodone.

My second thought? I had just screwed up big time. It was after five and I still had to go back to the office for my walk of shame. Dumb, dumb, dumb.

Margaret was still at her desk, smirking like the spawn of Satan.

"You're here late," I commented.

"I wanted to be sure to give you these messages before you . . . *left*."

Garbage. She just wanted to savor the last few minutes of my employment. I took the pink slips from her and went to the elevator. A month away from her made it almost worth it. Almost.

I had one message each from Liv and Jane. One

from my sister, who'd thoughtfully called to say she'd wired the money to me. Margaret must have loved taking that one. The last was from Dr. Wong, Juror Number Eight. His seven o'clock appointment had cancelled, and he wanted to know if I could come earlier. I called and confirmed the time change, then started packing my briefcase.

Not a lot to pack. In fact, the only thing I decided not to leave behind was a nearly full bag of coffee. I didn't mind giving Cami my cases, but an eighteen-dollar-a-pound bag of Special Blend Arabica was a different matter.

I called Liv and let her know to expect a package from me but not to open it. She was relieved to hear I'd be spending the night at Patrick's place.

Jane said roughly the same thing when I spoke with her. Intentionally, I was dragging my Betsey Johnson heels. Hoping beyond hope that Margaret had something better to do than lie in wait for my Walk of Shame.

Apparently not. Her beady little eyes followed me out the door.

With no time for dinner, I stopped for coffee. It wasn't the first time a Frappucino had doubled as an entrée for me. I stopped at the Western Union office on Australian Avenue and stood in line with my downtrodden brethren, suffering dirty looks as I sucked on my six-dollar frozen coffee.

When it was my turn, I stepped up to the smudged Plexiglas and spoke to the attendant through the speaker embedded in the glass. A few minutes later, I locked the stack of crisp bills in my glove compartment and headed for Dr. Wong's office.

"Office" was a bit of a stretch. I knew the guy had a Ph.D. from Stanford, so how come he was practicing out of a strip mall? I definitely had the right place—his name was stenciled on the door: FRANK WONG, CLINICAL PSYCHOLOGIST.

As soon as I walked in, I smelled the musty odor of water damage, poorly masked by a sickeningly sweet cherry odorizer. No receptionist. Or maybe she was just gone for the day. "Hello?" Dr. Wong appeared in the hallway, smiling and offering his hand.

"Nice to meet you," he said after we shook hands. "I have to return a call. Would you mind giving me five minutes?"

"Of course not."

He turned and went to one of two doors off the hall, closing it behind him. The waiting area was sparsely furnished with a few mismatched chairs and a bookcase. The only magazines were local apartment locators, so I went over and tilted my head to peruse the titles of the books in the bookcase.

Knowing Yourself. Loving Yourself. Finding Yourself. "Killing yourself," I muttered. There was something decidedly creepy about being in a shrink's office. Shrink, Jr., technically, but that didn't make me any more comfortable. There was nothing wrong with me that a little shopping couldn't cure. "Little" being the operative word, given my newly hosed over employment situation.

Wong's five minutes turned into ten. He came out, apologized, then ushered me into his modest office. Unpacked boxes were stacked discreetly in the corner. In addition to the boxes, his desk seemed out of place. It was high-end, polished, and didn't seem to fit with the worn chairs and cheap prints. The wall behind him was littered with framed awards.

"You used to teach?" I asked as an ice-breaker.

"Yes," he said, his dark gaze as annoying as his single-word response.

"Teacher of the Year," I commented, pointing to the certificate from a private Christian college in northern Florida. "Impressive."

"It was an honor."

"Why'd you leave teaching?"

"I recently decided to go into private practice. I specialize in adolescent behavior issues."

Something about his answer didn't sit well. Why would someone leave excellence for mediocrity? Why was I trying to analyze a therapist? Taking out my pad, I did my whole "reason for talking with you" thing. I had it down pat, so I moved quickly on to the questions.

Like the others I'd spoken to, Wong agreed that the jury was a diverse group but that in the end they had all agreed Dr. Hall had not committed any malpractice.

"I heard you helped the others understand some of the complicated medical procedures?"

He shrugged. "I have a little experience with transplants, so I was able to answer some of their questions."

"What kind of experience?"

"A friend of mine needed a liver transplant. I educated myself on the process."

"Was it successful?"

Pain flashed in his eyes. "He was deemed an inappropriate candidate and removed from the waiting list. He died two years ago."

"Before the law changed?" I was educated, too.

He nodded. "Very good, Miss Tanner. Yes, he had AIDS, and before the law changed, doctors, hospitals, and insurance companies could legally refuse to perform transplants on patients they considered too high-risk to waste the limited number of organs available."

"I'm sorry."

"So am I."

"I take it you weren't—"

"Out of the closet?" he finished bitterly. "I mean, I wasn't passing or anything—just discreet. I had hoped to keep my sexual orientation private."

"Why?"

"I worked at a very conservative college and didn't have tenure. I knew they'd manufacture a reason to terminate me if they found out. Turns out I was right."

"They found out?"

"A little over three months ago."

"How?"

"I didn't ask, and they didn't tell."

"Has anything else strange happened?"

"Strange? No. Just a run of bad luck. You know what they say, when it rains it pours."

"Lots of rain lately?"

"Just after I lost my job, the brakes failed on my car, and I almost had a nasty accident. Now my clients keep making excuses to stop seeing me. If this keeps up, I'll have to consider relocating and starting fresh."

I leaned forward, resting my palms flat against his desk. "Doctor, I know Stacy told you about her concerns."

"Yes. It struck me as . . . far-fetched."

"Kind of like having your job torpedoed, your brakes tampered with, and your ability to make a living evaporating? All in the same time frame as the deaths of three other people?"

He looked scared, and rightfully so. "The mechanic said the brake line could have been severed by road debris."

"But your job? And now your practice? Do you think road debris is responsible for those, too?"

"I'm a gay man who treats teenagers. It isn't completely out of the realm of possibility that some parents would be uncomfortable with that."

"Do you tell your patients?"

He shook his head. "No. I mean, I would, under certain circumstances, but it hasn't happened so far."

"What circumstances?"

"If a child was conflicted about his or her sexual orientation, I might draw on my own life if I thought it was appropriate. Do you know the percentage of gay teens who commit suicide?"

"Yes. It's roughly the same as the percentage of your fellow jurors who've been murdered."

"When did the first juror die?"

"In February."

"Well, my . . . *troubles* began in December."

Okay, that didn't fit the pattern. Unless . . . "You got fired in December. When was your car accident?"

"Last week of January."

"So, if you are a target and bad things continue happening, maybe the killer is still working on the right plan for you."

"Plan?"

"Yes. Some way to kill you that wouldn't seem suspect."

"But why? I'm no threat to anyone. I barely have friends, Miss Tanner, let alone enemies."

"Something about the malpractice trial. Please think. Maybe you saw Dr. Hall with someone?

Overheard him say something? Ran into him in the men's room? Holy shit!"

"What?"

"Men! You're all men. So far, the killer has only targeted men."

"What does that mean?"

"I don't know yet," I said, practically jumping out of my chair. "But I think you should go, um, hide or something."

"Hide? You put the fear of God in me, and all you have to offer is 'hide'?"

"I'm a paralegal, not a superhero. Just keep yourself safe."

I jumped in my car and called Liam's cell before shifting into DRIVE. "Why would the killer only be afraid of the men on a jury?"

"Is this the setup of a bad joke?"

"No." I shared the information on my recent meeting with Dr. Wong. "What do you think?"

"I think you're on a caffeine high and taking a pretty big leap in the logic department."

"Wanda and Paula haven't had anything weird happen to them."

"Or they have and they lied."

"Why are you urinating on my theory?"

"Urinating?" he repeated with a deep, sexy chuckle. "You can say 'pissed,' Finley. You won't offend my tender sensibilities."

I'd like to kick you in your tender sensibilities. "So I'll talk to the other men on the jury. Will that convince you that I'm onto something?"

"It'll convince me that you're psychic."

"Very funny."

"I'm serious. I just got a call from a cop friend of mine. Juror Number Eleven, Daniel Summers, was just found dead."

*Behind every great solution lurks
an even bigger problem.*

Sixteen

"Dead how?"

"Um, he's no longer breathing?"

"Liam, stop being a pain in my ass and tell me what you know."

"He took a header down the stairs at his condo."

"He was pushed?"

"I didn't say that."

"But it does follow the killer's pattern of arranging accidents."

"Or the guy was clumsy, or drunk, or distracted, or—"

"Why can't you ever give me a single, supportive, specific answer to any of my questions?"

"Okay, try this. I can specifically tell you that there were prints on the note pinned to your door."

Hot damn! "Whose?"

"Not in the system."

I pounded the heel of my hand against the steering wheel to vent some of my frustration. "What does that mean?"

"It means the person whose prints are on the note has never been fingerprinted."

"Well, that sucks."

"But, based on size, they probably belong to a woman or a kid."

A kid? God, had I totally lost all objectivity? Was my wishful thinking true, then? It really had been just one of the neighborhood kids playing a prank? "So what happens now?"

"You're dating a pilot, right?"

"How did—? Never mind. Yes, why?"

"What we have ourselves in right now is what he'd call a holding pattern. Patience, Finley, patience. Chill out for a while. It doesn't look like either one of us is going to get anything new tonight."

Speak for yourself, I thought. *Patrick is waiting for me. Besides, I am patient.* I waited almost ten minutes after hanging up with Liam, then I dialed Dave Rice, Juror Number Five's, phone number, thinking I was getting pretty damned good at this investigation stuff. Unlike Liam, I was not going to sit on my butt—which still smarted—waiting, at the mercy of others. The phone began to ring.

"I am so getting the hang of this," I said, mentally preparing myself for yet another professional, productive interview. "I am proactive. I am personable. I'm effective."

"Hello?" a man's brusque voice answered.

"Mr. Rice, this is Finley Tanner."

"Who?"

"Mrs. Evans called you and—"

"Leave me alone."

Click. I glanced at the phone. That was harsh

and rude. I debated for a few seconds, then hit RE-DIAL.

"Look," he growled, a half-ring into the call. "I have nothing to say to you."

"Don't hang up!" I knew I had to talk fast. Something told me my window of opportunity was slamming closed. I rushed through the history of the suspicious deaths, then broke the news about Daniel Summers. "You're in danger, Mr. Rice. We have to meet so I can—"

"Lady, I don't have time for you. Don't call here again."

I listened to the sound of the dial tone for a few seconds. That hadn't worked out as planned. Okay, I'd give him a few minutes and try again. Maybe after the reality of what I'd said set in, he'd be more inclined to hear me out.

I pulled into a convenience store and watched five minutes tick off the dashboard clock before I called back.

"Hi," a woman's voice practically sang. "You've reached Dave and Jenny. We can't come to the phone right now, but leave us a message."

The voice was a little familiar. It took me several seconds to realize that the strong, vibrant voice was a better version of the woman I'd spoken to earlier in the day. Obviously she had a cold or something, because when compared to the tape, she'd sounded like crap.

I tried the number three more times. Still no Dave Rice. He was screening, the bastard. Man, I hate that. I mean, I don't have a problem being the screener, just the screenee. Plus, with Daniel Summers, um, no longer breathing, you'd think Dave Rice would be a little more cooperative. At the very least, he should be taking precautions.

Since I was only a few blocks from Jane's office, I decided to drop in. That, and I hoped she might be in the mood for a drink. I needed one, and I had some time to kill before I met with Harold Greene, then hunted down Nurse Callahan. I wasn't totally comfy with the idea of going home, and Patrick wasn't expecting me until after midnight.

Oh, yeah, and if she had time, I was hoping she could give me her take on the financial stuff Liam had dropped by my job.

Former job? Hell, what do I call it?

Jane was in her office, burning the evening oil. Actually, she was burning a cranberry candle—I recognized the scent immediately. Plus, classic Bob Dylan tunes were blaring so loudly the framed paintings along the corridor were rattling in time with the bass.

I didn't understand Jane's love for the Dylans. Along with Mumbling Bob, the musical equivalent of poet laureate for the sixties' generation, Jane also had a thing for Dylan Thomas. Okay, confession time. I don't get poetry. Yes, it can be lyrical, and the language is beautiful, but if I have to buy a book of poems, then a companion book to explain what the poems mean, well, hell, I'd just as soon skip right past that to something that doesn't require a dissertation-level clarification.

Jane's dark hair was twisted into a clip, and she was so focused on the calculations before her—and harmonizing to the lyrics of "Ain't No Man Righteous"—that she didn't notice me in the doorway.

When she finally did glance up, she started, flinging her mechanical pencil across the room. "Jeez, Finley," she grumbled, grabbing a small remote and lowering the volume. "How long were you standing there?"

"Long enough to know that"—I cleared my throat to deliver a proper, whine-nasal-mumble Dylan impersonation—"sometimes the devil likes to drive you from the neighborhood."

"Screw you."

I practically collapsed into one of the leather chairs opposite her cluttered desk. I always thought accountant types were supposed to be neat, orderly, and organized. Not Jane. I was surprised she could find her own hand in all that chaos.

Removing her half-glasses, she peered over the edge of her desk and said, "Great shoes."

"Thanks. Want to go have a drink?"

She looked tempted but said, "I can't. The fifteenth is right around the corner and I've got two dozen more returns left to prepare."

"My treat?"

She immediately cast me an accusatory glance. "You can't afford to treat during a suspension. Save your money and my time. Just come right out and tell me what you actually need."

"Twenty minutes," I said, pulling the folder out of my purse.

"I can give you five."

"I lost my job today," I reminded her in a pathetic tone. "I might have a killer after me. By the way, he struck again a little while ago."

Jane perked right up. "What happened?"

"Someone pushed a juror down a flight of stairs."

"This is scary stuff. I think you should tell Patrick to take you away until they catch this guy."

"Step one is telling Patrick about all this, period."

"He doesn't know?"

"He did read about my arrest in the paper when he got home this morning."

"Why didn't you fill him in on all the other things?"

I shrugged. Truth was, I wasn't sure why running into the safe haven of his arms *wasn't* my first and only choice. "He was on a flight. I'm seeing him later. I'll tell him in person."

Jane eyed me, openly suspicious. "What gives? I mean, I know you've been wavering on the whole Patrick thing, but I thought the big points in his favor were his kindness and his stability. Isn't that exactly what you need right now?"

Lifting my hair off my neck, I held it while I stretched the stiff, tense muscles around my shoulders. "It is what I need," I readily admitted. "I mean, I'm scared I might be blowing my whole relationship with him for . . ."

For what? A chance to have wild, meaningless, fabulous sex with Liam? The same Liam who is still boffing his ex and thus far hasn't shown one iota of interest in me?

Dropping my hair, I raked it back into place with my fingers. "Ignore me. I'm just having a weird day. Weird week, weird month. Hell, weird everything."

"Perhaps it's time for you to admit that you aren't Buffy the Jury-Killer Slayer?"

Smiling at her teasing, I couldn't do anything else but agree. "It probably is, but until then, explain these to me." I handed her the envelope, and she pulled out the copies of Hall's bank statements and other financial documents.

"How did you get these?"

"They fell from the sky," I lied, not wanting to put Jane in any kind of ethically compromising position. While she looked at the pages, I took out my phone and hit the REDIAL button. Still no answer at the Rice residence. "Can you just tell me if there's anything out of the ordinary about their spending habits?"

Jane peered at me over her glasses. "In five minutes? No."

"But, Jane? I—"

"It will take me a little longer than that." Opening her desk drawer, she pulled out her purse—a really adorable Dooney and Bourke tassel bag that I hoped had a sister or a cousin who would find its way to the outlet store sometime soon. Jane handed me a twenty-dollar bill. "Nature's Way Eatery is two blocks down. Grab me a tofu burger, add sprouts, hold the onion, and a bottle of water. Get yourself something, too. If I know you, you've had a gazillion cups of coffee and nothing else."

"That really hurts, Jane." I snatched the bill out of her hand. "Here I am unemployed and you're mocking my lack of food."

"Bullshit. There is no correlation between your job status and your lousy eating habits. Your body is toxic from all the caffeine and sugar. Go." She shooed me away with her hand. "You need a salad, some roughage, something with some nutritional value. Order something green."

"Irish coffee?" I wondered softly when I was safely out of earshot. It fit the criteria. It has green sprinkles on the top.

Nature's Way is the kind of place I normally cross the street to avoid. It's always staffed by people who know their HDL, LDL, and BMI by rote. I didn't know one DL from the other and could care less. The only three-initials thing I care about is BMW, not BMI. The employees at Nature's Way are always rail-thin, and most share the goal of someday running the New York City Marathon. They're missing the whole point of visiting New York. You can put on ugly nylon shorts and pin a number to your shirt anywhere. New York was meant to be *shopped*.

The restaurant smelled like freshly mowed lawn. Something green was whirling in a blender while another machine sucked in a carrot and dripped out thick orange sludge. No way I would drink that. If I was truly meant to have carrot juice, the carrot would be capable of being squeezed without help from a two-hundred-pound juicer.

The menu was one of those blackboards that created a rainbow effect when the listings were handwritten each day. Food freaks are nutsy when it comes to freshness. Me, I like the occasional preservative. I want to know the cooties have been chemically and completely annihilated before I put anything in my mouth.

I placed Jane's order, then hunted for something that didn't sound too disgusting. I almost leapt for joy when I saw they had grilled portabella sandwiches. That would taste good even on the seven-grain, stone-ground, dry-as-dust roll.

I asked the counter person for a bottle of water for Jane and a Diet Coke for me. She was fine with the water, but blanched and lectured me on the evils of any beverage containing aspartame. I swear, her haughty attitude made me want to wait for her in the alley, wrestle her to the ground, and squirt a whole container of Cheez Whiz down her pristine throat.

Before the food—and I mean that in the loosest

sense of the word—was ready, I called Dave Rice again. Still nothing but the chipper request to leave a message. I didn't bother.

I thought about my earlier conversation with Liam. Okay, I thought about Liam's incredible body, then eventually got around to our last conversation and figured I should probably get my hands on a copy of the trial transcripts. If we really were going back to square one, I had to reread them and look over the exhibits entered into evidence.

I had a pretty good feeling that Sara Whitley had a copy, or if not, could get me one. Especially if she was, as I suspected, so sloshed she'd agree to almost anything. Not that I wanted to take advantage of a genteel drunk, but it was all for a good cause: saving my life, and my job. I gave her a call. One drink too late. Sara was so far inside the bottle she was pressed between the layers of glass. Trying to get anything out of her was useless. I'd try again in the morning.

I did have some of the exhibits. Well, Liv had them. I could get started there. I knew the overnight mail guy was always at her office by ten. I'd retrieve them and at least have something constructive to do in the morning other than obsess over my mandatory meeting with Dr. and Mrs. Hall and/or wait for Liam and the cops to decide how and why the latest juror died.

Until my job-related spanking was over, I'd have nothing but time to read the trial transcripts. At least the complete numbing of my brain cells would distract me from my shopping suspension.

I returned to Jane's carrying two white bags from Nature's Way and a brown one from the liquor store where I'd stopped to get my soda. She dove into the food with a lot more gusto than I.

"Your change is in there, too," I told her. "Thanks for . . . dinner."

She smiled. "Someday you'll thank me for caring about your health."

As I struggled to swallow the dry bite of sandwich, I knew today wasn't that day. "So, anything hinky in Hallville?"

"What do you know about a five twenty-nine?"

"It's one less than a five thirty?"

Jane grinned. "See this?" she said, laying some monthly statements in a row atop the other piles on her desk. She'd circled entries on four of the six statements. "A five twenty-nine is a limited-use custodial account that permits the designated trustee—"

"In English, please?"

"Someone's been raiding the daughter's college account."

"Since when?"

"Early December." She went on to explain, "A five twenty-nine is supposed to be used for college tuition and expenses. Making these cash withdrawals—that clearly weren't legitimately being used for those purposes—racked up some hefty fines and penalties."

"Where did the money go?"

"Impossible to know. The trustee—either Dr. Hall or his wife, they're listed as either/or signatories—authorized the withdrawals, then had the money put into his business account. Then electronic payments were made from that account to the Hall's personal account."

"So he was blackmailing himself?"

She shook her head. "A day or so after the

money funneled through his medical practice to his personal account, it was withdrawn. In cash." She added, "The smart way. No transaction ever exceeded ten thousand dollars, so no flags went up to the banks or the IRS."

"How do I find out where the cash went?"

"Someone has to tell you. There's no paper trail. Unless you can find the person who deposited the same cash amounts in roughly the same time periods. Then the Halls' bank might be able to compare the serial numbers of their cash on hand to the cash deposited in the blackmailer's account. It's a long shot."

My head hurt. "So, you'd have to know finances to know how to do this, right?"

"Maybe," Jane hedged. "I mean, anyone with enough motivation could figure out how to do all this. It isn't like the rules are secret."

"But you'd have to know Hall had the five twenty-whatever, though, right?"

She shook her head. "That's what threw me. The Halls have several other accounts with more than enough money to cover the amounts taken from their daughter's college fund. And they wouldn't have been paying outrageous penalties if they'd cashed out a few CDs or dipped into their money markets."

Wrapping my half-eaten sandwich in its paper wrapper, I sipped my soda.

"What are you going to do?" Jane asked.

"I don't know. I guess I need to find the black-mailer."

"Any ideas who that is?"

"Actually, yes."

* * *

"Nurse Callahan didn't show up for work?" I asked the woman seated behind the information desk wearing a peach apron over her clothing with a big smiley face pinned above her brass nameplate.

"I believe she called in sick. Would you care to leave a message?"

How was I going to accuse the woman of blackmail if she didn't have the decency to be where she was supposed to be? Helen Callahan was my best suspect. It explained almost everything. She was one of the nurses who'd treated Brad Whitley as well as his organ donor. She would have had access to the drugs that had shown up on the not yet complete lab tests. And she had worked with Dr. Hall for years, so she probably knew all his dirty little secrets.

The one thing it didn't explain was the murders. Why would she need to kill jurors? I was still missing something. A *big* something.

I'd deviated from my original plan and raced to the hospital in hopes of catching the nurse early in her shift rather than waiting until its end. I scribbled my name and cell number on a message slip, handed it to the volunteer and walked back to my car. I didn't think I'd get a call from Helen Callahan any time soon. Not if she was busy, off on a killing spree.

I had no way to track down the nurse, not without cold-calling about thirty numbers from the phone book. Hell, with my luck, she probably wasn't even listed, which meant I could spend hours chasing my tail. And now I was late for my appointment with Harold Greene.

Maybe Liam would have better luck. I called him as soon as I was on the way to see the last male juror on the list. "Hello?" It was a sultry female voice.

"Um, hi. I'm sorry, I must have dialed incorrectly."

"Hey, you're that paralegal, right?" she said cheerily.

"Yes."

"This is Ashley. We met the other night at the Blue Martini."

"Hi." I sounded so lame I cringed. Then I felt a surge of anger. Liam was supposed to be at the lab waiting on my results. I could even buy him stopping at the police station, checking on any details in the death of Daniel Summers. But no way could I come up with a scenario that required the presence of the ex-wife.

"Finley, right? Oh, honey," she said as she sighed heavily, "Liam told me about your day, about getting fired and everything. You must feel just terrible. Why don't you come over here and join us? I've already done my thing on Liam, and he's a whole new man. I'd be happy to do you, too."

She wanted to "do" me? What does that mean? She'd "done" Liam. I had a pretty good idea and a pretty vivid mental picture on that one.

"Finley, honey? Are you still there?"

"Yes. Yes I am. Thank you, Ashley, but I'm not comfortable with having you . . . do me. I'm not really into that. When Liam can, have him give me a call. Okay?"

"He's right here. Hang on."

I wanted to snap the phone closed and pretend this conversation had never happened. Too late.

"Hi."

I hate you, Liam McGarrity. "Yes, well, um."

"You're stammering."

"I thought you were staying on top of things at the lab." *But, no, you've been on top of your ex-wife, you so-not-divorced jackass.*

"I've had a long day. I needed to relax, and Ash has incredible hands."

My mouth opened as I screamed silently. Then I said, "Thanks for sharing."

His laugh only irritated me more.

"When you're finished with your personal time, please call me back."

"I am finished. I'm just putting my pants back on now."

"I don't want to have this conversation," I said through gritted teeth. "I don't want to know intimate things like that about you."

"What's intimate? Ashley is a professional masseuse," he said. I could hear him choking on his own amusement. "She just gave me a wonderful massage. I believe she offered one to you as well. Not interested?" The mockery in his tone was loud and clear.

Not when I thought it was a lesbian come-on, no. Now I just feel like a jerk. "No, but do thank her for me." My mom always stressed that good manners could smooth over any awkward situation. I hoped she was right about this one.

Quickly, I told him about the money and the AWOL nurse. "Dave Rice is dodging me. Maybe he'll talk to you." I gave him the number. He promised to see if he could speak to Mr. Rice and track down Helen Callahan while I went to see Harold Greene.

Greene answered the door wearing a T-shirt and a pair of paint-stained shorts, with a giggling child clinging to each of his legs. He was a big, burly African-American man who looked like he could snap me like a twig.

"I'm Finley," I introduced myself, then looked down at the kids with their matched set of dark eyes. "Hi, guys."

The children looked at me for a second, then ran screaming and crying for their mother.

"Sorry. They're shy."

"Not a problem," I assured him. My smile faded. "We need to talk about the Hall trial."

"Let's go around back," he suggested.

I followed him, feeling the heels of my fabric-covered pumps sink into the soft ground. *Great, just great.*

We went over the now familiar ground of the Hall trial, and I didn't learn much of anything new about the testimony or the exhibits. Harold Greene did mention a lot of hang-up calls in the past few weeks. His wife just had their sixth child, so he'd been home on paid leave for the past three months. Six children was excessive, but three-months paid leave was impressive as hell. Especially to me.

"But nothing strange?"

I watched him search his memory. "We heard a car drive by in the middle of the night a coupla times."

"It's a pretty busy neighborhood."

He rubbed the stubble on his chin. "Well, this particular car drives along without headlights."

Now we were getting somewhere. "What kind of car, do you know?"

"Boxy. A sedan. Dark. Blue or black."

I made a note to check the makes and models for cars owned by all the jurors. "Taking time off

after the baby might have saved your life," I said.
"The killer hasn't been able to get to you."

"I've got a week's more leave coming. Should I take my family away from here?"

I looked into his dark brown eyes and said, "Yes."

"What about Dave? Is he leaving?"

"Dave Rice?"

Harold nodded. "He and I kept in touch after the trial. We do some side jobs together. He's a great guy."

"Really? He's hung up on me. Twice."

Harold hung his head. "Dave's having a rough go of it. He worked for one of the largest cabinet manufacturers in the Northeast for nearly twenty years. Then, one day, they just closed the plant. Not only did he lose his job, but Dave found out all his savings were gone, lost in some sort of swindle by upper management. He and Jenny had two kids about to start college and no money in the bank. He took a job with the home center down here. Didn't pay nearly what he'd been making, but with that and the side jobs, they were getting by."

"Were?" I asked.

"Until Jenny got sick."

That explained why she'd sounded so bad on the phone. "Is it serious?"

Harold nodded. "Breast cancer. She had it before and beat it, but this time, well, who knows. She's taking some experimental treatments, and Dave, well, he needs to believe she'll get better. Said he saw miracles happen all the time when he was a medic during Desert Storm. I hope he's right. Jenny's a fine woman, and Dave's a real stand-up guy.

"It's been hard on them, what with it spreading fast and the HMO claiming the cancer was a pre-existing condition on account she had it before, when his insurance was through his other company."

"How fast?" I asked.

"She was diagnosed just after Halloween last year. Started treatment right after the new year."

I was pretty bummed when I arrived at Patrick's place, a little earlier than expected. I kept thinking about the irony of Dave Rice being a juror on a medical case and now sitting by helplessly watching his wife die because some HMO bean counter wanted to save a few bucks.

Patrick kissed me softly and wrapped me in his arms, and it felt wonderful. After savoring the familiar comfort of his embrace, I took him by the hand and led him to the sofa. "I've got a lot to tell you."

We spent the better part of two hours discussing the pros and cons of my theories. He voiced concerns for my safety but seemed to accept and respect my need to see this through. Of course he did. Patrick was all things wonderful and considerate. *He'd* never date his ex-wife or have her come over for intimate massages. And as long as I'd known him he'd never had a *"thing,"* either.

"I'd say you more than earned your gift," he said, gently brushing his lips against my forehead. He went into the bedroom, then returned with a pretty blue and gold box from the Antwerp Spa we'd visited during the early months of our relationship.

Even after all this time, he'd remembered how much I'd raved about the emollient lotion and decadent warming gloves that were part of the spa's signature offerings.

"Thanks," I said, running the tip of my finger along his jawline. "You are incredibly sweet."

"And you're wounded," he said, his voice tinged with regret.

"We can work around the Boo-Boo wound."

His eyes sparkled. "Really?"

"Really," I insisted, tucking myself under his arm as we moved into the bedroom. Making love was just the diversion I needed.

He'd unbuttoned the top two buttons of my blouse and was feathering my neck with warm, moist kisses when my cell phone rang. Normally, I would have ignored it, but, then, I'd passed my number out to all of the jurors I'd met and felt a responsibility to answer.

Patrick nibbled on one earlobe while I held my phone to the other. "Hello?"

"You sound breathless."

"It's late."

"I found Dave Rice."

Unintentionally, I shoved Patrick away a little harder than intended, sending him stumbling back onto the bed. I mouthed an apology.

"Good work, Liam, where is he?"

"St. Mary's Medical Center."

I felt a chill dance along my spine. "Is he dead?"

"No, but his wife is."

Is it still the end if it doesn't feel finished?

Seventeen

My morning was a regular topographical map—peaks and valleys and a bunch of crap I didn't understand. Patrick, my rock, my stabilizer, the pillar of compassion, announced over he-ran-out-and-got-my-favorite-kind of coffee that he was going ocean kayaking for the day. Of course, then he pulled a typical man-move. He brought out the pained, hangdog expression as he said, "If you really need me to, I can cancel."

Well, there are only two possible responses to a statement like that. Option one is to say, "Hell, yes. Cancel the plans you made without knowing I'd be panties-deep in a murder investigation, and stay with me." But that was selfish, needy, and pretty much conveyed the message that I was incapable of dealing with my own problems—ones I had, in fairness to him, at least partially brought on myself.

So I went with option two. "I'm fine, really. You've been working without any real breaks for almost a month. Go and enjoy yourself." I meant maybe half of that—the part about him deserving some leisurely downtime. I found myself deeply offended that he'd enjoy himself while I was in danger.

I took a shower, dried my hair, and decided I had to go home to change. Facing a second day in the same outfit with only touchup cosmetics at my disposal was enough for me to overcome my lingering fears of a killer on the loose. Almost.

So I ventured the three miles back to my apartment, checking my rearview mirror every thirty seconds or so for signs of a boxy, dark sedan.

The evil, snarky part of my personality wanted to call Liam, even though it was barely past nine, just to interrupt any postcoital bliss he might be experiencing.

I had the perfect excuse. I needed information on suspect vehicles. I had pretty much convinced myself it was the thing to do, when I turned into my complex and found Liam leaning against his car. A car, I might add, he'd parked in my assigned spot.

He had a videotape and the newspaper I paid to have delivered in one hand, and a 7-Eleven paper cup in the other. At least I outclassed him in the coffee department.

He gave me a pretty thorough once-over as I walked toward him, then his lips curled into an annoying smirk.

"Well, well, this is a first. Finley Tanner without the spit and polish."

Bite me. Please. I pointed at his car. "Well, well, *that* is a violation of the complex's posted parking regulations. I'll go spit and polish myself while Redmond's tows it away."

"Long night? Oh, wait, we're not supposed to be

interested in each other's intimate details. I believe that was your stated policy."

God, the man had the ability to make my blood boil! I was torn between a strong desire to smack him and, well, just plain old desire. Could I have had a psychotic break and not know it?

Peak, valley, peak, valley. I needed more coffee.

"What's on the tape?"

"Starbucks' drive-through from the morning Marcus died."

"Great," I said as I put my key in the lock. Much as I hated to admit it, I was glad he was there. Having a tall, dark, obscenely handsome man around did have its pluses. "I think I know what kind of car we're looking for."

"Because you called the Psychic Hotline?"

No, because while you were over at Ashley's, having hot oil rubbed all over your body, I was working. "Some of the people I interviewed mentioned seeing a suspicious car." Okay, only one of them, but he didn't need to know that.

When I saw the huge basket in the center of my table I was almost moved to tears. Liv probably put it together—baskets were a specialty of hers. I knew Sam, Becky, and Jane had all kicked in to make it special.

Pulling the gift tag free, I opened it, and Liam read it over my shoulder. "Happy Suspension." Tugging the pretty pink and lime-green ribbon loose, I discovered a wealth of treasures. Foremost among them, my laptop.

"When did losing a job become a gift-giving occasion?" Liam taunted. "Hey, maybe Hallmark should consider starting up a line of appropriate cards."

"You are way too cynical, and probably don't have friends as considerate and devoted as mine."

"Yeah, like the pilot? Ocean kayaking while you're investigating several homicides, is he? There's devotion for you."

How did he do that? "How could you *possibly* know where Patrick is spending his day?"

"I know things."

Infuriating man. I knew he wasn't going to tell me. I continued looking through the gifts, pretending I was not at all flummoxed by his presence. My laptop seemed to be in perfect working order and had a note taped to the bottom stating that the e-mail from AfterAll had been sent by a single-use account from one of the Internet cafés. My friends had donated some other great stuff as well. There was a Starbucks card, probably loaded with enough credits to last a good portion of the pay-free month, and books by two of my favorite authors—a steamy action-adventure and book three in a series about an Italian shoe company. Liv had also tucked in the express-mail package I'd had delivered to her office. Finally, there were a dozen single-serving boxes of Lucky Charms. My friends rock.

"I'm going to change my clothes. You can set up the film fest."

I stripped and told myself I was putting on a bra and thong set from my special-occasion collection because I could, not because Liam was in the next room. Since I had my two o'clock with the Halls, I opted for Anne Klein all the way. I paired a flirty black skirt with a black and pink jersey camisole, then slipped on my only pair of full-price Max Azria pumps—a Christmas gift from my mother. A careful application of Mac cosmetics, and I was good to go.

Liam's second once-over of the day was more thorough and practically made my knees buckle. The air between us seemed to crackle and sizzle, and for a second I actually thought he might cross the room and kiss me.

Patrickpatrickpatrick.

We watched the tape at least a dozen times. Several dark, boxy sedans passed through the pickup window and/or the small portion of the parking lot visible from the position of the camera.

"That wasn't much help," I remarked as I went to brew a fresh pot of coffee. "Sorry you wasted a trip over here."

"I have other bits of information, too."

I turned and gave him a dirty look. "Why do you drag everything out in bits and pieces?"

He was completely unmoved by my unguarded display of irritation. "I'm just helping you hone your patience skills."

"Stop helping me, and tell me whatever it is you have to say." I started moving items from my Liz bag to my Chanel purse.

"Okay," he said, pulling the notepad from the back pocket of his jeans. "Marcus had a high concentration of alprazolam in his system when he died. The common brand name for that is—"

"Xanax. I know. My mother claims I'm the reason she needs them. An anti-anxiety med that can cause drowsiness."

"Marcus had enough in his bloodstream to cause a freaking coma."

"So isn't that enough to go to the police?"

"It will be after I go to his family doctor and get an affidavit attesting to the fact that the man did not and never had taken that medication."

I felt positively giddy. "Yes!"

"I'm meeting Stacy at his office at three."

That put a hurting on my giddy. "So I still have to go to the Halls and suck up?"

"Your call. I wouldn't. Then again, I'm not the one who wants her job back."

"Well, you are getting proof that Marcus was murdered, but I already have proof that Hall was being blackmailed."

"And, unfortunately, we don't have any proof that one is related to the other."

"You'd have to be as dumb as a stick not to see the connection."

"D.A.s are funny that way," Liam said. "They won't sign off on arrest warrants for prominent cardiologists without bulletproof probable cause."

"How do we get that?"

"By identifying the blackmailer."

"Any possibility they have big black 'B's tattooed on their foreheads?"

"Nope. Now, on to our next topic."

"Jeez, Louise!" I tossed my hands in the air. "Would you mind handing me a memo or something so I'll know how many 'topics' we're going to cover?"

"Next to last one. Daniel Summers, the juror who bit it yesterday?"

"Juror Number Eleven."

"No autopsy yet, but the preliminary X-rays showed two distinct and separate skull fractures."

Resting one hand on my hip, I asked, "And now you're going to tell me that the finding is inconclusive because he could have hit his head on more than one step?"

"Nope. One fracture was horizontal, at the base of the skull. The other was a contra-coup fracture at the right front temple."

"Meaning?"

"The first fracture is most commonly caused when someone is hit from behind with something long and cylindrical, like a pipe. According to the forensic blood evidence at the scene, the vic smashed his head against a concrete slab, which most likely caused the other fracture. Or . . ."

"I hate when you say that."

He grinned. "Or Mr. Summers fell and fractured his skull against one of the wrought-iron railings. Then managed to get up, climb the stairs, fall again, and fracture his skull a second time on the decorative planter."

"So his death will definitely be investigated as a murder, right?"

He nodded. "I'll call my guy on the force and have him check to see if anyone reported a boxy, dark sedan in the area at the time of the murder. I'm also still trying to track down Nurse What's-Her-Face."

"Callahan," I supplied before realizing he'd said it just to get a rise out of me. Too bad. I wasn't about to let his warped sense of humor spoil my exuberance. "This is great." I was going to get my job back, and I was thinking Dane now owed me an apology, a raise, and a big freaking bonus. "What should I do?"

"Go see Dave Rice."

My heart skipped a beat. "His wife died last night. I can't go bother him at a time like this."

"Trust me, he'll respond better to you in person."

"He hung up on me. Twice."

"Because he couldn't *see* you."

"Meaning?"

"It's a lot harder to tell someone to kiss off in the flesh."

"God, you're asking me to be like those slimy reporters who shove microphones in people's faces twenty minutes after their kid got hit by a train. Can't you do it?"

"Nope. This is definitely woman's work. Buck up, Finley. You can handle it." He stood and headed for the door. "Oh, and call me before you go inside the Halls' house."

"Why?"

"So I can listen in. Just dial my number and put it on speaker."

"You are so not inspiring confidence in me."

"That comes with time," he said, then added, "a component of patience," and left.

"Patiently go screw yourself," I grumbled as I poured myself a big mug of coffee and went to my computer.

On the upside, I'd won both the Betsey Johnson dress and another link for my Rolex on my eBay auction. On the downside, I had twenty-four hours to pay for the items. So, after downing the pot of coffee and eating one box of Lucky Charms, I headed out for the first of what I was pretty sure would be two very unpleasant tasks.

It took me less than twenty minutes to reach Dave Rice's house. It was in a small community off Route 1 just south of Jupiter. Dreading every second of my assignment, I approached the front door slowly, hoping my knees and my hands would stop shaking before I had to face the grieving widower.

No such luck.

Dave Rice opened the door. His expression was vacant, his eyes red and ringed in dark circles.

"Yes?"

"Mr. Rice, I am so sorry to bother you today. I'm Fin—"

"I know who you are." He sighed heavily, then stepped aside for me to enter. The house smelled of disinfectant, and what had once been a family room had been transformed by the addition of a hospital bed, several IV poles, and assorted other machines.

At least fifteen pill bottles sat on the bar separating the sickroom from the kitchen. We went into a sunny nook, its cheerfulness seeming like an affront to the grief I read in his eyes. A plain file folder sat in the center of the table. He placed his palm on it and slid it across the glass top, positioning it in front of me. "I think this is what you're looking for."

Opening the folder, I saw it contained a single document. A pharmacy bill. Not for Brad Whitley, but for the heart donor, Ivy Novak. Even after several passes, I wasn't clear on why or how this was supposed to help me.

"I know I did the wrong thing," he said, glancing off into space as he spoke. "I knew it then, too. Maybe I should have said something."

"About?" I prompted.

"I was a medic in the first Gulf War. My job was pretty much making sure the wounded kids were bandaged and as pain-free as possible so they could be transported to the hospital in Germany.

"Ivy Novak's injuries were severe. She was going to die. Her organs were shutting down, and once that happens, they're no longer viable for transplant. Dr. Hall had to make a judgment call. With a new heart, Brad Whitley had at least a chance.

"I honestly believed the doctor did the wrong thing for the right reason. I still do. That's why I voted to absolve him of any wrongdoing."

"But?" *What wrong thing?*

"My wife got sick. We'd lost our savings, and our HMO said that since she'd been cancer-free for less than five years, they weren't responsible for any of her medical bills."

He stood and grabbed two of the pill bottles. "This one"—he paused to hand it to me—"is three grand for a thirty-day supply. And this one runs about fifteen hundred a month. Impossible for me to swing when I was earning twelve bucks an hour at the home center. Jenny thought I was earning the extra money doing side jobs. I couldn't tell her what I'd done. What I'd set into motion."

"What did you do?" I felt a sudden stab of fear. What if I had it wrong again, and Dave Rice was the killer?

It was like he'd read my panic. Tears spilled from his eyes. "I didn't even know they were being killed until Mrs. Evans called me."

I relaxed a little.

"I never meant for anyone to get hurt. I was just trying to save my wife."

He dissolved into wrenching sobs. I tried patting his back, getting him water, but he was well past any consolation I could provide. He pushed the folder at me. "Take it and go."

"Is there someone I can call?" *The police?* No, that seemed harsh; the guy was in his own personal hell. That could wait.

So, taking the folder, I left him to his grief. I had ten minutes to get to the Halls' place on Singer Island. I grabbed the phone and called my sister in New York. My call was transferred to an operator.

"Dr. Tanner, please."

"Dr. Tanner is in surgery. Can she call you back?"

Crap, what good was having a surgeon for a sister if she was in surgery when you needed her? "Um, yes, have her call her sister as soon as she's free. It's very important." My next call was to Liam.

"I'm at the Halls' gate," I said, switching to the speaker phone. I quickly repeated an abbreviated version of my encounter with Dave Rice.

"Can you fax me what he gave you?"

"Gee, sure, I keep a fax machine in my glove box for just this kind of situation."

"Sorry. No big deal. I'm sure there's someplace with a public fax machine nearby. As soon as you leave the Halls' place, you can take care of it. I'm sure the Evans' family doctor can explain whatever's on that bill that's worthy of blackmail."

"I could show it to Dr. Hall."

"Wrong answer. Never show your cards to a suspect."

"I can see the daughter." I whispered for some stupid reason. I was still in the car, so she probably thought I was babbling to myself. "She's watching me."

"Go do your thing," Liam said, his voice calm. "Make it quick. Keep it simple. Then get the hell out of there."

The Halls' home was pretty much what I expected. Tasteful, with formal and informal spaces designed for entertaining. Vases of freshly cut flowers adorned nearly every table. The daughter, Zoe, with the typical surly teenage attitude, had me wait in the foyer while she got her parents.

My attention flitted around the room, picking up little details here and there. The art looked like they could be originals. The rugs were antiques. I figured that the custom crystal light fixture over my head ran somewhere in the neighborhood of thirty grand.

None of that was as interesting as the letter on the foyer table. It was from the Friends' Academy Office of Academic Standards and Student Affairs.

As a former private-school girl, I knew about those letters. Zoe Hall was in danger of failing one or more of her classes.

"Miss Tanner, please come with me." While Zoe's manners were above reproach, the request still came out sounding more like, "Screw you and the horse you rode in on."

Meredith and Kent Hall sat at opposite ends of an ornate Louis XV sofa. At first, I thought that might be some sort of body-language way of letting me know there was dissension in the ranks. But, no, it was only to accommodate Zoe, who slipped comfortably between them. Actually, she sat slightly closer to her father than her mother.

Photographs in polished silver and gold frames lived happily among various porcelain figurines, also French. Most of them were of Zoe. Zoe goes to school; Zoe goes to the zoo; Zoe graduates from something; Zoe as a Candy Striper; Zoe on horseback. It was definitely an only-child mambo.

"I came to apologize for any inconvenience my actions may have caused your family." Couldn't get much shorter or sweeter than that.

"Zoe," Meredith said, patting her daughter's knee. "I had Cook make tea. Would you please bring it in?"

Zoe looked like she'd rather spit on me, but she dutifully exited the room.

"That isn't necessary," I said. *I hate tea. Tea is for colds, flus, and the British.*

"I do hope you realize the gravity of the situation you've incited," Dr. Hall commented.

I noticed his cheeks redden and figured that wasn't a good sign. "Yes. But in my defense, I never mentioned your name to the police. I guess they just made that assumption because I had some files pertaining to the malpractice case in my car at the time of my arrest."

"That matter is closed," Meredith reminded me just as Zoe returned with the tea.

Worse than tea. Rose-colored herbal tea. It smelled a lot like the eau de toilette one of my step-grandmothers gave me every Christmas.

Zoe poured with practiced grace. Obviously, among her many talents, she'd also studied Emily Post. "Thank you," I said, accepting the toilet water. It tasted worse than it looked. She filled the three other cups, then rejoined her parents.

"Your timing couldn't be worse," Meredith said. "Zoe is interviewing at colleges. She plans on following in her father's footsteps, and we don't need that scandal revisited. Not when it could affect her future."

I gulped the tea even though I knew better. "Well, then, Zoe, I wish you all the best, and again, I do apologize."

I started to stand when Dr. Hall said, "I assume, then, that we won't be hearing any more rumors about your . . . activities?"

"Rumors?" I repeated. "Heaven's no. From now on, I will only deal in facts."

The Halls seemed satisfied. I was just hoping the perspiration I felt dripping down my cleavage didn't show.

"Are you insinuating you have some relevant facts?" the doctor asked.

I could hear Liam groaning in my head. "Relevant facts? That's—" My cell phone played the siren sound, alerting me of a second call coming through. My guess was Liam was dialing in to give me a graceful way out. "Please excuse me," I said, putting down the cup and reaching into my purse.

I clicked the ACCEPT INCOMING button and said, "Hello?"

"It's Lisa. What do you need?"

"Hang on." Covering the mouthpiece, I looked at the Hall family and apologized again. "This is my doctor, and"—I made sure to make eye contact with Dr. Hall—"I really don't want to keep her on hold. Thank you for the tea, and thank you for seeing me."

"But—"

Ignoring Meredith's half-hearted protest, I practically ran to my car. By then, Liam was trying to beep his way through my call with Lisa. Sliding my key into the ignition, I fired up the engine and practically squealed my tires as I rounded the horseshoe-shaped driveway to make my escape.

"Finley!" Lisa said curtly. "I don't have all day."

"Okay, okay," I said, blinking to clear the spots from my vision. Obviously, my performance for the Halls had caused my blood pressure to spike. "If I read you a list of medications, can you tell me what they're for?"

"How long is the list?"

"Not very. Please?"

"Go."

I managed to hold the page against the wheel, splitting my attention between the road and the overly long, unfamiliar words. I read the first six, struggling as my vision seemed to be getting worse.

Lisa confirmed they were typically medications administered to improve organ function. "Is this a transplant donor?"

"Yesss." I heard the voice slur.

"Fin? What's wrong?"

"One more," I managed, swallowing as I fought to pronounce the last one. "Me-per, mepreri—"

"Meperidine?"

"Yesssss." I was really feeling woozy, so I steered on to the narrow shoulder of the road.

"It's a pain-killer."

My fogged-in brain barely processed the concept. "Why would you give a donor a pain-killer?"

"You wouldn't. Brain-dead people can't feel pain."

Oh God. "That's what he knew."

"Fin? Where are you?"

"Sing—Singer Island. Need help."

"How long have I been here?" I asked Becky, who just happened to be the first person I saw when my eyes and my brain were finally back in sync.

"Four hours. You've been in and out. Mumbling. Not making a whole hell of a lot of sense for the most part. There's a line out in the waiting room. We've been assigned specific shifts until visiting hours end."

"Dr. Hall?"

"I'll have Liam come in and bring you up to speed on that, but you might want to turn up the volume on the TV."

"He's in jail?" I asked Liam a minute later when he stepped into my hospital room. Flicking through the television stations, I was dying to see Dr. Hall doing the perp walk, hands and feet shackled. Would he be humiliated or overcome with remorse? Who cared? Hopefully, he was going to go to prison and spend the rest of his days being some gang member's bitch.

"He's being questioned. Then they'll probably file formal charges. And, by the way, you were right about the car. The Halls bought an S-Class Mercedes, midnight blue, the week before their daughter's birthday. How are you feeling?"

"Good. *Really* relaxed," I added with a grin. "Ready to get out of this hospital."

"Patience," he reminded me. "You're here for the night."

"Swear to me they didn't cut my clothes off. Do you have any idea what that outfit cost me?"

"You worry about the strangest stuff. Hall almost killed you, and you're concerned over a skirt and top?"

"Well . . . yeah."

"You better be grateful for your twelve-cup-a-day coffee habit. The high level of caffeine was the only reason the alprazolam didn't stop your breathing and kill you."

I shuddered, then looked up and said, "There he is. Wait!" My stomach fell into my feet. "He's not handcuffed. What's the deal?"

"I'll make a few calls," Liam said as he jogged from the room. He came back twelve agonizingly long minutes later, his eyes glistening with anger. "Son-of-a-bitch has an airtight alibi for Vasquez and for Marcus Evans."

"How airtight?"

"Out of town, teaching transplant techniques at other hospitals. There's, like, a hundred people who verified his alibi, plus the airlines and hotels where he stayed."

"But he could have killed the others, right? We know he was in town when Daniel Summers was murdered."

"Banging Nurse Callahan. That's why she called in sick. Apparently the two of them have been having a fling for years."

"Then why wasn't he charged with killing Ivy

Novak? My sister said she wouldn't have needed a pain-killer if she was really brain dead."

"He's claiming it's a mistake. The pain-killer only shows on the pharmacy bill, not the OR notes."

"It has to be him," I said, crossing my arms as anger simmered in every cell of my body. "Dave Rice all but came right out and told me he was blackmailing Hall to cover his wife's cancer treatments."

"Hall claims that was just a charitable act on his part."

"Then get Dave Rice in to talk to the police."

"That's going to be hard."

"Why?"

"He blew his brains out right after you left him."

I felt a stab of pain. "And you believe that?"

"He left a note. The handwriting was verified by his two sons and exemplars the cops took from his house."

"What did the note say?"

"Two words—'I'm sorry.' "

"Everybody's sorry, but no one's responsible? Can't the police search Hall's house? He put something in that nasty-ass tea they made me drink."

"They searched. Nothing."

"Who is that good?"

"Hall's got a genius-level IQ, and his wife is no slouch, either. She graduated with honors from Wellesley. The daughter got the smart genes, too, though it appears she's been slacking off recently."

Some imaginary bell must have sounded because my mother appeared in the doorway, hugging a large bouquet of flowers in one hand and a linen hanky in the other.

"That's my cue," Liam said before slipping out of the room.

The parade continued until eleven, when the nurse emphatically refused to let anyone else cycle in. I had flowers from Patrick, Liv, Becky, Jane—who also smuggled in a coffee—and a huge spray from Dane-Lieberman. So I was guessing my suspension would be lifted soon, if not immediately, but they were crazy if they thought flowers would be enough.

The drug I'd been given at the Halls' hadn't totally worn off. The only things keeping me from falling into a much needed sleep were anger and frustration.

I knew I'd been dozing in and out, mainly because every time I opened my eyes the images on the television had changed. I didn't see a clock anywhere, but I kept reminding myself that I needed to call Lisa and thank her. Calling 911 from two thousand miles away had probably saved me as much as the coffee.

I wanted coffee but was happy to settle for water. Feeling pretty awake, I decided I'd grab my Styrofoam pitcher and do a little self-service refill. I was sure the night nurses had better things to do than play waitress for me.

Barefoot and holding the slit in the back of my hideously ugly hospital gown, I strolled down the corridor. After about five minutes, I finally found a small room with an ice dispenser and some water. With my pitcher filled, I went back to my room. By the light cast through the partially opened door and the silent images on the television screen, I poured myself a drink. That was when I heard the sound.

Whipping around, I noticed the hypodermic needle first and Zoe Hall second. My instant reaction was to toss the ice water in her face, then grab her wrist and hold on for dear life.

Zoe was eighteen, and both taller and stronger than I was. I, however, was an exceptional screamer. Though it took a few minutes, orderlies finally arrived and subdued the girl. Since I was still relatively new at the whole "someone tried to kill me" thing, I simply crumbled to the floor and watched mutely as she was dragged, flailing, from my room.

Patrick was away again. Liam had disappeared since our last conversation at the hospital. I'm so pathetic I can't decide which of them I miss more. It's a week later and I'm back at my desk. Correction, I'm back at a better desk. I got a modest raise, back pay, and an office with a view of the street instead of the parking lot. Dane didn't apologize, though he did send a welcome-back e-mail. At least he was consistent—he was, is, and always will be an asshole.

This morning I read that Zoe Hall's attorney—who, coincidentally, is Jason Quinn, the same Jason Quinn who threatened Dane into practically firing me—was going to plead temporary insanity. "Good luck with that," I scoffed. It was a tough defense and, in my opinion, an impossible one given that she'd planned and executed her crimes nearly perfectly.

I did feel a little sympathy for her parents. Apparently, Zoe had overheard one blackmail call and knew only that it was a man who'd served on the civil jury. She didn't know that her father not only recognized the blackmailer as Dave Rice, but that he was ready, willing, and able to pay for Jenny's cancer treatments. Zoe's desire to protect her father had simply spiraled out of control. But *crazy* isn't the same as *legally crazy,* so I hoped the girl liked bright orange jumpsuits because I figured she'd be wearing one for years and years to come.

I was just on my way out to the copy room when I nearly collided with Liam. He looked as good as ever and smelled wonderful. And, being the cool, calm, aloof, professional woman that I am, I couldn't even coax a simple "Hi" out of my throat.

He practically backed me into my own office. "I see they gave you new digs. Nice."

"Bigger, better." *Babbling.*

"How have you been?"

"Great. You?"

"Busy. I've had a lot of things lately."

He didn't sit down. Instead he just kept inching closer until I felt my hip hit the edge of my desk. Those incredible eyes were fixed on mine. "Do you need something?"

"Yep."

His head dipped fractionally, and his gaze dropped to my mouth. Time froze. He froze. I freaked.

Oh, to hell with it. If I could fend off an attacker, I could ask a simple question. "Well, are you?"

"Am I what?"

His warm, minty breath tickled my skin, and I felt a flush rush to my cheeks. Liam was still close in, his mouth no more than a few inches above mine. "Well, um, are you going to kiss me?"

"No."

I blinked. "This feels like you're about to kiss me."

He smiled. It was slow, crooked, and very sexy. "That's just one of the differences between you and me, Finley."

"What?"

"I'm very, very patient."

Acknowledgments

Unlike in the movies, where the author—usually seen in his or her New England seaside cottage typing on a vintage Underwood—easily completes the novel that simply flows effortlessly from his or her fingertips, writing this book was truly a labor of love, complete with struggles, dry spells, and a pretty daunting learning curve.

This book wouldn't be a reality without the encouragement of my agent, Kimberly Whalen. Nor would it be a reality without the support and excitement of my editor, Audrey LaFehr, and the amazing people at Kensington Books. Thank you for welcoming Finley into the world.

Thanks to Richard Berjian, M.D., for his medical advice. Thanks to Martin B. Lessans, Esq., who patiently taught me the duties and responsibilities of an estates and trusts paralegal. If I've made any legal or medical mistakes, it wasn't the teachers, it was the student.

For Cherry Adair, Leanne Banks, and Traci Hall, who propped me up when I didn't think I could take this step. These women are the most talented and generous plotting partners a person could ask for. Thank you all for giving me the courage to take this leap of faith. Thank you even more for being honest without ever being cruel, for being encouraging without being patronizing, for celebrating the sale with my beautiful and treasured pink briefcase, but mostly for being there when I needed you, day or night. I love you like sisters.

Thanks to Joanne Sinchuk, owner of Murder on the Beach, the very best bookstore in all of south Florida, for graciously allowing Finley and her friends to hang out in your store.

Thank you, Mom, for all the hours spent sticking Post-its on the hard copy of my manuscript. Who knew one daughter could make so many typos? Thanks to Connie Chesley, opera diva and dear friend who continues to help me breathe life into Finley's mother. Thanks to my great friends Amy Fetzer, Maureen Child, Kathy Pickering, Kathleen Beaver, and Karen Harrison.

And last but by no means least, my family, Bonnie, Eric, Kevin, Maris, Russ, Mara, Ray, Claire, Ronnie, Dottie, Linda, Mark, Rebecca, Jonathan, Justin, Grace, Ron, Blysse, Paige, Anna, and Alex.

If you enjoyed
KNOCK OFF,
read on for a special preview of
Rhonda Pollero's next fun and sassy mystery
starring everyone's favorite new amateur
sleuth: Finley Anderson Tanner!

KNOCK 'EM DEAD

A Kensington hardcover on sale in March 2008.

*As it turns out, there is something a guy can't
live without.*

One

I was having an erotic dream about a seriously hot
guy with blue eyes, and black hair—*not* Liam Mc-
Garrity—a so-wrong-for-me man who can turn me
into a quivering pile of hormones with a single
glance. And definitely not my perfect-in-every-way
boyfriend, Patrick, when the knocking started. It
was loud and insistent.

Some impatient someone wanted my attention
at this ungodly hour of—I slitted bleary eyes at the
bedside clock—five-twenty A freaking M. On a Sunday, no less. This better be good.

I groaned heavily, missing my thousand-thread-
count sheets even before I'd tossed them aside.
Patrick was just back in town, so I was dressed in a
cotton tee and matching boxers. No sense wasting
the good stuff when I'd spent the previous evening
watching the *What Not to Wear* marathon I'd been
storing up on my new DVR. A gadget I'd only been
able to afford after Visa upped my credit limit.

Bam. Bam. Bam.

"I'm coming, damn it!" Three quarters asleep, I pulled on my robe, and started out of the bedroom, stubbing my toe against the bedframe in the process while whoever the idiot was at my door kept right on knocking. Like I hadn't heard the first ninety-nine knocks. Me and all my neighbors.

I winced, hopped, and cursed, not necessarily in that order. The banging on my front door became more urgent. In the few seconds it took me to hobble through my darkened apartment, flipping light switches along the way, I mentally ran through some possibilities.

Could be Sam, my upstairs neighbor and friend. Soon-to-be former friend if he was the one on the other side of the door.

Patrick was a more remote possibility. He flew cargo for FedEx and often arrived and/or departed at off hours. But we were two years into our relationship and he knew me well enough to know I wouldn't appreciate an early morning drop-in. Not when I'm at my most visually vulnerable pre-shower, hair, and makeup.

Definitely not my mother. Even if she needed me urgently, she'd send a messenger before she'd break protocol. She doesn't even use the telephone other than during the socially acceptable hours of ten AM to ten PM.

I got up on tiptoes to peer through the peephole. Though the figure was silhouetted by back lighting from the parking area, I recognized my friend Jane Spencer instantly.

Fumbling with the safety chain and flipping the deadbolt's lever, I yanked open the door so fast that Jane's balled fist caught me square in the center of the forehead.

I stumbled backward, my head now throbbing along with my toe. "Jesus, Jane! What the f—"

"*Ohgodohgodohgod,*" she babbled, closing the door and gripping me by the shoulders as I teetered.

I'd met Jane at the gym almost six years ago. Though we were total strangers, we'd agreed to pretend to be friends in order to take advantage of the gym's two-for-one special. I don't like to think of it as a scam so much as the broadest interpretation of the term *friend*.

My friendship with Jane is now a reality, and we get together whenever possible. My attendance at the gym is spotty at best. Jane, on the other hand, works out religiously, hence the reason her accidental blow had me seeing stars.

"I'm okay," I lied, shrugging off her hold. Moderately pissed, but okay. Then my vision cleared and I looked at her. Really looked at her.

Her dark brown eyes were red, puffy, and filled with a kind of abject terror I'd never seen in my calm, reasonable, rational friend. Though she looked a lot like one of the Pussy Cat Dolls, Jane was an accountant and investment broker. A geek in sex-kitten clothing.

She was covered in deep crimson blood.

Wet deep crimson blood.

It was matted in her hair and soaked through the right side of her thigh-skimming, aqua La Perla negligee. The streaks of partially dried blood continued down the side of one leg to her bare foot.

My brain dealt with the blood first. Why she was outside, in the middle of the night, in her nightie, could wait for later. "What happened? Did you have an accident?"

Jane's fingers trembled as they snagged in the crusting blood in her hair.

I followed her as she walked stiffly into my living room, leaving single-footed, reddish-brown marks on my tile and carpet as she moved, her hands hugging her bare, blood-streaked arms.

"He's dead. There was so much blood . . ."

My initial hope that maybe she'd picked up some run-over animal, or something had evaporated. "He who?"

"Paolo. He's dead. Oh, God, worse than dead."

Paolo? The name didn't register. Nor did the concept of worse than dead. It's one of those absolutes, like being pregnant. You definitively are or you aren't.

"Back up," I insisted, gently lowering her to the sofa. I grabbed the pashmina throw draped over the back of the couch and wrapped it around her shoulders. Taking her hands in mine, I knelt in front of her. "Take a deep breath and start from the beginning."

She swallowed audibly and nodded. "Paolo was my date. You know, from that meet-a-rich-guy introduction service Liv represents?"

Sure, I remembered it. Olivia Garrett, one of our mutual friends who owns an event-planning company, had been hired by a very exclusive, very expensive dating service to create 'fairytale fantasy dates' for available men and women of means. Liv had persuaded the owners to waive the whopping five-grand membership fee for Becky and Jane.

Becky Jameson and I work together at a law firm in West Palm Beach. She's an attorney in the Contracts Department, while I'm a few rungs down on the professional ladder. I'm an estates-and-trusts paralegal.

Because of Patrick, I was blissfully exempt from the freebie. Jane was willing to give it a try. Becky was not. If I remember correctly, her exact words were, "I'd become a celibate lesbian before I'd go out on a buy-a-guy date."

Back to dead Paolo. "So he was your date and . . . ?"

"Heart Association fundraiser at the Breakers. Cocktails after. Then he drove me home. He had chilled champagne waiting in the limo and by the time we got to my place I was feeling pretty good. So, I invited him up for some coffee and we, um, you know. At least I think we *you knowed*."

"You don't remember?" God, sex with Patrick was methodical, but at least it was memorable.

"We must have," Jane decided with a small shake of her head. "Why else would I be wearing my get lucky lingerie?"

Good point. "And then?"

"I woke up and there was bloo—"

"You fell asleep?"

"Apparently," Jane snapped. "I know, total breach of first-sex etiquette, but I must have had more to drink than I realized, and the guy was gorgeous. Anyway, he was on one side with his back to me. I thought he'd breached too, and was fast asleep, so I shook his shoulder."

I felt her shiver before she yanked her hands free of mine.

"He was ice cold, and then I went to move closer to him when I felt the wet sheets."

"Gorgeous and incontinent. Interesting combination."

Jane glared at me. "I tossed back the covers and there was blood everywhere. It was exactly like that producer guy in *The Godfather* who wakes up with the horse head in his bed.

"I think I crawled over him or—maybe it was around him—and I see this big knife in his chest. I pulled it out, rolled him over, and was about to feel for a pulse when I just happened to glance down and see . . ."

Jane looked like she wanted to vomit. Her skin bleached white and her eyes squeezed shut for a second.

"And saw what?"

"It was gone."

"What was gone?"

"*It,*" Jane repeated succinctly.

"*It* it?" I felt disgust churn in my stomach along with serious confusion. "So what? The police showed up, took your statement, and then just let you leave? Dressed like that?"

"I didn't call them."

I practically leapt to my feet. "*What?*"

"Everything was so bloody, and I'd just touched a dead guy. I was terrified and not exactly thinking straight. It isn't like I've ever awakened and found a man with his privates cut off in my bed before. Plus, I didn't know if the killer was still in my apartment, so I just grabbed my keys and jumped out the window."

I blinked. "You live on the second floor."

"The jump wasn't bad. The landing was a bit of a bitch. So what do I do?"

"We call the police and then we call Becky." I reached for the phone, changing the order of the calls in my mind.

Becky answered in a groggy, guttural voice. "Hello."

I don't think I stopped to breathe as I quickly told her the tale of Jane's date, culminating in the discovery of Dickless Paolo.

She mumbled a few curses, then said, "Call the police and stay put. I'll be there in thirty minutes."

"Okay."

"Finley?"

"Yeah?"

"I don't want either one of you to say a word to the cops until I get there. Understand?"

"Not a word." I glanced over at Jane, who was now curled into a fetal position at one end of my sofa. I had a feeling the cops would expect more than a 'no comment' when they got their first glimpse at Jane. "Do we tell them our names?"

"Name, address, age, occupations, all fine."

"Jane is covered in blood. I'll get her cleaned up and she can—"

"No. No shower, no change of clothes. Nothing to compromise the forensics any more than they've already been compromised. Why didn't she call the police?"

"She wanted out of her apartment."

"Then she should have driven to the sheriff's office." I heard Becky's frustrated sigh. "Why didn't she think?"

"How am I supposed to know?" Cupping my hand over the mouthpiece, I whispered, "She's totally freaked out. Stop lecturing me and get over here."

I'm not sure if I said good-bye to Becky before calling the cops. Yet a few seconds later, a calm, monotone voice came on the line. "9-1-1. What is your emergency?"

I shot a quick glance over at Jane's huddled form on my sofa. "I, um, well . . . I need to report a . . . a, um, bloody friend."

"Do you need an ambulance, Ms. Tanner?"

"How'd you know my name?" I pushed a strand of my disheveled hair off my forehead. "Forget that. What I mean is, my friend was in some sort of . . . See, she had this date and it didn't go well."

"Ma'am, what *specifically* is your emergency?"

"Specifically? I think I need to report a murder."

"Who has been murdered, ma'am?"

"Paolo."

"Is that a first or last name?"

I rolled my eyes. What difference did it make? Was she going to send help or carve the freaking headstone? Jane was pretty useless, so I gave what limited information I had, including Jane's address so someone could check on Paolo.

"I've alerted the sheriff's office. Please stay on the line with me until help arrives."

I did as she asked, though it felt weird holding the receiver to my ear when we weren't talking to each other. Maybe 911 should invest in Muzak or something. Anyway, it seemed like days passed before I heard sirens and the screech of tires. I hung up, opened my door, and counted no fewer than a dozen sheriff's cars careening into the parking lot in front of my apartment. In a matter of seconds, several of the officers leapt from their cruisers and crouched behind their squad cars, guns trained in my direction. I was blinded when they turned their mounted spotlights on me.

Through a megaphone or radio or whatever, a disembodied male voice boomed through the pre-dawn quiet. "Lace your fingers and place your hands behind your head. Get on your knees. Slowly."

"But I'm—"

"Now!"

Squinting against the harsh light, I dutifully followed instructions. My pissed-off meter went into the red zone. The cement was rough, painfully digging into my bare knees. As if it wasn't humiliating enough to be assuming a position I'd only seen on episodes of *Cops*, I heard my neighbors whispering as they stepped out of their apartments to investigate.

Jane came up behind me.

"Hold your position, Ms. Tanner," the male voice instructed. This time his tone was compassionate as he spoke to Jane. "Let us subdue the suspect before—"

I rolled my sightless eyes. "I'm not the suspect, and she's not Finley Tanner. I am. I'm the one that called you." *Morons.*

Oh, and like I wasn't already mired in Suckville, a photographer's camera flash strobed where the cops had busily set up neon yellow crime-scene tape to cordon off my parking lot.

Getting the police to understand that I wasn't an imminent threat to society was a lot like trying to bathe a cat. But eventually, I was allowed to put my arms down and get to my feet. Much to the disappointment of my neighbors. My complex is a pretty laid-back place, so the commotion was a really big, if personally mortifying, thing.

Finally, two plainclothes detectives stepped forward, escorting Jane and I, with two uniformed officers trailing us inside my apartment. The female detective motioned to the deputies with her head. Leaving me helpless and annoyed as the officers dispersed, one went into my kitchen while another strode toward my bedroom. "Where are they going?"

Ignoring my question, the female detective instructed Jane and I to sit on the sofa. She was African-American, with skin the color of a caramel latte. She wore utilitarian navy slacks and a plain, white cotton blouse. No jewelry, unless you counted the silver-toned grommets on her sensible shoes. Or the gold badge clipped at her waist. I didn't.

The male detective came over to me and caught

me by the elbow. There wasn't anything the least bit chivalrous about the gesture. Using my right arm like a rudder, he quickly got me to my feet and escorted me into the bedroom, pushing the door just shy of completely closed.

The detective stood next to my dresser, stiff and devoid of expression. He reminded me of the guards outside Buckingham Palace. Not that I've ever been to see the Queen, but it is on my list of things to do and places to go.

Reading the gold nameplate above the badge dangling out of his right shirt pocket, I locked eyes with the detective. I didn't even attempt to soften the contempt in my tone. "Detective Graves, Jane's in shock or something. Maybe you should—"

"EMS will check her out," he said. He asked me for identification, then reached into his back pocket. He pulled out a small memo pad and took a nub of a pencil from inside the spiral binding. I grabbed my purse off the nightstand and pulled my license from my wallet.

My thoughts were fractured, racing in every direction. Jane, Paolo, blood, and the inappropriate memory of finding the pink Chanel wallet at the outlet mall. So what if the clasp was broken? It wasn't like I passed my wallet around, so my secret was safe. No one, not even my closest friends, knew that I'd been reduced to buying factory seconds. But I couldn't think about that now. Jane's predicament was far more pressing than my tenuous financial situation.

He dispensed with the standard questions— name, age, et cetera—all while comparing the answers to my driver's license. "Please tell me your version of tonight's events."

"Version?"

"Yes, ma'am," he answered, pencil poised. "Approximately what time did Miss Spencer arrive?"

"Before I had a chance to make coffee," I said. I wasn't trying to be snotty, I just couldn't help myself. The detective had coffee breath and it didn't seem fair that he'd gotten his while I was expected to provide lucid answers without an ounce of caffeine in my system.

His single, bushy unibrow pinched between his chocolate-colored eyes. He was also African-American; but unlike his partner, his complexion was very dark. He either worked out religiously or had a serious steroid problem. His neck wasn't a neck so much as a thick stump. His biceps and oversized chest strained against the fabric of his blue oxford shirt. And his tie was at least five seasons out of date and knotted wrong. The thinner black-and-gray striped strip hung pathetically about two inches below the front flap. In fact, now that I had an opportunity to look at him, I realized he'd worked out so much that his body no longer fit conventional clothing. The waistband on his slacks bunched beneath his cinched belt. Because of the bulk of his thighs and calves, the seams on his khaki slacks were stressed almost to their breaking point.

While some women find musclebound men attractive, my brain goes in only one direction. If a guy's pecs make it impossible to lower his arms completely to his sides like a normal person, how does said guy aim to pee?

"The time?" he prompted.

"Five-twenty."

"You noted the *exact* time?"

"Cursed it, actually." I glanced through the slit in the door, trying to catch a glimpse of Jane. I couldn't hear her conversation with Detective Sensible Shoes, but every so often the muffled sound of Jane hiccupping wafted into my room. "She's really distraught, Detective. I know she needs medical attention."

"She'll get it," he said. "Now, if we could get back to your statement?"

Raking my fingers through my hair, I was about to give him the abbreviated version. Screw Becky's advice. In fact, screw Becky, she should have been here by now.

The radio clipped to his belt crackled, and an almost unintelligible voice said, "One-Eight-Seven confirmed at 636 Heritage Way South."

Graves grabbed the radio, depressed a button, and asked for more details. "Hispanic, approximately 5'10". According to his wallet, the vic is Paolo Martinez. Palm Beach address. The ME hasn't gotten here yet, but COD is definitely multiple stab wounds and . . . uh . . . mutilation."

"Mutilation?" Graves asked. For the first time real interest seemed to kick in.

"Yeah," the voice on the radio answered. Like Jane, he seemed to have a difficult time describing the injury. "There's been an, well, um, a—"

"For Chrissake," I cut in, my hands slapping against my sides. "The killer cut Paolo's penis off."

"Yeah," radio voice agreed. "What she said."

"Signs of a struggle?"

"Negative. We've been unable to locate the missing, uh, er—"

I glared at Graves. Why was it so hard for men to say the word, yet so easy for them to adjust it in public whenever the mood struck? Amazing. "Penis."

"Yeah. We haven't found it."

"Keep looking," Graves said.

I thought about that assignment, repulsed as I imagined how it must feel to be the one assigned to find the penis.

Graves asked me all sorts of pointless questions. *Did I know Paolo?*

No.

Was the deceased Jane's boyfriend?

Heck, no.

Would I characterize Jane as a violent person?

Hell, no.

Graves seemed frustrated by me, my answers, or both. He left me under the watchful eyes of the uniformed officer as he slipped into the living room. Balancing on the edge of the bed, I leaned to the right, hoping I might be able to catch bits and pieces of the huddled conversation between the detectives.

Silently, I tried to send Becky an urgent telepathic message to move her ass. Especially when I saw the vacant look in Jane's eyes. Hearing a knock at my front door, relief washed over me—but it was short lived. Instead of Becky, two paramedics lumbered in, carrying what looked like large red tackle boxes.

I stood, only to have my progress blocked by Officer Useless. "Keep your seat, ma'am."

Kiss my seat, and don't call me *ma'am*. "I don't understand your problem," I muttered.

"Standard procedure," he said, as if that explained the whole divide-and-conquer thing they had going on.

"She's a dear friend who has suffered a terrible trauma. I'd simply like to offer some moral support."

"I can't let you do that, ma'am."

I swear, if he 'ma'amed' me one more time, Paolo wouldn't be the only one in Palm Beach County missing a certain body part.

The EMS guys checked Jane for injuries, flashed

penlights in her eyes, and then declared her injury-free.

"Like hell," I yelled loud enough so the group in the other room could hear me. "Look at her, she's obviously in shock."

"This will be a lot easier on everyone if you calm down, Ms. Tanner," the officer insisted.

"Why the hell should I?" I asked emphatically, standing up and tugging at the edges of my robe.

The officer opened his mouth to say something just as Detectives Steadman and Graves slapped handcuffs on Jane.

"Have you all lost your minds?" I demanded as I pushed past my official babysitter. "Why are you handcuffing her? At best she's a witness; and at worst, an almost-victim."

"Stand back," Graves warned in a very official tone.

"But!" I started to argue, then realized I had nothing convincing to say beyond, 'vacant-expression Jane is my friend and I know for a fact she would never de-penis a guy.'

My phone rang then, and I was torn between answering it and muscling my way through the throng of cops to save my glassy-eyed friend as she was being led toward the door. Counting paramedics, there were six of them and only one of me, so I went for the phone.

"Yes?" I snapped into the receiver.

"The whole parking lot is cordoned off. They won't let me past the police line."

I added this bit of information to my growing list of irritations. "Hey, Kojak," I called to Graves, who had one hand on Jane's bound wrists and a brown paper sack in the other. He glanced in my direction as his latex-gloved minion was depositing my pashmina into an evidence bag. "We're being denied our right to counsel."

"You and Ms. Spencer will be afforded an opportunity to make a call from the station," he replied blandly.

Me? What had I done? What had Jane done? Shit. "Our attorney is right outside. Her name is Rebecca Jameson and I happen to know she has every right to be present during arrest and questioning."

Both he and his partner gave me that 'you're a real pain in the ass' look. Not that I cared. I just wanted Becky here to put an end to the idiotic notion that Jane was in any way responsible for Paolo's death.

Graves made a call on his radio, and within a matter of seconds, Becky was rushing through the door. In the forty-seven minutes since I'd made the frantic call to her, Becky had obviously been busy.

I was a scrunchie and a bad shoulder tattoo away from looking like a skanky warehouse shopper. Jane was a zombie: a barely conscious, bloody, La Perla–clad mess. Becky, however, looked polished and professional.

Her red hair was twirled into a loose knot, secured by a couple of lacquered chopsticks in the same shade of coral as her blouse and wedge sandals. With her cream jersey skirt, she had the perfect casual business look of a no-nonsense attorney. I'd berate her later for taking the time to accessorize and applying a full complement of makeup; but for right now, I was just glad she was here.

I'd known Becky since our freshman year of college, so I recognized the look of horror that flashed briefly across her face when she saw bloody Jane cuffed and surrounded by sheriff's deputies.

She introduced herself, conveniently leaving out the part about being a contracts attorney who hadn't seen the inside of a courtroom since her moot court assignment as a third-year law student. "Who is in charge here?"

"That would be me," Detective Steadman said, stepping out of the small group. She didn't offer Becky her hand. "I'm the lead on the case, and this is my partner, Detective Graves."

Graves nodded, then walked out on my patio when his cellphone rang. His part of the conversation consisted of a series of grunts—lots of 'umms' and 'uh-huhs' and 'reallys.'

"Do something," I mouthed to Becky.

"Unless you have cause to hold Miss Spencer, I want the handcuffs removed now."

"That isn't an option," Steadman said without inflection.

"Why not?"

"Miss Spencer is under arrest on suspicion of murder."

Suddenly my babysitter twisted my hands behind my back and slapped handcuffs tightly around my wrists. "Ow!"

Steadman's expression didn't so much as flicker. "And I'm taking Miss Tanner in as well."

"For what?" I practically screamed.

"Accomplice, material witness, assaulting a witness after she was told to stay in the bedroom. Take your pick," Graves said, his dark eyes flashed something that looked annoyingly like pleasure.

Steadman turned to Becky and added, "You have thirty seconds to vacate these premises. Based on evidence found at Miss Spencer's home and the blood trail here, I'm designating this apartment a secondary crime scene."